the
demon
queen

WHEEL OF CROWNS
BOOK FOUR

the
demon
queen

BRANDI ELLEDGE

Published by Aelurus Publishing, November 2019

Copyright © Brandi Elledge, 2019

Cover design by Molly Phipps

ISBN 13: 978-1-912775-35-4

www.aeluruspublishing.com

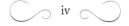

dedication

This one is for Caity-

You bring happiness, entertainment, and love to my world. You never cease to amaze me. I am so proud of you. Now, go let that light shine.

acknowledgements

To the most amazingly awesome people in my life that love me unconditionally. God for giving me the following people to acknowledge. Matt my awesome husband who feeds me and loves me. Cole and Caity for allowing me to be an uptight overprotective helicopter mom. Who me? Whatever. Later in life you can send me your therapy bill. For Mom and Dad or mainly just mom because I've already told you dad you don't get a shout out until book five. So mom, love you big time.

To my aunt B and aunt Pam for being the best aunts in the south. My cousin Brook for beta reading my books and loving them. Tacha, Tony, my sweet little precious Andrew who plays archery and Fortnite with me, Hannah Chelle, and Beth. Love you crazies.

To my best friends for always being super proud of me and laugh when I'm salty and extra.

To the Aelurus Publishing team: Rebecca Jaycox, who understands my potential and will not let me settle for anything less than fantastic. You're extraordinary. To Katherine for being an amazing proofreader. You rock and one day I'll tell you that in person. And for Jeff Collyer for making all of this happen. Blessed to be part of this fantastic group.

chapter one

I wasn't a natural-born killer, and that was my biggest problem. Well, one of several. There was always a hesitation within me. That's why others considered me weak, but I would find a way to shed this so-called weakness like a snake sheds its skin. Or I would die trying. Literally. What was my numero uno weakness? I was not evil enough. I cared a little too much about things someone in my position shouldn't even consider, much less care about. So what should I do? I just needed to work on my weakness for humanity like a problem. If it were a problem, then there had to be a solution. Did I have issues? Of course, I did, and every single one of them led back to my psycho father, so really if there was anyone to blame for my faulty wiring, it should be him. Somewhere along the way, he broke me. Yep, here I was, a broken doll. A badass doll, but still broken, and in need of a mental health evaluation. I wasn't exactly sure what my diagnosis was, but I knew it'd be hard to pronounce.

I crossed my arms and thrummed my fingers on my stomach, as I stared up at the ceiling. My advisor cleared his throat, and I continued to ignore him. This was the meeting I called, which meant I could do as I please, and not addressing his last question seemed to be a good start.

"Carmen, how about we start with the crown?"

My fingers automatically traveled to the black beast of a crown I wore on my head. I really did need to take the time to get it sized. It was hard to take someone seriously when their crown regularly fell over one eye. "What about it?" I asked, weary.

Fobby, who was the new right-hand man to the crown—I had fired the last two—shifted uncomfortably in his seat, as I studied his ruddy complexion. He looked like he wanted to have a heart to heart with me, but was scared. His self-preservation skills were at an all-time high. Good for him.

"Ugh. Fobby. Dear sweet, Fobby. This is where you tell me how well I wear the crown, how great of a ruler I am, and how everyone fears me. Then maybe you should come up with a slogan for me like, 'Carrier of death.' No wait, that sounds like a disease. I can already hear the jokes on that one. Also, I need new ideas on how I can promote fear better."

"But Princess, that's part of the problem, isn't it? Your ancestors never had to tell tales of their horrendous acts or 'promote' themselves—they were just innately feared." Maybe he had a point, or maybe I should fire him, as well. "Princess, might I say that I don't feel like you are the intended ruler."

"Excuse me?" I bolted upright, causing my crown to fall on my forehead. "And it's Queen to you, you weaselly worm."

Fobby's arms flapped about him in distress. "Please hear me out. I think the others are perhaps planning to dethrone you. I'm worried they will lump me with you when they try to take your crown. Plus, your uncle suggested—"

"My uncle?" I seethed. That man had done everything he could to unseat me from the throne. I knew it was only a matter of time before he succeeded. I studied my soon to be ex-advisor. He was a fire demon, like most of the other demons in this God-forsaken place. Red skin, black horns, and beady eyes. The only difference was Fobby looked like a nerd. A demon nerd. He was thin and weak, which was a rarity in the male fire demon species. His voice didn't boom when he talked but almost wheezed out of his body. Pathetic, really. And the worst thing was he was dumping me. Who was pathetic now?

I held up a hand to stop him from speaking. I made him nervous, and he made me sick. "Fobby, quit your whining. I don't plan on getting overthrown, you dweeb."

Poor Fobby started wringing his hands. Pathetic, I tell you. "I would have to disagree."

With a flash, a smoky wisp uncurled from me. Resembling hands, they wrapped around his throat and slowly began to tighten. His eyes rounded in fear.

"Now Fobby. Tell me exactly what is on your mind and what you've heard, or I'll kill you right here and now. Remember, I'll know if you're lying."

"As you know, I have been advising you for two months now, and still no one respects you like they did your father. You almost act human," he said the word with disgust. "You rule with soft hands, and that brings me to another point I want to drive home. You're a smoke demon. Not that there's anything wrong with demons who take human form, but you don't even have your true form. It's like you want demons to laugh at you. Your attitude is so flippant, as if you truly don't care what your underlings think of you, and to be quite frank with you, some of the demons truly don't think you're evil." He almost whispered the last word.

"Are you serious?" My wisp tightened around his throat. "First of all, I am aware I don't have my true form, but I assure you I am just as powerful without it." I was sure as hades not as powerful as I could be, but I'd fake it 'til I made it. "Also, I might appear flippant because I don't care what you or anyone else thinks of me. Sorry if your small, trivial brain can't understand you are beneath my cares. To be honest with you, I'm shocked you can breathe unassisted. And second, me not evil? Why just the other day, I put six demons' heads on spikes for everyone's amusement. If that doesn't scream, 'let the good times roll', I don't know what will."

Fobby cleared his throat. "Yes, but some say it was because you caught the demons about to harm a small child, and you flew into a fit of rage."

Truth. "Lies! All of them. I killed the poor sods because I was bored."

My advisor gave me a doubtful look. "I'm not sure—"

"Fobby, I'm the Queen. Do you hear me? The Queen, and it's about damn time you, along with everyone else, looked at me as such."

Obviously, the nerdling wasn't having any of it. "You rescued a kitten the other day. In front of demons, mind you. It's hard for them to respect someone so …"

"Go on, finish that sentence. What were you going to say, Fobby? Weak?" My wisp tightened around his throat until he could no longer breathe. He fell to his knees as I decided what I should do with him. Maybe if I beat him bad enough, it would help my image. Just as I was reaching for him, a knock sounded on my private office door.

The door swung open without invitation, and there stood my uncle Maligno, with a malicious smile on his red face. His black horns were long and proud and ramrod straight with agitation. Oh goody. He came looking for a fight.

"I'm hoping I'm not interrupting anything important?" he said with a knowing smile.

I glared at Fobby who was now crawling on his knees away from me. He better keep his mouth shut. "No worries, we were finishing up. However, Uncle, from here on out, I expect you to wait after knocking until I give you permission to enter."

"Oh, of course. How rude of me." He gave me a mock bow. "Please excuse me, your highness, but there was a situation I thought you should know of immediately."

"What is it?" I pushed out between gritted teeth.

A smile lit his face. "A teenager was brought to the underworld. A thirteen-year-old girl who will one day become a witch."

"What? Why is she here?"

"Oh, I'm sure the demons weren't thinking when they brought her here." His tone implied differently. "But since she is here, we thought we would have a little fun torturing her before we ended her life, and since you are the queen, we thought you might want to do the honors."

Bile rose in my throat. Torturing an innocent young witch was not on my bucket list. To decline was one thing, but to deny the demons their fun would show them how weak I was. Could I let an innocent die, though? No. I looked into my uncle's smug face. This was yet another test, one which I would not pass. Perhaps today would be the last day of my reign, but I'd go out swinging.

"You are to release the young witchling immediately. No harm shall come to her by a demon's hand."

I tensed as his horns straightened even more. My uncle was unaware but the truth was, without my true form, my power quickly became depleted. None of them knew exactly how powerful I actually was, and my great poker face was the only thing keeping me alive. I refused to break eye contact with him, and finally he bowed his head in submission.

"Yes, niece. I'll make sure to relay your message verbatim."

Oh, I was sure he would. The story of how the Demon Queen saved the life of one of another faction would be top news. It was only a matter of time before I was overthrown. He left just as abruptly as he'd come. Fobby was in a corner, shaking his head. I felt myself about to become unglued. I paced, letting out a string of curses. Every once in a while, I threw in an adjective.

The door to my chambers flew open. Was this it? Did my uncle bring reinforcements? I found myself readying for battle. The goal would be to destroy as many as I could before they ended me. The only problem was no demons stood on the other side of the door. What the hell was that flying towards me? Oh, this was hilarious. Surely, my uncle Maligno, didn't send this wee little creature to take me out—a fairy wearing a suit and tie. This had to be some kind of joke or an illusion. I mean, really, how did a fairy even end up in Hell? The tiny being blew something pinkish into my face and I gagged. Fobby backed up into the corner, as I wiped tears from my face. I couldn't breathe; what was that stuff?

"Do not worry, Queen. I vow my potion will cause you no real harm. It's only intended to clean up that vile language of yours. I just can't work with someone who curses so much. My good friend, Kimball, once said, 'profanity is the effort of a feeble brain to express itself forcibly.'"

There I stood, mouth agape, staring at the small creature. "What the fox are you talking about?" My brows drew together. "Fox." I clenched my fist and tried again. "Fox. Oh, for fox's sake, what the hey have you done to me? Oh, shirt, this is bad."

Fobby glanced nervously around before he crouched down. Fear leaked out of his pores, the little foxer. What the hey? I couldn't even mentally swear. The fairy was dead. I would find out why he was here—or how he even got here to begin with—then I would kill him. Today was quickly going down the shirter.

chapter two

U naware of his impending doom, the fairy gave me a polite smile before taking in his surroundings. He huffed a deep sigh of resignation before he mumbled something under his breath.

I tensed, as the fairy, who was dressed like a lawyer, flew to a stop directly in front of me.

"Who the hey are you?"

"Ah, your manners are outstanding, but nonetheless, I shall greet you properly," the fairy's overly cheerful voice chirped. "I'm Tally, and I'm on a special assignment. I'm here to help you in any way that I can."

Say what? "I'm sorry. We're not taking applications at this time. Try back, like, never."

The small fairy flapped his wings in agitation. He carried a miniature briefcase that looked as ridiculous as the pinstriped suit he wore. "I couldn't help but overhear that exchange you had with the red man. That was intense. But just so you know, I'm someone who doesn't take kindness as a sign of weakness." He zoomed in an inch in front of my face and without glancing at Fobby said, "Fire this poor excuse of a demon, and let's get to work, shall we?"

I looked over at Fobby, and he appeared just as clueless as I felt. His eyes rounded in shock. Oh, the gossip mill was going to be lit today.

The fairy smirked. "That blabbering idiot"—he pointed to Fobby—"will never understand the potential you have. You could become the most powerful queen that a faction has ever had, so go ahead and kick him to the curb. We've got work to do. Chop chop."

Was he bossing me around? What the fox was going on? Never mind that he spoke of a power that didn't exist without my shell. I studied the small creature in front of me. To kill or not kill, that was the question. My calendar was free. I could schedule in a quick killing, but my gut said hear the fairy out. He would live. If anything, he could stroke my ego for the limited amount of time I still had on the throne. "I'm intrigued to know why you're here."

"As I've previously said, I've come here to help. I'll tell you exactly how when there are not prying ears nearby."

My eyes flashed to Fobby. "You're fired. If anyone asks you, tell them it's because you sucked at being an advisor, and you didn't enjoy my wit. If you don't say that, maybe you'll find your head on a spike, too."

Fobby, the pathetic coward, started to run from my office but Tally intercepted him. Blowing some translucent powder in Fobby's face, he told my former advisor, "You will not remember me."

Fobby sprinted towards the door, never once looking back. The fairy had just saved me from the gossip mill and being the butt of all jokes today. My previous interactions with fairies were limited. They stayed in their lane, and I stayed in mine. So what would bring this fairy here? What was this little man's game?

I gave the fairy all of my attention, and in return he studied me. We didn't get many visitors in the underworld. Why would he come here willingly? The answer was he wouldn't. The fairy had shaggy blond hair and light green eyes. He was attractive, if men the size of caterpillars were your thing. The way he sized me up made me uncomfortable. It was almost as if he was trying to determine if I was worthy of some task. I was really getting tired of that look.

My teeth gnashed. "So, what exactly has brought you to the underworld?"

"I am here to help you secure your crown." Tally flew over to the couch and plopped down. He opened his briefcase and took out a pad and a pen. I waited, half pissed and half amused, as he made several notes on the paper. "I hear you have a nasty temper. With that being said, if you should agree to work with me, I have one stipulation that I'll share at the end of this meeting."

Apparently, my temper wasn't as bad as it should be. "I'm losing patience. Why are you here, bug? I need the specifics."

"The Oprah version is I was sent here by someone extremely powerful to help you dissect yourself, so you will be able to find your true identity—who you are really meant to be. Think of me as a life coach who has a vast knowledge of moral philosophies or a fashionable therapist."

Oh-em-gee. Did someone send me a shrink? It was one thing to joke to oneself about the lack of mental stability, but it was a whole different thing when others talked about your mental health condition. "I will kill you. Do you know who I am?"

"Yes, way to prove me wrong on the whole temper thing, and of course I know who you are, but do you know who I am?" He gave me a snobby look. "I come from the Fae King's inner ring. I am his trusted advisor."

"Um, whoopee? Am I supposed to be impressed because I missed that email? Maybe I should check my spam folder."

His little fingers started to scribble even faster. Curiosity was killing me, so I leaned in to see what he wrote, but he held the pad up so I couldn't see. He flashed me a snarky little smile. "Sorry, I can't share my thoughts with you."

"Um, you just shared plenty with me, but what's to stop me from killing you and taking the pad? After all you are in my domain, my personal headquarters to be exact, and yet you dare to be rude to me."

"You could kill me, but you're not going to. It would start a war with the fae realm, and who has time for that?" He had me there. My calendar was full. He scooted back, so he sat up against the couch. "You see, I have personally been sent to you by the Fae King himself on the authority of the best soothsayer in the world. So, this …"Tally made a motion between us with his hands. "What is it that the kids say? This is so happening."

"Best soothsayer? You mean, Ariana?" My heart sped up.

"The one and only." He popped his suspenders. "And I'm here to help keep your scrawny behind on the throne. All you have to do is open up to me and agree to a few things. Keep in mind, our discussions will not leave this room." Oh, this had to be a joke. A fairy who was a therapist, swooping in to save the mighty Demon Queen. I was full-on laughing, but the bug just talked over my hysteria. "According to Ariana, you need me in order to get over this little hump you're going through, and even though you are great at self-sabotaging, I think you will come around to my way of thinking, and take the help that is offered to you, or you might not ever get what you truly desire."

Was he talking about my body? My shell? If he came on the authority of Ariana, he had to be talking about my true form. I could tell he was by the way he nodded at me, a knowing gleam in his eyes. That sobered me up. My shell was the one thing that would ensure I stayed on the throne. The way the bug grinned at me, he knew I'd have to listen to what he said now. It irked me to no end that everyone knew how badly I wanted my real body back. That made me vulnerable. Part of it was vanity, but dang it to hey, the other part was I was sick of jumping into bodies. It was gross. As soon as I donned the human form, it felt like it was constantly slithering over my bones, never quite settling into place, and I was never truly powerful. Not that I could admit that to anyone.

"So you were sent to help me retrieve my shell?"

"In a roundabout way, yes. So would you like your true form back?"

Duh. I went to the long mirror hanging between two tall bookcases, and studied the body I currently inhabited. Honestly, I'd done worse but still. Ugh. I picked up the short, reddish-orange hair that felt like straw. If only someone would've told poor Becky she was over-processing the strands. I was currently rail-thin and almost six feet tall. I literally looked like the scarecrow from the Wizard of Oz. The only way I could get bodies now days was due to the high rise in opioids. At least Becky overdosed on molly and not meth like Harold, the last body I'd possessed. That man had no teeth. Like none. I couldn't enjoy a good juicy steak for days. A long time ago, I had decided to only jump into bodies if the human was about to die. If a demon jumps into a body and doesn't evacuate within three days, the human dies. So in my mind, if I jump into an expiring human, then there's no harm. My weakness didn't allow for me to be a murderer of humans.

I gave one more look at the human form I was currently wearing, albeit not very well. I really did want my body back. After all that was my goal.

As if hearing my internal thoughts, Tally said, "Think about it. You would never have to jump into another fragile human body again."

"Okay, bug. You have my attention."

"Ariana said I would. Eccentric room, by the way."

I scoffed as I looked around my office. Back when it belonged to my father, everything was dark and tacky along with massive. The desk, bookcases, and furniture were black and gigantic. Nothing was out of place, and everything about the room screamed "I am King." It was boring as fox. Now, there were Guns N' Roses, Def Leppard, and Van Halen posters plastered to the walls. I painted the desk blood red and got a matching black velvet couch and cozy chair. I placed the chair in front of the fireplace, so I could be comfortable when talking to all of the guests I never invited back to my chambers. I wasn't really a people person. Regardless, the fairy said eccentric, I say cool as shirt.

"So," he said, "this is how it's going to go. I'm going to help you, and you are going to have to accept my help. Take a moment and decide if you are comfortable with allowing an outsider like myself to advise you with more than just queenly duties, but your life in general."

I didn't like the condescending tone he took with me. I could squish him with the heel of my boot and be done with this. Could I even trust someone from the fae realm when I couldn't even trust the demons I ruled? But Ariana had vowed to me a while back that she would help me with my body. The soothsayer was crazy, but she wouldn't break a vow.

I paced the length of my office. Upon father's death, I threw out all his souvenirs and trophies. Then I put what the bookshelves deserved—books. My fingers trailed down the spines. I guessed my collection was a little strange, considering who I was, but the Queen of Demons or not, I loved me some romance novels. There were a couple of classics, from Charles Dickins to Jane Austen, scattered amongst the romance books, just to make people think I had a little bit of class, but the trashy romance was where it was at. That and holiday movies. I was a sucker for the Hallmark channel. Obviously, being sappy was a massive part of why I was having a hard time ruling. No demon wanted a tenderhearted, mushy, sappy queen. I could have weekly stoning or beheading sessions earning their respect, but if I rescued one tiny little kitten, suddenly we had a mutiny on our hands. But if I had my shell back, I would be unstoppable, and the subjects would know that. The whole supernatural community would know that.

Appearing annoyed, as if I was wasting his time, Tally said, "So, what will it be, Queen? Will you allow my presence here, so we might work on some of the issues you are facing when it comes to ruling?"

I looked over my shoulder at the small fairy. The first person to call me by my title in months, and it was a dang fairy.

My mind was made up, but I decided to let him believe I weighed my options. I didn't want him to know how truly desperate I was. "Let me think."

I hid my smile, as he released a dramatic sigh. I strolled to the middle of the room where there was a huge oval carpet that covered blood spots that belonged to yours truly. This chamber had also served as a torture chamber for yours truly. Every morning and every night, my dear ol' dad would beat me. Sometimes Maligno would come to participate. How I hated them both. I could have washed away the blood, but Father, dear, chose not to during his reign, and I decided to go with the family tradition. It reminded me of where I came from and where I would never go back. I would never again be someone's whipping post. I did, however, decide to cover most of the blood. Talk about literally sweeping your baggage under the rug. Maybe this was why I for real needed a therapist.

A true Demon Queen would not harbor resentment or be bitter at what she'd done to survive; instead, she would be proud she was a survivor and I was proud. I didn't feel remorse for what never was. I was also secretly thrilled I had been present to watch him die. If anyone deserved death, it was him. So therefore, I didn't entirely understand why I felt so empty. Was my father a terrible person? Absolutely. Did he deserve to die? He sure as hay did. Was I depressed? Why, yes, I was. Zoloft couldn't even conquer these emotions right now. I was the unbeloved queen over demons that I didn't even like, and I wanted my stupid shell back. I was feeling a little unbalanced. Maybe I needed a voice of reason. If Ariana sent this fairy to me, he couldn't be all bad.

"I agree to let you help me, little man, but if I decide you aren't to be trusted or no longer worthy of my time, I will crush you like"—I gave him a saucy wink—"a bug. Do we understand each other?" He tilted his head in agreement. "Tell me what exactly we need to work through."

For the first time, he looked a tad uncertain. "I wasn't fully briefed. Apparently, if I knew the whole truth, then the mission, which is you, would be compromised." His face turned ruddy. "I might have a bad reputation as a gossip." I couldn't help but laugh. "The soothsayer didn't say that she didn't trust me to tell you all the reasons why I needed to be here, but I could tell …" He gazed at the carpet with embarrassment.

"Listen, Fairy, I think me and you will get along just fine. My favorite hobby is people watching at Wal-Mart. So, you have the edges of why you were sent here? Maybe we can piece the puzzle together slowly."

"Yes, I was told to get you to open up to your feelings."

"Good luck with that."

"Queen, if you are in agreement with working with me, I need to talk about the one stipulation I need from you."

"What's that?"

"You have to take a vow to not kill your uncle."

I got up to pace. "No, no way. I've had this plan ever since I saw him lead my mother to her death. No. He's dead, and he'll die by my hand. I've already promised your stupid soothsayer that I'd wait until I had my shell, but that's all I can do."

"Then I'm afraid you will never retrieve your shell."

I grew deathly still. My blood pounded through my veins. Did I want my shell bad enough to forsake my vengeance?

"Did you know that whenever I was bad and my father and uncle were bored with the beatings, they would lock me in a time freezing machine. Supposedly, it was for the fun of it, but it was really because it hurt my mom. A demon doesn't stop maturing until their late teens. I was three years old for one hundred and fifty years. Of course I didn't know it. I have no memory of it, but when they finally released me, my mother wept for days." There was a look of shock on Tally's face. "That is nothing compared to what I have truly endured, and you're wanting me to give all my vengeance up?"

He nodded. "It does seem unfair to ask of you, but I have been told that without that vow you—"

"I know. Ariana won't help me get my shell back. Can you tell me why?"

He shook his tiny head. "Sorry, that was the part I wasn't privy to."

"I need time to think."

His green eyes held sympathy. "That's understandable." He tapped his pad several times with the end of his pen. "Just make sure you don't take too much time. I was informed that we needed to hurry."

I was stressed and needed some space just to think. I knew the clock was ticking. I could almost hear the other under lords planning my demise right now. Surely, Ariana the all-seeing wouldn't have sent this fairy to me if I was to die tonight? I mean, wouldn't that have been a waste of time on her part? I glanced over at the fairy, who polished his shoes with his thumb. Plus, there was a council meeting in an hour I had to prepare for. If any of the under lords, especially my uncle, thought I was apprehensive, they would behead me. Without my true form, it wouldn't be extremely hard to kill me. I took a deep breath. I didn't need to be raw going into that meeting.

"Tomorrow is soon enough to talk. I'll let you advise me if it means I'll get my shell back, but I need to think on the other part of the deal. Now, if you will kindly show yourself out, I will have Markee take you to your quarters, where you should be relatively safe."

"It's important that no one know I'm here to help you secure the throne."

Duh. I gave him a nod as I rang a bell for my new secretary: I fired my father's old one. The fairy looked like he was about to argue but decided against it. As soon as Markee agreed to show the little man where he could sleep during his stay in the underworld, I fell back onto the couch and wondered how a foxing fairy was going to help me unleash my inner evil. Ariana wouldn't break a vow. This fairy had to be the answer to my problems, so why did I dread our next meeting?

chapter three

I had planned on telling Tally my decision. It was going to be a hard no from me. I didn't need my shell that badly. I had spent years planning my revenge. I couldn't just let it go. Not even for my true form. As soon as I entered my study, I knew something was off. A sharp pain had me gasping. I slapped a palm to my neck and felt blood coat my hand. Another pang knocked me to my knees. I looked up to see the fairy flying in front of my face, holding onto a poison dart. He shot me? The weaselly traitor shot me! This body could die. I would only have a few hours to find another body, or I would be forever dead. Was he working for my uncle this whole time? What the frog nog? My eyes rolled back in my head. I was losing consciousness fast. When I woke, I was going to find a new body and then kill that centipede.

I moaned as I cracked my eyes open. My mouth felt so dry, and I had the mother of all headaches. I lay in my office on the rough carpet that totally messed with my Feng Shui. As I moved, coarse orange hair fell over my face. How was I still in the body of the poor soul that resembled a scarecrow in her former life? This human body should have died from the poison.

A throat cleared from one of the only armchairs in my office. "I'm guessing you have questions?"

I sat up glaring at Tally. "I'm going to kill you. But first I'm going to play with you until every bone in your stupid body is broken."

He grabbed his yellow notebook and made humming noises as he scribbled. What the fox, dude? He should be pissing himself not humming, "Mary Had a Little Lamb." That was the only thing saving him from me ripping his head from his shoulders. I was in shock.

"Sorry I had to go to such drastic measures to prove a point, but this was my two birds, one stone approach. You see, we need to talk, because we are really on a time crunch, and I also needed to remind you how vulnerable you are in this human body. The darts, by the way, were a sleeping potion, not poison. I didn't destroy your body. You're welcome."

"I'm not thanking you," I nearly screamed.

"One wouldn't expect gratitude from you, but you are still welcome, nonetheless. Now, let's focus on healing you from the inside, so you can focus on the outside. Your shell. The first thing you have to do is take that vow not to kill your uncle." I pushed back the rat's nest from my face but didn't say anything. "Carmen, if they attack you in this weakened state, a human shell, you're dead anyway. What do you have to lose by taking the vow?"

"Everything. My revenge." He started to say something, but I held up a hand. "Look, I don't need someone to diagnose me."

"No, you don't." His green eyes bored into mine. "You know what else you don't need? A bunch of enablers. Right now, you have two types of demons surrounding you. Ones that are terrified of you and will do whatever you say, not out of loyalty but out of fear, and the other type is trying to undermine you as we speak. Get over yourself, take the vow, and rule like you were intended."

I broke eye contact. He was right. My uncle was one of those demons planning my doom right now. I lay back down on the rug and threw an arm over my eyes. "The end result will be me finding my shell?"

"Yes, Ariana and the Fae King need you to be the ruler of demons."

I snorted. "The devil you know and all of that."

"Something of that nature."

"All right I vow to not kill my uncle if I get my shell back."

He clapped his hands in excitement. "Okay. Good. Fantastic. Now, let's get you to open up." Maybe I would rather die. "So, how about we start with why you insist on working in a space full with what I am assuming is your blood?"

I didn't lift my arm from my face. "It's a reminder, of what my father and uncle did to me, and the people I've loved he has taken from me and all that I've lost." Tally was quiet. "Is this where you tell me I have survivor's guilt? Because I can promise you, I do not feel any guilt that he died and I didn't."

"You did witness it, correct?"

"Yep. Then I stepped over my father's still-warm corpse to collect my crown. The one my brother tried to take from me by planning my demise numerous times. The Werewolf King and Queen offed him. Good riddance. One less person I have to worry about stabbing me in the back."

"You live in a lonely world."

"Wow. Way to cheer me up. Good thing I'm not paying for this session." Plus, I already knew that.

"I heard ever since you took the crown off of your dead father's body, you have refused to remove it. I hear that you even shower with it."

I snickered. I didn't shower with it, but let them think whatever they wanted to. The fairy flew in circles around the office before landing on the corner of my desk. I peered up at him, waiting for him to make his next point.

"Tell me why do you think you're in such a slump right now."

I thought about his question and decided to answer it with complete honesty. "Because I'm not him. No matter how hard I try, I will never be my father."

The fairy gave me a disgusted look. "And why would you ever want to emulate that man? He was a wretched soul. You should thank your lucky stars you're not him."

Was he joking? My father was feared by all. Maybe the fairy didn't understand how dire of a predicament I was truly in. I voiced the thing concerning me the most. "Sometimes, I hesitate to make a kill that should be easy. And worse, sometimes after I've killed, I have … I have guilt." I said, almost choking on the word.

The fairy's mouth dropped open, and his wings flapped double time. "A demon with a conscience?" He started pacing all over my open folders lying on my desk. "This is why they sent me to you, and this is why you are in a slump." He chuckled.

Lucky for me, I was in reaching distance of the desk. I sat up and flicked him across the room. "Not funny, ass-hole."

He rolled himself into a sitting position, wiping the tears from his eyes. "I'm not laughing at you. It's just I assumed you were a head case, teetering on insanity, and instead I find out that you're a good demon. This is fantastic!"

"Fantastic," I snarled. "No, fantastic would be governing a body of demons that actually listens to me and respects me. In order to keep these demons in line, I have to instill fear in them. Which usually means someone has to die. Having a conscience is going to make me a horrible ruler and might even be the death of me. I have to fix this."

His head cocked to the side. "Fix your good side? You want to be evil?" When I didn't reply, he said, "Ahh, I see. It's interesting how you view yourself. Have you ever thought that it might be the good side in you that will save us all?"

I snorted. "If I lose this crown, I won't be saving anyone. I'll be dead."

"So, let's not lose the crown." The fairy gave me a mischievous smile. "I'll vow to help you to secure the crown, but in return I need you to let me help you how I see fit."

"If not allowing me to cuss was a precursor of how you will help me, no thanks. I have no urge to be a goody-two-shoes. Not to mention, being good will get me buried."

"I'm not saying you have to be Mother Teresa, but let's aim for somewhere between Gandhi and … and … and … well, you."

I should be offended but I wasn't. He was asking me to reach for higher than average on the moral calculator of life. He had jokes. So cute. "Um, why don't you try to loosen up a bit? Lose the bow tie and every once and a while throw out an F-bomb, or is that too scandalous?"

The poor fairy turned crimson, as his hand patted down his immaculate attire. "I'm sure we can come up with some sort of an arrangement. Now, can you give me a proper tour of this place, so I can see what we are working with, and while we're at it, maybe tell everyone to stop trying to eat me?"

I gave my first laugh in what felt like a century. "Sure thing, beetle."

"Another bug joke. And here I thought you weren't lame."

I stood up and walked to the door. "I'm just full of surprises. Now come on, and I'll show you the different levels of the underworld."

He fidgeted with his bow tie before nodding. It'd be interesting showing my home off to someone not born of this world. I wondered if he'd be impressed or disgusted. Only time would tell.

The architectural layout of the underworld could be compared to an ant farm or an intricate spider's web. Sometimes, I actually felt more like the insect caught in the web than the spider, but I was working on remedying that. There were black onyx tunnels zigzagging and intersecting repeatedly. The outer rings were where most of the lowly demons resided. The inner rings were for the more powerful, primordial demons. The closer to the center of each level resided an under lord, and that area became more lavish. The floors went from dirt to different shades of marble. The wealthy and the higher-level demons lived closer to the under lord in charge of that specific area. They handled their level's problems and then reported back to me weekly on how they were faring. Unfortunately, the under lords were not impressed with my new title and had expressed concerns, although not vocally. At least that was the word on the street. Here recently, they hadn't been showing up to the weekly meetings. Another thing I needed to fix as soon as I got my shell back.

Tally followed me through the tunnel leading from my chambers.

"It would take us weeks to walk each level, so if you don't mind, I will teleport us to the different levels." Without waiting for permission, I gently grabbed the shrink and took him to level one.

After several levels were viewed, I could tell by the disdain on his face he wasn't impressed with Hell. Trying to see things through his eyes, I had to admit the underworld was a tad depressing. Darkness flowed from every corner. There were torches every eight feet, but it brought no warmth. Instead, when the flame flickered just right, you could see tiny demons slithering along the walls. They were following us, intrigued, but not comfortable enough to announce their presence.

"There are twelve levels and twelve under lords that rule each level under my command. So far, I haven't found a demon I trust. Call me paranoid, but I believe everyone is currently planning or hoping for my beheading."

Tally landed on my shoulder. "Maybe you should nuke all twelve of them and start over. A culling, if you will."

"I could, but I believe that would cause the kind of upset I might not be able to handle. Especially in a human body. I need my shell. Also, aren't you Mr. Ethical?"

"Yes, but sometimes people can't be saved. All I sense here is pure evil."

We walked in silence for a while. I noticed Tally taking it all in. There were several different types of demons in the underworld, but he seemed to strongly dislike what we called the fire demons. Like my uncle and Fobby, they were red with complimentary black horns jutting out of their head. Tally should be afraid of them. My father had been a fire demon, and I wasn't sure if I'd ever emotionally heal from the trauma his rages had put me through. Lucky for me, I took after my mother, who'd been a smoke demon. Most of the demons we passed flared their nostrils at the fairy in aggression, and their horns became straight. Tally's wings fluttered nervously, as he probably recognized he looked like a tasty little morsel. The smoke demons wore human shells and were less obnoxious in their desires. Then, of course, there were the shadow demons. They were the size of my index finger. Most of them were more tricksters than they were vicious demons. Every demon we passed bowed their head at me, even if their eyes conveyed disrespect. They all took note of the fairy on my shoulder, and that was the best I could do for him. No one would touch him now. Not unless they wanted to dance with death. I could tell by the fairy's body language he was disgusted with this world, and truth be told maybe I was too, but I was next in line for the throne, and I was born to rule and rule I would.

chapter four

Two weeks had gone by, and I thought even the fairy was bored with our sessions. Plus, both of us were feeling the turmoil in the underworld. We knew that any day now my uncle would strike. Honestly, I wasn't sure why he hadn't yet. During the past couple of weeks, we'd talked about every sordid detail of my past: my feelings on my abusive, murdering father, and how I felt when I'd watched him murder my pet, my childhood friend, my mother. How the hey did the fairy think I felt? Jeez.

"Have you come to terms with why your father did these horrid things?"

I blew on my nails that I had just finished painting black as I halfway listened to the fairy. "To try and ruin me because he knew I would one day be more powerful than him."

Tally nodded. "Do you feel like you inadvertently caused your loved one's death because your dad was trying to get to you?"

"Well, no, I didn't. Not until you suggested it." I went to sit in my chair in front of the fire. "What the fox do you want me to say? That it's my fault my loved ones died? That if I had never loved, then they would still be alive?"

"I just want the truth from you. Whatever that may be."

I glared at the fairy. "Okay. Maybe I do hold myself accountable for their deaths. But do you know who I hold the most at fault?" Tally shook his head. "My uncle."

Tally's eyebrows rose. "Not your father?"

"Oh, sure, he was the one landing the blows but it was my uncle that was pulling the strings. He was never as powerful as my father but he was a hay of a lot smarter. When I was little I would always catch him watching me. Around the age of seven I realized that my father was the fire but it was my uncle that was the gasoline. He would feed on my father's doubts and fears of always remaining on the throne. It was easy to do considering that every demon around could tell how powerful I was even at an early age. I was also different."

"Different how?"

I shrugged as if none of this bothered me. "I'm not blood thirsty. I don't crave death. Don't get me wrong I've never backed away from a fight but I have never craved the battle."

"You clearly loathe your uncle and don't get me wrong it's justified, so why didn't you kill him? I mean he did have a hand in every death of your loved ones including your mother's."

"Because it was him that built the maze. Your soothsayer made me a promise a long time ago to help me with getting my shell back. She told me then not to attack any of the under lords until I had my shell." I rested my head on the back of the chair. "Now, she's changed the rules again. I will never be able to exact my revenge."

"Revenge is not everything."

I rolled my eyes and almost told him maybe he should pick a different profession. Clearly, he wasn't getting me. Then we talked more about my feelings. We broached the subject of my brother and how he had planned my death. Did I feel lonely? Ostracized? Well, no shirt, Sherlock. I had no family or friends. At one point, everyone I'd ever been close with either tried to kill me or died. Leaving me alone. I thought it was safe to say loneliness was a companion of mine.

In full on snark, I asked, "Not that I don't like our little chats, but when do we get to focus on my shell?"

"We're done," he said. Tally stacked all his pads together and put them back in his briefcase, and a sickening feeling filled me to the brim. He was leaving. I wouldn't let him know that somewhere throughout the last couple of weeks I'd grown attached, or that he was literally my first friend since I was six. I would wave him off and not shed a tear. I was good at saying goodbye.

"What do you mean 'we're done?' You were supposed to help me retrieve my shell," I shrieked.

"There's that nasty temper. You're also moody and a total smart aleck, but you have potential. There is enough good in you that might tip the scales in our favor."

"Whoa. What are you talking about? Good will get me killed. It's like a disease infecting my whole body. I need help with getting rid of my conscience, not talking about my stupid feelings. Feelings are for pansies." I pumped my fist in the air. "I can say pansy! Hey, yeah. Now, in all seriousness, when are we going to call up creepy soothsayer and ask her for my dang shell?"

Tally's green eyes twinkled with mischief. "Actually, she got in touch with me yesterday. She was waiting until everything aligned just right. I have been given permission to give you a gift." He held up a hand. "Before you get all excited, it's not your shell, but it will get you one step closer to retrieving it. So, go change into something less …" He wrinkled his nose at my all-leather outfit and crown. "… Demon Queen and perhaps find something quieter. Shoot for small, Southern-town attire."

"I'm sorry. I threw out all of my knitted sweaters and overalls, so leather will have to do, and it'll be a cold day down here before I remove my crown." I felt a little bit of excitement and worry over venturing out. "Where are we going? I don't know about leaving the throne unattended for too long. Everything right now is so unsettled."

"We will be back before you know it."

My eyebrows arched. "We?"

The fairy winked at me. "Oh, yes. I have a feeling you will need me to guide you on the right path for some time."

"What path would that be? Talking about my feelings and being a good person? No, thanks."

I would never tell Tally the truth … that I was happy I had someone to talk to. Someone who might stay around for a while.

I pulled on my black, high-heeled boots then stuffed a couple of daggers down in them for good measure. "Okay, I'm ready to go. Tell me where to take us."

The fairy shook his head. "You look like a transvestite hooker."

I cocked a hip out. "Like a well-paid hooker or one that just barely makes a living?"

He laughed as he gave me the directions to a small place on the outer banks of North Carolina. He was right; I was going to stick out like a sore thumb, but I was never one to turn down a gift.

I took in the little beach house where I had teleported us. This place held my gift? Surely, this was a joke. The house was tiny, but I guess one could say it was cozy, if you were into small homes, warm fires, and the smell of baked apple pie. It was pale blue with white shutters and had an ocean view, but other than that, I couldn't see the appeal or why there was laughter coming from the inside. I mean, people who craved a homey atmosphere? Phew, such losers.

Tucking away my jealousy, I clambered up the steps.

"Knock on the door before any of the neighbors see us," the fairy whispered in my ear.

"Don't want to be caught with a hooker, I take it?" I mumbled, as I rang the doorbell. "You'd never make it as a politician."

A beautiful brunette opened the door. She had big brown eyes and an all-American look to her. She was probably as sweet as the apple pie I smelled. There was something about her ... she had power, but what I was feeling from her was low-level. I guessed she was a witch. Her mouth dropped open as she looked from me to Tally.

Her voice was like molasses. "Hun, we have visitors."

A man who appeared in his early twenties came strolling around the corner, wiping his hands on a dishrag. No wonder women across the nation bought all of those home and garden magazines, especially if this was what being domestic looked like. Ring that dishrag, baby. Holy amazeballs. He was six feet plus of pure awesome. His hair was so blond it was almost white, and his eyes were a startling shade of blue. He was magnificent, like right up there with unicorns dancing over rainbows magnificent. Looks aside, he was noteworthy just from the fact that I couldn't get a read on his power level. He was definitely part of the supernatural club, but how powerful he was, I hadn't a clue. His easy smile that was more beautiful than a thousand suns dropped as he studied the both of us. I wanted to boo but I contained myself.

His voice was clipped. "Can I help you?"

"May we come in?" Tally asked. The fine specimen started to say no, but Tally cut him off. "It's important. Ariana sent us."

There was recognition with the soothsayer's name. The man's eyes bounced back and forth between Tally and me before he nodded. "Show them in, Sarah." His voice expelled no warmth.

The intriguing man and his beautiful girlfriend sat on the couch, as I chose a chair facing them. Tally sat on the arm of my chair.

The man asked, "Why are you here?"

That was a good question. I looked pointedly at Tally, waiting for the answer.

"Austin is your name, correct?" The man gave a terse nod. "Great." Then he gave me a smile as he pointed at the man. "This is your gift."

There was a lot of commotion after that sentence, as chaos erupted around us. Sarah started screeching at Austin about big decisions not being discussed as a couple, and how trust and communication was everything in a relationship. I tried not to barf on the wood floor while wondering what in the world was Tally's game?

chapter five

Sarah glared. So much for being sweet as apple pie. She pointed a finger at me. "She looks like a meth head. I mean, are those sores on her arms? And is she even a she?"

Oh wow. I couldn't believe she was making fun of my human body. Dude! Beggars can't be choosers. Jeez.

The man shot daggers at me with his eyes while trying to calm down his hysterical girlfriend. "No, that's a smoke demon. I'm guessing she has taken over some poor soul's body," he said, eyes drifting over my body, "because this body doesn't seem to fit her well."

Okay, that was it. I had had enough. "Well, first of all, you'd be partially correct, probably on all levels. Except for the girl being a dude thing. This body is for real a girl. And no, she wasn't some poor soul." I pointed at Sarah. "Mary, there, is correct. Becky, the body I'm currently housing, was on drugs but not meth in particular. The night she OD'd she left her two small children in some rat-infested apartment just to get her next fix. She would have sold them if she had thought about it or had the right connections. She was within thirty seconds of dying before I jumped into her body."

Sarah leaned forward in her seat. "It's Sarah, not Mary."

"Yeah, so that's what you got from all of that? The children, did you say? I called protective services and had the kids go stay with a loving grandparent. Trust me they will be better off, but thank you for asking of them. Your concern astounds me."

Tally gave me thumbs up. What in the hay? He could probably jump in at any time and clear this up, but my suit-wearing shrink had a flare for theatrics.

Sarah was on a roll. She was so pissed her face was beet red. "He is not yours, demon whore!"

That was it. I was going to kill her. "Tally, I command you to let me cuss again. I'm going to need to use a few dirties as I'm creaming her face."

Tally shook his head. "No."

"What do you mean, no?" I hit my fist on the chair in frustration. "Son of a benching shirt-hole," I snarled. "Do you hear that? That sounds utterly ridiculous." Tally rolled his eyes. "Okay fine, I'll just have to send her to the underworld with positivity and good thoughts as I'm pummeling her into the ground, but everyone in this room will know what I'm really wanting to say."

Austin's didn't look worried in the least, as his head tilted in confusion. That was strange. He first glanced at Tally and then me. Popping my neck, I slowly started to stand, as Tally flew up and put his tiny body in front of mine, waving his arms.

"Whoa, whoa, whoa. Everybody settle down." He straightened his bow tie. "Listen, the Queen of Demons has a lot of good qualities, but managing her anger is not one of them. Please be mindful of how you speak to her."

Well, that grabbed everyone's attention. The man studied me with interest. "You are the queen?"

"Darn skippy. The one and only. You can bow now, monkeysmukers, and while you're there—"

"And," Tally quickly interrupted me, "we are here because you, Austin, can help the queen retrieve her true shell."

Oh, so this was the guy I had heard rumors about. A couple of months ago, my path had crossed with the soothsayer, and she had said someone named Austin might be able to help me with what my heart desired.

Ugh. Mary was talking again. "Why would he do that?" she scoffed. "To make a demon more powerful? I think not."

I ignored her as I observed Austin. Could this be who the soothsayer was talking about? I doubted it. Yes, this male was strong, masculine, hot as hades, but he wasn't radiating power, and if I was going to get my shell back, I needed someone oozing with power.

Tally said, "Austin, I think you'll find it in your best interest to help the queen because if you do her this favor, she will be indebted to do one for you."

"Whoa! I think your suspenders are too tight. Don't put words in my mouth, little man."

It was Tally's turn to glare. "Do you want your original form back or not? Think about it. You would never be forced to inhabit another body again."

He had me at 'original form', but I just made a carry-on motion instead. I was a queen and shirt. This was me being blasé about the whole thing.

Austin crossed his arms in front of his body. "And what could I possibly need from a demon?"

Tally smiled like he knew he had already won whatever game it was he played. "The most powerful demon to ever live would help you secure the key."

Um … what? Why would I do that? Half of the supernatural community was out fighting for the keys. I had my own battles in my own backyard; why would I want to involve myself in another battle?

"How did you know I was searching for the key?" Austin asked in a deadly tone. I sat back in my chair, folded my legs underneath me, and mentally clapped with glee. I loved it when shirt hit the fan.

"Easy, big guy," Tally said. "I'm friends and advisor to the Fae King and have a great rapport with a soothsayer."

"Yeah, I hate to break up whatever negotiation is going on here, but how do you think this guy can get my shell back?" I said. "I mean, you would have to be pretty sure of yourself in order for me to vow my help."

The man leaned forward in his seat. "But would you vow to me your help in securing the key if I could get you your shell back?"

I was so over this whole conversation. "Yeah, if you could. But if is a pretty big word."

"It's only a two-letter word to me." He smiled, lighting up the universe. "Go ahead and vow it, because not only will I get you your original body back, but then we will secure the key."

Mary/Sarah screeched, "You can't take help from her. She's a demon. They can't be trusted."

I shrugged because Mary had a point. Austin smiled at his disgruntled girlfriend. "Yeah, but babe, a vow is a vow, and I'll make sure she doesn't double cross me."

I almost laughed, such arrogance in that statement. What part of the most powerful demon in the world did he not understand?

"So, you both are witches?"

Sarah looked miffed. "I'm a witch, and Austin is technically born of the witch family tree, but he's so much more." She started open her mouth to expand, but Austin squeezed her leg. Interesting. She turned to him and begged, "Please tell me you're not seriously thinking of helping this hideous creature?"

"Awesome," I said. "So Mary, why don't you go—"

"Carmen," Tally shouted. "Can I talk to you for a second?"

I jumped to my feet. "Why? So we can talk about my feelings? Or how I should really try to dial back my anger? Enough is enough. I don't know this chick, and yet she wants to judge me. Fine, but I'm going to rearrange her face."

"Carmen," Tally snapped.

I glared at my therapist. "What if I told you I think it would help sort through some of those issues I've been having?"

Tally seemed to weigh what I said. He drummed a finger on his chin while he pursed his lips. My shrink was so dramatic. I loved it. "No, and listen, we need them as badly as they need us, so don't screw this up."

Sarah sat as far back in the cushions as she could possibly get while Austin just casually took in the scene. Obviously, he wasn't afraid I would hurt his girlfriend, so that made me wonder for the second time what power he hid.

I sat back in the chair with a huff.

"So, Carmen, do we have a deal?"

I looked at Austin. "That's Queen to you, and I vow to help you find the key if you retrieve my shell for me."

Vows were unbreakable. Punishable by death if broken. Rumor had it the soothsayer herself would send out fallen angels to extract payment if a vow was broken. I expected him to take a moment to really weigh his options, but he just gave me a smile instead. "Deal."

Sarah threw up her arms, making choppy motions like a ninja on drugs. Austin leaned in and whispered calming things into her ear. I may or may not have groaned loudly.

Tally clapped his hands together. "We will talk about how we are going to retrieve the shell as soon as we get back to the queen's chambers. The three of us leave now."

That got Sarah's attention. "Make that four. My boyfriend will not be going alone with that creature."

Austin clenched his jaw, a telltale sign his girlfriend's screeches were getting on his nerves, too. Why was he even with her? Yeah, she was beautiful, but she was equally loud and obnoxious. Maybe she had a trust fund. That made me laugh and caused Tally to give me a cautionary glance. He probably thought I was having homicidal thoughts.

Sarah clutched her pearls to her chest. "Is she crazy?"

I tilted my head to the right like I was listening to someone. "What, Lola? Huh? No, you can't take over, silly. Remember the last time I let you gain control? You murdered everyone in the room. You're going to have to take a backseat on this one." I slapped my forehead. "Oh great, now the Cajun wants to come out and play, but I can't let him because we will all end up shirt-faced and will literally waste the whole day playing beer pong." I made my body convulse. "Damn it, Lola! I said, not now."

"Austin," Sarah shrieked. "Who is she talking to?"

After a few moments, I pretended I was wiping a sweaty brow. "Duh," I said, "I'm talking to my multiple personalities. Doesn't everyone have at least a few?"

Sarah looked horrified while Hotness just stared at me.

Tally groaned. "Really, Carmen? You are not helping the situation at all."

Whoopsie. I gave a little smirk, as I watched a rattled Sarah rub her pearls and draw her knees up to her chest. Personally, I thought I was hilarious.

Poor Sarah was still shell shocked, but Austin sat there and listened with interest as I explained where my shell was held. He acted confident, but I knew how difficult it would be to retrieve my shell. My father and uncle had it locked in a safe in the underworld in an enchanted maze. They couldn't physically destroy my shell because they weren't powerful enough. But had they made it so I personally could never retrieve it? Yep, they sure had. Mother sucker shirt humper.

Tally waited patiently while I tapped my foot on the hardwood floors. We stood by the entrance as Sarah made an overnight bag. Finally, she emerged and locked up what appeared to be her house. Apparently, Sarah and Austin weren't in the "roomies" status of their relationship yet. Austin grabbed Sarah's hand, and I grabbed him by his oh-so-muscular shoulder, along with Tally, and transported them to where the shell was. My domain. The underworld.

chapter six

I f everyone was wary of a fairy living in the queen's quarters, then the demons went a little ballistic when I added a witch and whatever the hey Austin was to the mix. Word spread like wildfire that the crazy queen had finally gone around the bin. What these ash-holes didn't know was I already resided in crazy town. I was just better at hiding my crazy than most. I held a mandatory meeting with the twelve under lords. Just in case some of them decided not to show, I sent a message around the levels, letting the under lords know those who didn't come would lose their head to a spike. I call this method "motivation 101" and it usually worked.

We had arrived early for the meeting held in the center of level six in an onyx room. I headed to the black throne sitting in the middle of a raised stage. There were a couple of chairs on either side of my throne. Austin and his girlfriend, upon my instruction, sat to the right of me while we waited for everyone to arrive for the meeting. We faced a long rectangle table and twelve empty chairs. The under lords were really testing my patience. They weren't certain of how powerful I was without my shell, so they acted out in little acts of defiance. Trying to test me daily. Soon, they would figure out I wasn't as powerful as all of them combined, and if they chose to band together, they could bring me down. I sighed as Sarah whined again. The girl had not stopped yapping since we'd arrived. The air was stale. The floors looked dirty. Her hair now smelled like smoke. The horrid demons kept looking at her, and she wanted them to stop. She didn't feel safe. They should have never agreed to come here.

After a few minutes of hearing her benching, I felt like I was about to blow. Even poor Tally had put some distance between himself and the whiner. I sat on my black throne, my crown cocked to the side, contemplating murder. I mean, Austin was a very attractive man; it's not like he wouldn't be able to find another girlfriend. I might actually be doing him a favor.

As the under lords started to file in to sit in their assigned seats at the large, rectangular table facing the throne, I leaned into Austin. "Muzzle your girlfriend, or I'll have to do it for you. She cannot disrespect me in front of these demons."

He gave me no lip but instead offered a half-smile and a salute before he whispered something to Sarah. I had a few moments of blissful silence. Austin sat up straight, as he studied each of the under lords. His gaze continually came back to the under lord from level eleven—Maligno, my uncle. As my eyes clashed with my uncle's, we both understood it was only a matter of time before one of us attacked. Who would be the first to strike? He finally broke eye contact, and my uncle's lips slightly curled when he noticed Austin's gaze. I glanced at the man sitting next to me. He was becoming more and more interesting by the minute. Something at the back of my head struggled for information that wasn't there. Like puzzle pieces that wouldn't fit together. Who exactly was Austin?

I whispered, "Do you know my uncle?"

His electric blue eyes jerked to me. "Personally? No."

Without my shell, I couldn't tell if that was a lie, but it felt like one.

I'd table that for now. I let the room grow quiet, as I acknowledged all twelve under lords, and they leered back at me. They were composed of various types of demons, but they had one thing in common: they were all evil. I felt it from where I sat. They searched for any weakness they could find. If they knew I planned to make a go of getting my shell back, they would all unite and just try to kill me now.

Two of the demons on the far left loudly discussed my ordered release on the young witch they'd captured. Their thoughts on my actions held a few unkind adjectives. I pretended to ignore them, which was more than I can say for Austin. He hung onto every word, and whether the demons cared they had a captivated audience was beyond my knowledge. I had to choose my battles if I wanted to win the war.

I cleared my throat. "I've called this meeting today to let you know who these people are who have graced us with their presence. This is Austin and his girlfriend, Sarah, but feel free to call her Mary. They are here to spell my quarters from enemies. Spread the word. Also, let everyone know if they try to hurt either of my guests, I will kill them outright. Do I make myself clear?"

There were a few mumbles. Then the under lord from level four spoke up. "Why would you need someone to cast spells around your quarters? Do you not feel safe, my queen?"

The last part came out as more of chuckle, causing several of the under lords to laugh. I really hoped I wouldn't have to use my powers, but I couldn't allow the demon's taunt to go unchecked. I extended my hand. With tired eyes, I watched as black smoke turned into a wisp, uncurling itself from my fingertips and slowly crossing the room until it wrapped around the demon. It encased him like a cocoon. My smoke dragged him across the table he sat behind and across the floor, until he was directly in front of me. I stood from my throne, and with my bare hands, I broke both of his horns from his head. He howled in pain, and I did my best not to flinch.

"I do not think it's a surprise there are a few of you trying to undermine my authority." My gaze landed longer on my uncle before I made eye contact with the rest. "But please know this, it will take more than just a few of you to bring me to my knees and even then, I will bow to no one. Do I make myself clear?"

The demon before me nodded, along with the other eleven under lords sitting behind him. I let the smoke tighten briefly around him before flinging the demon across the room. That was it. My power was almost depleted from that little show, but I couldn't let them know that. None of them knew exactly what my power range was in this borrowed form, and I aimed to keep it that way. Head held high, I sneered. "Meeting's adjourned."

After everyone had filed out, I caught Austin studying me with his startling blue eyes.

"What?" I asked.

"Nothing. I was just thinking if you're that powerful without your shell, maybe it's not a good idea to make you more powerful than you already are."

I wagged my finger in front of his face. "Nuh-uh-uh. A deal is a deal. In fact we need to get started now." I was too weak without my shell, and that little stunt I just pulled proved it.

Austin nodded. "I agree. In fact the sooner we get you your shell, the sooner we can go after the key."

He sounded so sure of himself. "I have a book. It belonged to my father. It talks about the enchanted maze. It's vague, but there might be something in there that will help you if you would like a look at it."

He shook his head. "No, thanks. I think I'll be just fine. In fact this will all be a piece of cake."

Seriously? I released a heavy sigh, as I shifted the weight of my crown. It was a pity he'd probably die. What sucked worse was I wouldn't get my shell back.

Ever the gentlemen, he helped Sarah stand from her chair. She tossed her silky hair over her shoulder and gave me a once over. "You disgust me."

"Well, good, Mary. Then my job here is done. We couldn't have you full of joy and cheer down here in the underworld, now could we? It would ruin our image."

She stormed off in the wrong direction. I couldn't help but chuckle when Austin had to track her down and point her in the right direction. Some things I would never understand. I straightened my crown for the umpteenth time as I left the throne room.

chapter seven

The four of us gathered in my chamber. I had a feeling Sarah would not like this next part, so I let Tally take the lead, as I sat down in front of the fireplace and held my hands to the roaring fire. I let my eyes almost fully close as I studied the three of them through this poor soul's lashes. Becky had no eyelashes. No eyebrows. But dang if she didn't have hair coming out of her chin. I plucked three stubbly hairs just this morning.

The fairy settled onto an armchair facing the fire while Barbie was like a leech on Ken. Never letting him out of her sight, it was apparent there was some separation anxiety there. They wouldn't separate, and it was giving me anxiety.

Tally cleared his throat. "The tension in this place is at an all-time high. We need to go into the enchanted maze sooner rather than later to retrieve the queen's shell. This is where we will need to separate. I'll stay behind to watch Miss Sarah."

Sarah stuck out her bottom lip. "No, Austin. Don't leave me. Take me with you."

"It wouldn't be safe." He gently pulled her hands from his thigh. "It'll only be for a day. Maybe not even that long."

I rolled my eyes. No one besides the Demon King, my father, and his brother had made it through the maze. It was a forest of magic spells that my uncle had set in place to ensure I would never be able to retrieve my body. If Austin was willing to risk his beautiful hide to find my shell, who was I to stop him? But the arrogance in which he treated this mission could not bode well for us. I must not get my hopes up.

Sarah was practically wrapped around Austin, like a gigantic suction cup. She was so clingy I had to hold down my bile. As three pairs of eyes glared at me, I realized I had said this out loud. Sarah tapped her foot on the floor. Was she waiting for an apology? Well, this was about to get awkward.

"I'm sorry that you are so clingy."

"Oh, that's it!" Sarah took two giant steps towards me. Fire danced in the little witch's hand. I never stood up but waited for her to get closer to me. When she was a foot away, I reached out with my hands and smothered the fire before she hurt herself. She was sputtering. I almost felt bad for her.

"Um, dude. Born of fire and all that." She was breathing so hard I was scared smoke was going to come out of her nostrils. "Maybe you could try another trick?" I suggested helpfully. At her look, I clucked my tongue. "Oh, dear. That's all you can do is create small balls of fire?"

"You are ugly. It doesn't matter how powerful you are, you will never find anyone to love you." There was probably a lot of truth to her words. "From what I hear, your own father and brother couldn't stand the sight of you so much they tried to rid the world of you."

Both Austin and Tally started to speak, but it was too late. I was pissed. With a wave of my hand, I moved her body across the room and into a chair. I mumbled a few Latin words, and she was rendered mute and immovable. With that little burst of power, I was completely tapped out, but it was worth it. Her eyes frantically looked to Austin.

"No, this is where I rule, little witch. He can't help you. This is how it's going to go. Your boyfriend and I are going to see if we can retrieve my shell and when we get back, you will be free, but mark my words, you don't want to get on my bad side. You think I'm ugly now? Beauty is only skin deep, but I'm rotten to the core. My ugly will give you nightmares, so do yourself a favor and behave."

My eyes darted to Austin, who stood there with his hands crossed in front of his broad chest. He gave me a tiny nod. "Your house, your rules."

Sarah stood there with her mouth agape. Not to identify with the cray-cray, but I could kind of understand her confusion. Austin didn't want to defend his girlfriend? Demand that I release her? I cocked my head to the side. Nothing seemed to add up when it came to the mouth-watering, power-hiding male standing before me. He was just another anomaly in my life, but maybe I would find out his secrets soon.

Tally broke my train of thought. "I will watch her for you."

I took several calming breaths before I nodded my thanks. I strapped my weapons, my two favorite blades, to my back and headed for the door with Austin trailing behind me. We were both quiet as we left my chambers and traveled through a series of tunnels.

"The entrapped forest is actually on this level—level twelve. I have a question. Why wouldn't you take up for your girlfriend?"

"Excuse me?"

"You heard me. Is it because there is trouble in paradise, or is it because you don't want me to know how powerful you are? Or is it something I'm missing entirely?" When he was quiet, I continued, "Most would intervene on behalf of a loved one. Even the weak ones that don't have much power, and yet you let me force her in that chair and restrain her. Why?"

His blue eyes cut to mine. "What if I said it's because you are queen and I'm not stupid?"

"Then I would have to say neither am I. You don't have to answer my questions. I'll eventually find out the answers, anyway."

"Speaking of questions, is it true that a young witch found herself trapped here, and you ordered her release and safe return to her family?"

"She was too young to eat." I snapped my teeth together. "Everyone knows you have to wait until adulthood before the meat gets juicy."

"Hmm," was all he said, as he followed me down a narrow staircase. "You seem so old for your age." I glanced over my shoulder, and he gave me a once over. "How old are you? Thirty-six?"

"Remember, this is not my body. Looks can be deceiving." We turned down a black tunnel and came to a stop in front of a golden door. "I'm theoretically hundreds of years old, but since I was locked in a chamber that froze time on several different occasions, I've collectively only fully lived nineteen of those years. When I was eight years old, I was put in the chamber for two hundred and twenty-three years." He had a look of horror on his face. "The chamber froze my mind and body, so it's not like I knew how horrible it was. Not until I saw my mom. When I was released, she held me like I was priceless. It gutted her I was in there for so long. Smoke uncurled from my body and crushed the machine. That was the night my father took my powers and killed my mother." Austin acted like he was about to ask questions, but I was dragging up memories I couldn't think about at the moment. Or ever. The pain was too deep. "Social hour is over, champ. If you don't mind, can you show me why the most powerful soothsayer in the world thought you could help me?"

His lips curled back into a sexy smile. "Sure thing, Highness."

He wrapped his hand around the golden knob and pulled the door open. My mouth dropped in shock. The door was encrypted with riddles. Ones he didn't answer. The door should have released a poison, saturating his skin. He should be dead right now instead of winking at me.

"How did you …? How—"

"It's no fun if I have to tell you."

I reached for the door. His hand was lightning fast as he snagged me by the wrist. "Your curiosity will kill you. That door can't harm me because I'm immune to poison, but it can definitely kill the body you're in."

Witches weren't immune to poison. What was he? A sorcerer?

"Hurry up. That was just step one, and I don't want this to take all day. How many more steps do we have to go through before we find your shell?"

I gave him a wary look. Who the hey was this guy? "Twelve in total." As he would have known if he'd taken the time to read the book on the enchanted maze before we were in the maze. "So, we have eleven more," I mumbled. "The same amount as levels in the underworld." At least I thought we would have to get past twelve entrapments. But what did I know? I had never made it past the golden door.

The entrance to the maze was so narrow we were forced to walk single file. I had nothing better to do than to stare at his fantastic butt. He stopped so suddenly I almost ran into his back.

"Look, we have a live entertainment show, and we didn't even have to purchase tickets."

"What?" I asked. He was too big. Even with this human form being gigantic for a female I still couldn't see around him. The tunnel widened up ahead of him, but he blocked my view of whatever was before us. I peeked around Austin's massive shoulders and sighed. We came upon a small cavern resembling a lion's den, but unfortunately it wasn't lions squaring off at us right now. This was just great. At least the book I'd found in my father's chambers was correct when it listed out the order of dog droppings that was about to come our way. Step two of retrieving my body was getting through an elite demon guard. The best of the best. My powers were practically drained, so I'd have to rely on my combat skills. Lucky for me, I was freaking amazeballs. The guards faced us, and goosebumps rose on my arms. Maybe if my father had the elite guarding him the day he'd died instead of my shell, he would still be here. He'd always possessed more brawn than brains.

The ten guards pulled wicked blades from their backs. I eyed Austin. Sure, he was muscular and well-built, but he was probably going to get gutted before we even made it to step three.

He shoved me behind him. "I'll try to protect you for as long as I can."

I shoved him right back. "Ha! That's cute. Move it over, blondie, and I'll try to make sure you don't die a slow, agonizing death."

I popped my neck from side to side. There was nothing like a good fight to get rid of some pent-up tension, but first I would attempt diplomacy. "Hello, boys. I am your Demon Queen. I'm sorry my father has locked you up in this dank place for so long, but lay down your weapons now, and I can promise you that you will feast tonight in the great hall beside me and my—"

Something hit me. I looked down to see a small blade sticking out of my shoulder. "Mother funchez—" I pulled the knife out with a moan. "You couldn't wait until I was done with my little speech before you threw a blade at your own dang queen. Which one of you little shirts threw that?"

I threw the blade with precision at the one on the far right. It hit him in the middle of his forehead. Not a kill shot, but it would slow him down. I took two steel swords from the sheath tied to my back and passed one to Austin. "Decapitate or remove the heart. Only way to stop them."

"Yes, I know."

I didn't ponder his words as two demons rushed at me. I crouched down and swung my sword low, getting one in the Achilles tendon causing him to topple over. I rolled the blade over in my hands and swung again, catching the other demon in the gut. I didn't have time to remove heads or hearts, as more demons began to attack. My goal was to wound badly enough that it would buy me some time to circle back around and make the kill shot.

Austin shouted, "Behind you!"

Going on instinct, I fell to the ground and rolled to the right. The sword of an elite demon came barreling down, missing my head by an inch. I hopped to my feet and found myself in a corner. Corners were not my friend. I needed to work my way out, or I would be dead. Or at least this mortal body would be. I glanced across the room, and Austin was engaged with three demons. I was surprised to see how easily he swung the blade. Focusing back on my predicament, I planned my next move. It was risky, but I was out of options. I threw my sword at the approaching demon. It pierced his chest but left me weaponless. I ran towards him and grabbed hold of the handle protruding out of him. I turned him in a semi-circle, using him as my shield and just in time. A blade meant for me sliced through the back of the demon I currently pulled my sword out of.

After I yanked my blade free, I wounded the demon still trying to attack me, and then I beheaded the demon recovering from getting run through twice. It just wasn't his day. Poor fellow. Nine more elite demons to go. I swung my blade at anything that moved after that. I cut arms, legs, and abdomens. They were all wounded but not dead … yet.

I worked my way back to the middle of the small opening. After a couple of swings, I found myself back to back with Austin. I was shocked to see how well we worked together. It was almost as if we had rehearsed it. I would slice a heel or take off an arm, and he would behead the wounded then we would rotate. It was amazing. After we had beheaded every demon, we leaned on each other's back, just taking a moment to catch our breaths and smile over our victory.

Austin cleaned off his blade on the heel of his boot. "You did really good. I'm impressed."

I gave him a saucy wink. "Ah, buddy. I don't have a speech or anything prepared, but here goes nothing. I would like to thank all of those that I fought today for being slightly worse of a fighter than me. My psychotic father who insisted on nightly beatings. In the long run, it made me super tough. You know what? No, I'm not going to thank him because he was a douche. Yay! I can still say douche. Stupid fairy probably doesn't even know what it means. Oh, and last but not least, a shout out to you, blondie. I thought you were doomed for death, but you surprised me, so kudos."

He blinked several times before he shook his head. "Are you always like this?"

"By this, do you mean wowing people with my awesomeness? Why then, yes."

I thought he hid a smile or his lips could have been twitching. "Come on, let's go."

We exited the cavern and continued on our path, which was extremely narrow. The maze was a long tunnel opening up wide at each stage like a python that had swallowed a volleyball. The labyrinth was dingy, dark, and smelled like mold. In my head, I might have romanticized the enchanted maze more than what it really was in actuality. Enchanted sounded so whimsical. Instead, it should have been named the rank maze. I chuckled to myself. I loved me. I was exhausted, but as the tunnel began to open up, more adrenalin started to pump through me. We were getting closer. Then again, we were just at step three, so I shouldn't get my hopes up yet.

chapter eight

The floor changed beneath us into a zigzagged stone pattern. The walls shrank even more, and I wasn't entirely sure the top of Austin's head wasn't grazing the ceiling. Just as I was about to make a claustrophobic joke, a gate came crashing down behind us. We could no longer exit the way we came from. A massive steel door was before us. In Latin there were words, questions, carved at the top of the door. At the bottom of the door were more Latin words letting us know that if we answered incorrectly, it would mean we would be trapped in between the gate and door until the puzzles were solved. Apparently, the maze had strong enough magic that trying to teleport out was not an option. That meant being forever stuck down here in the labyrinth until the witch died, and I killed myself from pure boredom.

Which had me asking, "Hey stud muffin, are you immortal?"

He said, "Yes," and then looked like he immediately regretted sharing that bit of information with me.

Most witches lived long lives but they weren't immortal. He must be a sorcerer, but then again, sorcerers were incapable of hiding their powers.

Austin had his hands on his hips as he studied the first door. "Instead of trying to figure me out, why don't you concentrate on our mission? It looks like our first riddle is, 'What is black as a demon's soul but not as deep as the ocean?'" The first was easy. In unison we both said, "Grave." Once we were allowed past the door, we smiled at each other.

The door opened, and we were past step three and faced with yet another door with another riddle.

The second door was a stupor. "What's a penny to receive but two to give."

We both crouched in front of the door tossing out potential answers when it hit me. I slapped my hands together. "I got it."

One of Austin's eyebrows lifted. "Yeah?"

"A penny for your thoughts?"

He nodded. "And if you ask my two cents …"

We had our answer. Austin placed his hand on the door. "The answer is thoughts."

I almost hummed and skipped all the way to step five, which was a magical bubble of sorts. Purple electricity shot from one side of the tunnel to the next. Austin put his hand on the wall. Sweat beaded his forehead as he closed his eyes and bowed his head. The purple bolts pinging from wall to wall slowed down and began to swirl around each other in a funnel. I watched in astonishment as the purple electricity seeped its way into the wall Austin currently had his hand on. I stuck a hand out. The energy had completely faded. Being able to calmly reroute that kind of energy was unheard of. He must be a sorcerer.

"How did you do that?"

He lifted a shoulder, as if what he had done was no big deal.

"Remember, it's no fun just to give answers." He kept walking down the tunnel forcing me to catch up with him.

"Seriously?"

A chuckle was his only answer.

I rolled my eyes. So, that was how it was going to be.

The tunnel widened enough for me to step up beside Austin. He was saying something, but the image in front of me held all of my attention, as it shocked me to my core.

"Mom? Is that you?"

My mom stood there, beautiful, just the way I remembered her. Her long, brown hair flowed behind her. Her pale skin was radiant. She reached out to me, and I felt my feet shuffling to her. I could hear Austin shouting my name but I ignored him. This was my moment with my mom, and I would not let anyone ruin it. As I started to enter into her embrace, I noticed her eyes. They had always been a light shade of brown, but now they were almost black, and the outside of her irises was rimmed with red.

"Mom?" I asked again.

Strong arms wrapped me up from behind. I tried to fight the aggressor off, but I couldn't take my eyes off of my mom. What if she disappeared? I couldn't lose her again. Someone shoved my head into something

hard. I realized it was a warm chest that smelled like summertime. It smelled like hope. Someone talked to me as they stroked my head.

"Shh. It's okay. You're fine now."

I broke out of his hold, looking around for my mom, but she was gone. I felt tears falling down my cheeks. "What just happened?"

"Not sure, but I heard you calling out to your mom. I couldn't see her, but I think that this was a desire spell. If you had touched what looked like your mom, it would have turned you crazy."

"Er." I swiped my tears away with jerky motions. "It would have made me crazier."

I pushed away from him, and after I got myself under control, I tried to take the focus off of me and my humiliating tears. "What did you see? What was the thing you desired?"

For a second, I didn't think he would answer. Finally, he said, "The key. I desire the key above all else."

Why did that ring false? "You saw the key? You're sure?"

He gave a shrug that looked funny on him, considering how wide his shoulders were. "Why wouldn't I see the key? Here is a fact: right now, the Lux are doing everything they can to save us. Save the world. While the Degenerates are hell-bent on destroying it. Demons are Degenerates."

"Are we?"

"Aren't you?"

I didn't answer because I didn't know how. Did I want the world destroyed? No. Was it my mission in life to save

74

the world? No. Up until this point, all I'd ever thought about was securing the crown and then retrieving my body. If I didn't want to let demons have free reign and have a hand in destroying mankind, wouldn't that mean I was not fit to rule? And wouldn't that mean I was weak? The one thing I swore I wouldn't be anymore. The silence grew heavy. I glanced up to see Austin studying me. I was shocked to see disappointment in his eyes. Whatever he was looking for from me, he obviously didn't receive.

Finally, he started moving through the maze again. "Come on. Let's get this over with."

Steps seven through ten were more magic that Austin somehow quickly disabled. If I weren't offended by his sudden prickly behavior, I would have congratulated him, or at least told him how impressed I was, but instead I just followed him to the next step.

On a golden stand was a velvet cushion holding a galvanized box. The whole area around the stand hummed with unrecognizable energy, but one thing was certain: my true form was calling to me.

Austin pointed to the box. "Is that your shell?"

I nodded. I was scared to blink. Maybe this was a trick? Maybe my shell would disappear just like my mom. Then I would be doomed. I started to walk towards it, but a hand snagged me back.

"No, you can't get close." He pointed to a faint circle that was drawn around the base of the stand. "Any demon who crosses the line will die. Human form and soul. I'll grab it for you."

"You can do that without getting hurt?" Fishing, I said, "Because you're a witch?"

"No, this is a powerful ring. I would think most witches, vampires, and werewolves would be disintegrated on the spot if they crossed the line." He turned to me and gave me a half-smile. "Did that answer your question?"

"Ha! I wasn't asking what you are." I totally was. "As long as you get me that shell, I don't care who you are."

He mumbled something about, "Let's hope so," but as he reached out to grab my shell and the tunnels didn't collapse, and my true form didn't evaporate, all I could think or feel was an overwhelming sense of joy. We did it. He did it. I would have my shell.

After a brief moment, he handed it to me and just like a fragile newborn baby, I cradled it against my chest, emotions flooding through me. Giving me some time, he stood off to the side and didn't say a word as I warred with my emotions. Why was I scared to put on my true form?

Austin finally broke the silence. "Not having your shell could be the end of your reign, the death of you, and yet you still yearned for your mother before anything else."

"So?"

"So, it just seems strange that a tyrant would crave love above all else."

I tightened my hold on the box. "Do you think of me as weak?"

He nearly bumped into me. "I didn't say that."

"How about you just mind your business?"

He raised his hands in surrender. "Easy. I didn't know it was such a touchy subject." He pointed at the box in my hands. "Aren't you going to get back in your own body?"

His demeanor was calm. Maybe he wasn't judging me. "I have constantly made jokes to soften the blow about my circumstances, but the truth is my dad took my true form away because he feared I would be more powerful than him. I don't really remember what I looked like, but I know he hated me even more in my shell. He never loved my mother or me." I held the box tighter to my chest. "What if I don't love myself?" That part wasn't meant to be said out loud.

Shock colored Austin's face before he masked it. "If you don't love yourself, how can anyone else? Let's start there."

I straightened my spine. He was right. I was a freaking queen; it was dang time I started acting like one. Love myself. Hey, yeah, I was going to get that embroidered on every pillow I had back in my chamber. I would love the hey out of myself.

I opened the box's latch. A transparent ball lay before me. Half of it was tinged black and the other half white, and yet neither of the colors mixed together.

"It's beautiful." A thought occurred to me. "I won't get to keep these clothes. Could you let me borrow your T-shirt and turn your back for a second?"

He mumbled something about a modest demon, and how he had officially heard it all now. I wasn't paying attention. I was too busy staring at my beautiful shell. Out of the corner of my eye, I saw Austin folding his shirt and laying it at my feet. I had a brief moment to take in his muscular form before he turned his back on me. Just as well. I didn't want to go down that rabbit hole. But if I did, I would have noticed he didn't have an inch of fat on him. Or how his muscles rippled when he placed the cloth at my feet. Or how blond hair trailed happily from his lower stomach to below his jean's line. But good for me, I didn't notice any of that.

I closed my eyes and concentrated on what was truly important—leaving the human body I had taken over months ago. I sighed like a weight had been lifted off of me when Becky collapsed to the ground. I should feel sorry for her, but the truth was she'd been evil before addiction ruled her life, and she'd hurt her kids. They were honestly better off without her. Once I was out of her body, the multi-colored ball I held in my hands rammed into me, pouring over me like water down a windowpane. The box hit the ground as energy flowed through me, and all traces of exhaustion washed away. This was the best I had felt in years. For the first time in a long time, I felt as if every molecule in me danced with pleasure while my shell and soul merged together in unity. My body arched as my chest tightened, as if it was sewing itself together. Minutes went by before the transition was complete. I stretched long and hard, reveling in my body before I put on Austin's shirt. While his back was still to me, I took a quick second to bury my nose in the soft cotton, letting his scent wash over me. Letting the hem drop, I frowned as I saw his shirt almost came to my knees. I was sort of hoping I would be a bit taller.

"Done yet?" he asked.

"Oh, yeah, sorry. You can turn around now." I looked over at Austin, who stood with his mouth open. He stumbled back, as if he had been sucker punched. Both hands interlaced behind his head, causing his six-pack to ripple as he looked up at the ceiling.

"No freaking way. Come on. Seriously?"

I watched in amazement/horror as he had a whole conversation with himself. He paced back and forth. Every once in a while he would cast a glance my way. I could hear him silently cursing Ariana. He said something about wayward plans and dancing? I arched an eyebrow, waiting for the rant to be over. Then he said that word again but it was Dansby. He stopped pulling on his hair. His face contorted with rage before his eyes caught mine again. Then his expression changed to … disgust?

What was I missing? This couldn't be good. Oh no. I patted my face. "What? What's wrong?"

He cleared his throat. "Nothing. Nothing at all."

"Am I hideous?"

"Huh? What?"

I pointed to my face.

"Your looks? You're worried about your looks?"

Uh. Kind of. Especially after that weirded out display he just put on. I rested my hands on my hips and just stared at him.

He finally answered me. "No. You might be vain but you're not hideous. Mary is going to flip."

I pumped a fist into the air. "So I'm smoking hot?" As he tried to give a casual shrug, failing miserably, I laughed.

I needed to see what he was seeing. I felt my cheeks for dimples and came up empty handed. Dang, I always wanted those, but at least this time around I had boobs. Beggars couldn't be choosers. We needed to backtrack our way through the maze. Since our mission was completed, all the connecting doors should be open, and as soon as we were close to the first golden door, I could teleport us to back to my chamber. Austin mumbled to himself again. Then two random thoughts hit me at once. First, there had been only eleven steps in retrieving my shell. That seemed way too easy, and second, Austin had called his girlfriend Mary instead of Sarah. Foxing hilarious if I did say so myself.

chapter nine

efore we could start walking towards the golden door and our freedom, the cavern walls started to shake. If the walls collapsed and I had to dig us out of here, I was going to be super upset. Then I realized whatever was about to happen to us was step twelve, and it was meant as a fail-safe to make sure that if I somehow managed to retrieve my shell, I didn't survive with it. The cavern ceiling crumbled above our heads, and our only exit quickly became blocked with huge boulders. The walls on either side of us were slowly closing in, as spikes jutted through the cavern floor.

As I dodged fallen rocks and spikes, I said, "Mr. 'this will be a piece of cake,' what's your plan now?"

The cavern wall behind where my shell had been disappeared, and there was nothing but blackness as far as the eye could see. A boulder fell from the ceiling, and unfortunately I couldn't dodge it in time without impaling myself on a spike. The impact from the rock hit the side of my head and shoulder causing my knees to

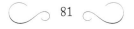

buckle. Strong arms scooped me up before my knees hit the ground. Blood dripped down my face and ran into my eye making everything blurry.

"We have to jump into the darkness," he said, just as another rock fell from the ceiling, barely missing us.

"Keep in mind my uncle designed this so you can bet he wanted us to jump."

He leaped over spikes and dodged the falling rocks. "We don't have a choice. We jump, or we become buried under the rocks, and before you make a decision, those spikes are coated with some form of magic even I do not recognize." I glanced at the spikes glistening with liquid. "We have to jump."

I tried to slide away from him, so I could stand on my own two feet, but his arms tightened around me. "No, Queen. We're in this together and if I jump, you jump."

He never took his eyes off of me as he flung us into nothingness. Things, or perhaps beings, snatched at my arms and legs as we continued to fall. I turned my head into Austin's warm, protective chest to keep my face from being clawed. Screams and shrills became louder as we continued our descent into the pits of the underworld.

In a moment of clarity, I knew where we were. The underbelly of the underworld, and this wasn't my domain. Underneath all twelve levels was where all souls went when their time had expired on earth. The only being who was allowed in the underbelly was Death himself, and even that arrogant ash didn't frequent these parts.

We finally landed with a thud. Souls flew past us at unimaginable speeds. As they lashed out at us, I tried not to cower with fear, as Austin stood and helped me to my feet. His hand gripped my forearm.

"I have a feeling I know exactly where we are." He shook his head. "I can't teleport. I wonder if I'll be able to use any powers?"

"No, you won't and neither will I. Perhaps you could have prepared for this if you would have read the book, but no, your cockiness has landed us right in the middle of irate souls who will probably rip our flesh from our bones thousands of times before we figure a way out of this mess."

A soul came too close, taking a hunk of flesh out of Austin's cheek. His jaw clenched in pain, but that was the only hint he gave it hurt. Blood dripped down his jaw and onto his bare chest. He jerked my arm to the ground, and we crouched just in time to avoid an angry soul.

"Right now is not the time to get in a discussion. We need to move from here. Focus. Souls, what do they hate? Water and light. We move until we find either one of those."

"Guess what demons hate? Also, water."

"You'll get over it."

He pulled me to my feet, and we started to jog over the thick dirt. The shrieks grew louder. A creepy iron gate was before us. He began to pull me through, but I jerked out of his grasp as a wave of despair and loneliness hit me so hard it stole my breath. Whatever was past the gate, I wanted nothing of it.

"Carmen, we don't have time for this."

"But don't you feel it?"

He gave a nod. "Yes, but every soul is now aware intruders are here. Look behind you."

Thousands of souls swirled around one another like hornets, forming a black ball above us. We would be consumed by them in less than thirty seconds. Austin extended a hand, and after one more glance at the screeching souls, I placed my hand in his. He tugged me past the gate just in time. The wall of souls hit an imaginary barrier, blocking them from following us. Their screams over their lost victory made me shudder.

An overwhelming sense of grief and anger pulled at me as I glanced up at Austin. "Well, we've avoided being ripped to shreds, but I can honestly say it might've been a better choice."

The soil we were on seemed isolated and quiet, but one look at his face, and I knew he was being slapped with emotions as well. Within a blink of an eye, a teenage boy stood in front of me. I immediately recognized him. He was from a Louisiana werewolf pack. When I was nine years old, my father had claimed me weak and soft. He and his comrades took me to Louisiana to show me what happens to the weak. They'd had no plan in mind, but when my father found the young werewolf too far away from his pack, he'd quickly come up with a sickening idea. They'd tortured that boy while the crickets chirped in the bayou. He'd pleaded and begged for his life as they laughed. When his soft brown eyes had met mine with a plea for help I couldn't give him, I'd humiliated my father even more by retching in the underbrush. Now, that boy stood in front of me with accusation in his eyes.

chapter ten

Austin steered me around the boy. "He's not real. Keep your feet moving."

I followed behind Austin, as the boy trailed behind me. His anger washed over me. Finally, I turned around. "I'm sorry."

He mouthed the words, "Are you?"

"Yes, yes, I am. I was nine. Nine. They were the most powerful demons in the world. What could I have done but join you in death?" My voice cracked. "I was a child."

Austin gripped my arm. "Shh. You're okay. There is no reasoning with these beings. They are not who they once were. We cannot talk to all of them without losing our minds. Keep moving."

All of what beings? My eyes whipped off of the boy's face to take a look around. We were surrounded by souls. Some I recognized, others I did not.

"Who are all of these souls?"

"I'm assuming," Austin said, steering us around a woman in her early thirties who glared at him while she

85

mouthed words we could not hear, "they are all people we have ended or have witnessed their death firsthand."

"Why are they so real? Why are they not like the souls who chased us?"

"Again just an assumption, but I believe these souls died in violence. It seems like they are locked into this state. Perhaps our minds brought them here. I'm not sure."

After I recognized a young witch who had tried to take my life and ultimately it had cost her hers as she'd died at the end of my blade, I decided to keep my head down and let Austin lead me through wherever we were. "Who was that woman back there?"

"When I had just turned eighteen, I was approached by that woman. She wanted me to join her against the Lux. She wouldn't take no for an answer. She could tell I was powerful, and if I refused to join her, she could not allow me to join forces with the Lux, so she followed me one night. She tried to run me off the road, and instead I ran her off the road. She didn't survive."

I did a quick scan of the people crowding in on us. Yes, I knew half, but the other souls must be what haunted him at night. Austin acted as if they meant nothing to him, but I could tell he was just as affected. He was just better at hiding it. For both of us to be so young, there was a lot of dead bodies left in our wake. Remorse and grief made my steps heavier and heavier, as we headed away from the souls trailing in an angry mob behind us.

Austin gave my hand a tug. "What's done is done. If you allow their emotions to assault you, then you might as well lay down and give up. Keep moving."

"How are you doing it?"

"I have never taken a life when it wasn't self-defense. Yes, I have been forced to kill, and somewhere along the way, I have grown good at it. But when a life is lost, it is just that. A loss for everyone. I regret their death, but I don't regret surviving."

I nodded. "I've never attacked first, either."

His eyes darted to mine in shock. It was clear he didn't believe my words but they were true. I had never drawn first blood. It was pointless to try and convince him. It was clear what he thought of demons, and after all that's exactly what I was. Instead, I focused on putting one foot in front of the other.

I tried to shake off the feelings of despair, but the cries and resentment kept hitting me with every step I took. It felt as if days had gone by, and just when I thought I couldn't take it anymore, we had reached an exit gate. A demon's worst nightmare lay in front of me. A girl just couldn't catch a break.

chapter eleven

Dingy water flowed north to south.

"Tell me no."

"We have to. The banks of the river will be littered with souls that literally want a piece of our flesh."

I looked at his face that was still raw. If he had healing powers, it was evident they would be of no use to him here. We were at the mouth of the river, and it seemed if we planned on escaping the underworld, we would need to swim against the current.

"Demons hate water."

He gave a small smile. "Yeah, I know. But if we want out of here, we've got to get a move on it."

Finding my courage, I jumped into the murky river first. It was icy cold. Just another thing demons hated. Austin's T-shirt billowed around my legs, making it hard for me to swim. Floating in the water, I knotted the ends of his shirt around my waist. The water was dark. I couldn't see my legs, so I felt confident that neither could Austin. I began to relax and was startled to realize I didn't hate treading water. In fact once I figured out which way to move my arms and legs, I found myself enjoying the feel of the water sliding over me. Austin stood on the bank with a look of puzzlement on his face.

"You don't hate the water?"

"I'm just as confused as you, bud." With little grace, I cut through the water to the edge of the bank. "And look at me, hotcakes. Swimming and shirt." I groaned. "The only thing that would make this experience better is if I could legit cuss."

Austin mumbled under his breath as he kicked off his shoes and stripped out of his jeans. I turned my head, but not before I caught a glimpse of muscular thighs pushing off the bank to dive in the frigid water. Kicking with those sturdy, powerful legs, he swam past me. With one last sigh, I swam after him. Hours passed before we took a break. Austin grabbed hold of a root jutting out of the bank. Snagging me by the waist, he held us anchored there for enough time for me to realize I was exhausted and cold. My teeth chattered, and just before I pleaded with him to allow us to crawl up the bank and take a quick nap, he was barking orders.

"Break's over. Swim like your life depends on it."

So we did. I lost all track of time. After several breaks and hours later, we reached the mouth of the river. I unknotted Austin's shirt, so it would fully cover me before I exited the water. My legs felt rubbery as I climbed the bank. Austin stood in front of me, shameless in nothing but a pair of skin-tight, black boxers, and honestly with a body like that, why would he have any shame? His hands were on his hips, as he studied our surroundings. He acted as if we had just gone for a fun dip in a pool.

Meanwhile, my wet hair hung about my shoulders in clumps, and I was freaking exhausted. At this point, I would willingly battle some angry souls before I got back in the dirty, cold water.

I followed the barefoot Austin as he made his way up to a narrow trail. I didn't know how much time had passed, but I knew it was enough for my thick hair to completely dry. Austin's shirt clung to me with sweat. My feet were cut open from all the sharp rocks I trod upon. At first I'd tried to avoid them, but somewhere along the way, I stopped caring. Austin came to a stop in what I had hoped was to take a break, but then my senses became aware. In front of us was a massive rock wall with a gigantic stone at the base. What was behind that stone had me grinning from ear to ear.

He grabbed a hold of the stone and pushed. His back muscles strained, as the stone finally began to move. To be so strong without his powers was amazing. He moved the stone eight inches, but there was still no way for him to fit through it. The boulder hit a crevice in the wall and wouldn't budge any farther.

My powers were still not accessible, but I knew home when I smelled it. Beyond that boulder was level six of the underworld.

I hurried past Austin. "I think I can squeeze through."

"Yeah, but I can't."

Turning my face to the side, I narrowly made it through the opening. My powers once again came alive. I flashed a smile as I said, "Stick your arm through the opening."

Once his muscular arm crossed into my domain, I clasped onto it and teleported us both back into my chambers. I squealed with laughter as I spun in circles.

"We did it! I have my shell. No more souls are chasing us. We did it. We really did." I stopped spinning once I realized Austin wasn't sharing in my excitement.

"You could have left me," he said in astonishment.

"Um, yeah, but I didn't and we're out." He crossed his arms over his muscular chest, as his blue eyes squinted at me. Was he angry? "You're right. I could have, and I probably should have, but you know what they say about hindsight being twenty-twenty, and you should have taken the time to read the stupid book. I guess we both screwed up."

"I don't like things that don't add up."

I might have been the queen of crazy, but I had met my quota of the day. I patted his masterpiece of a chest. "Okay, big fella. You don't want to celebrate then we won't. But I have got to see what mama looks like." I waved a hand in front of my body. "Stay or go, it's up to you, and before you lecture me on vanity again, I'm the Queen of foxing Demons, if I wasn't vain, something would be wrong."

Well, more wrong. I straightened his grungy T-shirt that was still slightly damp from my sweat and had dirt stains on it, trying to look as queenly as I could while I marched into my chambers. I wasn't going to let him steal my thunder. I had my shell and just survived a place that only Death, that handsome devil, could go. I was totally slaying queenhood.

chapter twelve

I stumbled in front of the mirror, gazing at my reflection. I had forgotten what my actual shell looked like. To be fair, I hadn't finished growing when it had been stripped from me. I studied myself in the mirror. My silky hair flowed past my waist in jet black waves. My eyes were the color of grey smoke, and they tilted just slightly upwards at the corners, giving me an exotic look. I pulled my full, ruby lips open with my fingers like a vet would do to a dog to see perfectly straight teeth. Small waist and enough boob to make up for that time I had to be in a man's body for a whole six months. Even being dirty and gross from the day's events didn't detract from the package. I was gorgeous, but more importantly I felt the power running through my veins. I would be unstoppable. Austin came up behind me and stared at my reflection.

I gave him a nod. "I know, right? If this was tinder and I was a guy, I would so swipe to the right."

I expected him to laugh, but he ran a hand over his face and shook his head before gruffly saying, "I've done my part. I retrieved your, um …" His blue eyes raked my body. "Your original form, and now you need to hold up your end of the bargain. We need to go after the key."

"Whoa, cowboy. Can't a girl have a second to enjoy her accomplishments? Do you have any clue how long I've waited for this moment? Let's put it this way. I couldn't even remember what I looked like."

He took two steps closer to me, putting his face over my shoulder, and as we both looked at each other's reflections in the mirror, I tried to figure out what had come over him. "You've ogled yourself for long enough. Now, we had a deal, and I would like to start right away."

Wow. It was almost like he was angry I'd gotten my body back. My shoulder brushed his chest, and I slowly turned around. I was small in my original form. Five feet three, so I had to tilt my head all the way back just so I could meet his eyes.

"I never said I was backing out of our deal. I just don't understand what the hurry is."

"Are you being serious?" He sounded disgusted, as he glared back down at me. "Of course, you're being serious. You're a demon. How else would you respond? There is a hurry to find the key, so that you know … earth freaking survives."

I arched a brow at his tone. Obviously, something had happened back in the maze, but I wouldn't ask questions because I was a Demon Queen and didn't care about someone else's tedious emotions. "For the earth to collapse, all forty-nine portals would have to be open, letting all of the banned Degenerates come back over. The Degenerates that are currently on earth don't have all the keys in their possession, so yes, they could open a few portals, and that would cause damage to earth, but not total destruction. Let's not be dramatic. Also, you're correct. I am a demon, but I'm also a queen, and I don't like the way you talk to me. Watch your tone or else."

Something flashed in his eyes before he gathered me in his arms in an … embrace? It was almost if he were about to kiss me. Confused, I tried to pull back from him, but then everything blurred. My stomach rolled, as a wave of nausea hit me. I blinked at my surroundings. He was still holding onto me as I realized exactly what the most strikingly handsome man in the world was. Dang, it! I was screwed, and by the smile on his face, he knew it, too.

He still hadn't released me, and I was thankful for the extra body heat. I would have to say being in the middle of nowhere in Alaska was a drastic change from the climate I was used to. I was freezing.

I glared at my captor. "Well, you have my attention. Can I have my power back now?"

He chuckled. "I wondered if you realized."

"That I'm without power? I'm not an idiot, you moron. Of course, I noticed. So, you can undo witch spells, teleport, big whoopee by the way, and you can obviously eliminate powers. Anything else I need to know about?"

He just shrugged. I fumed. How dare he transport me somewhere without my permission and strip me of my powers? That was unforgivable. My father had done that once, and I'd be danged if I let someone else take them again.

"You do realize my father did this very thing to me. He stripped me from my powers after years of tormenting me, freezing me in time capsules, and killing anyone who ever meant anything to me. Now, you are doing the exact same thing without even thinking."

"You need to understand what I'm capable of."

One day soon, he would know what I was equally capable of. I would have to kill him for this. Right after I kept my vow. Until then, I would play nice.

"So, can you only eliminate someone's powers by touching them?"

"Yes."

"And you have to remain in contact with them to eliminate their powers?"

"No."

Then why the hey was he still holding onto me? "Why are we here?"

"To get your attention. You might be the Queen of Demons, and you might be able to toss your authority onto everyone, but not me. There are several supernaturals out there that are no longer supernaturals because I have stripped them of their powers. I've dropped them off in places similar to these to teach them a lesson. They must figure out how to survive just like humans. Most don't make it. So before you try to hold your title over me again, remember this. Remember what I am capable of."

There was a tiny bead of sweat forming at his hairline. I was surprised it didn't freeze in this cold weather. Wait a minute. "It pains you to take my power, doesn't it?"

His eyes narrowed. "Why would you say that?"

"Answering a question with a question is basic deflection 101, buddy." I knew because I mastered the class.

He gave another shrug, letting me know I would not be getting anywhere in this conversation. The good news was at least it hurt him to rob me. I dropped my head to stare at his chest. Yep, he was a dead man walking. He just didn't know it yet. I would bury him in the pits of the underworld. Or maybe I would mount his head in my chambers, so everyone who came in would see the handsome beast I slew. It would be a reminder that no one threatened me and got away with it.

Austin wrapped his hand around my hair and gave a gentle tug, forcing me to yet again meet his gaze. His eyes traveled all over my face before he gave a bark of laughter. "There for a second, I thought you had feelings, and I had actually hurt them, but you're contemplating my murder right now, aren't you?"

I felt a smile start to come upon my face, causing his eyes to drop momentarily to my lips. "No. I would never have such evil thoughts, but just in case you do happen to expire, what would you like written on your gravestone?"

Whatever I expected from him, laughter was not one of them. "You've made a vow to help me with the key, so I should be safe until then at least."

In a rush, I felt my power returning to my body and soothing every part of me. Within seconds, it was like I could breathe again, but before I could say anything to him, everything blurred. When I teleported, it was easy for me and the others I brought with me. It was like we became part of the air, existing even if you didn't see us.

Austin's teleporting skills left something to be desired. It was like riding a rollercoaster running off of its tracks. He deposited me right outside of my chambers and took his sweet time releasing me. I could tell he enjoyed my discomfort because the more I wiggled the more he smiled. It wasn't that I didn't like being held by a gorgeous male, because who wouldn't? It was more the fact that we had just laid down the battleground rules and we were opponents.

"Gah," I gasped. "I wonder if all the ladies find your skills as lacking as I do."

"I've never had any complaints."

Good to see he was still cocky as ever. We both knew only one of us would survive after finding the key, and I aimed for that someone to be me. If he took my powers from me, he might as well drive a blade through my heart. It was the same thing in my opinion. My eyes roamed over Austin, assessing him. To be so masculine, and yet to move with the precision and grace of a panther, was a gift in itself. I was certain his stunning good looks helped out on more than one occasion, especially if you paired it with that sexy smile he handed out like tokens of gratitude to unsuspecting strangers. I was not susceptible to a handsome face, though. That in itself put the ball in my court. I bet Austin believed in dignity and in a fair fight, so that was an advantage I had on him. I fought dirty.

I wondered why he hadn't revealed his powers before he retrieved my shell. I assumed it was so our deal would be set in concrete. Maybe he thought I would rather not retrieve my body than to have to fight to survive later on. He would have been wrong. If I had known about his abilities prior to the enchanted maze, I wouldn't have made an attempt on his life. I was convinced he was the only one who could have given me back my shell. My eyes slowly traveled back up his body until they met his blue eyes, twinkling with suppressed laughter.

"Well, Queen, do you find me a formidable opponent?"

Gah, he was hot. I pursed my lips and tapped my chin like I was thinking. "I really find you lacking."

His eyes narrowed a fraction. I hid my smile as I slid past him and through my chamber door. I needed to change out of this grungy T-shirt, but first I had to say hey to my bug. I tried my best not to skip as I headed towards the main area that was large enough for parties. The area where I entertained none of my guests, but it was on my to-do list. Make friends and then entertain them. No, who was I kidding? That sounded like it would take way too much energy. Besides, demons didn't have friends; they were a weakness. But enemies I could do. The first being I saw was Sarah, who was still tied up and glaring, along with the fairy who was currently reading a magazine on my velvet couch.

With a flick of my wrist, I released Sarah from her bindings. Not noticing me, she immediately started spewing all kinds of derogatory things towards the Demon Queen. Tally put his magazine down quickly, realizing this was where the real amusement was.

"Where is she?" Sarah screeched.

I gave her a little finger wave. "Yoo-hoo! Mary, it's me."

At first she didn't recognize me, but when it dawned on her who I was, her fists balled to her sides as she tilted her head back, and better than any four-year-old I'd ever seen screamed, "Sarah. My name is freaking Sarah!"

My brows knitted. "Are you sure? Because you look like a Mary."

"Austin! Why are you in your boxers?"

I glanced over my shoulder to see him standing in his half-naked glory. Seriously, why? Couldn't he have taken two seconds to throw on some sweats?

"And why is she wearing your shirt?" Without waiting for an answer, she made a leap for me.

Stupid girl. Lucky for her, her boyfriend was there to intercept her.

He gave her a stern look before he glared at me. "Cut it out. You know what her name is."

I gave him an innocent, wide-eyed look that said, "Do I?" but he wasn't buying it. Sarah looked like one of those women from the show Snapped. Any minute something was going to push her over the ledge into insanity. Oh, how I hoped it was me behind the pushing.

Austin turned his back, and for the first time I noticed a tattoo on his shoulder blade. Gah, as if he needed to get any hotter. I tried to read the small writing, but he must have felt my eyes on him. He glanced over his shoulder at me. His eyes narrowed. Well, if he didn't want me looking at him, he probably should have put some clothes on.

I raised my hands in surrender. "Easy tiger. Just checking out the tat."

"What?" He sounded pissed. "Of course you were. And what do you think of it?"

Someone was a little sensitive about their ink job. Jeez. I pretended like I didn't hear his demanding, snappy questions. Like I needed to explain myself. Hello, freaks. Demon Queen here. When he realized I wasn't going to provide an answer, he pulled his girlfriend into a corner to have a little pow-wow with the psycho.

Tally flew over to me, hovering about an inch in front of my face. "Wowzer."

I winked. "I know, right?" I tugged on the hem of Austin's shirt. "At first I was worried that my original shell hadn't grown while being held captive." It would totally suck to have the mentality of a nineteen-year-old but stuck in an eight-year-old body, but thankfully that wasn't the case.

"I completely understand," Tally said before he flew a circle around the room, so he could listen to the lovebirds bicker. Gah, the fairy was such a gossip. I personally loved it. If you couldn't sit down next to me and talk mad trash about someone, we just couldn't be friends. "So, Sarah over there looks like she is about to lose her mind. I think she's even more upset that you came back in this body, and her boy can't seem to take his eyes off of you."

I looked over at the arguing couple. "No, I think you're mistaken."

"She just asked her boyfriend if he thought you were hot, and he stumbled over his words."

Did she? Had he? I hadn't heard. I shrugged, showing indifference. I mean, who cared if the sexiest man alive thought I was hot? As soon as I found the key, I was going to have to kill him. Whoops. I might have voiced that out loud.

Tally pointed a finger at my nose. "You're toeing the line between good and evil all ready, and you want to go and commit a murder? Don't you think that'll put you in the evil column? Tell me, Queen, what was the exterior color of your shell?"

Huh? "Um, it was half black and half white."

He nodded. "Of course it was, because you're equal parts good and bad. It's like ying and yang. You have created a balance within yourself. The first demon to ever do so, might I add."

As interesting as that was, I didn't want to talk about my good side, if I had one. I snatched him out of the air, careful not to damage his wings. I walked over to the fireplace, trying to give the arguing couple their space. Plus, seeing Austin trying to calm down his girlfriend left me feeling yucky. I was scared I would start gagging, and then everyone would be glaring at me again.

Sitting in a nearby armchair, I dropped Tally on my lap. "I don't have time for a session right now, doc. All I know is that man"—with the glistening abs—"over there plans on taking my powers from me the moment we succeed in finding the key. Just like dear ol' dad did. I can't let that happen. Not again. I've killed before."

"In self-defense." Tally rubbed a hand over his face. "Has it crossed your mind that maybe his prejudice against you is because it's hard to find a living demon that has an ounce of good in them?" He nodded at me. "Seriously, have a good think about it. Being the Queen of Demons, can you name one of your subjects that has a shred of decency?"

No, I couldn't, and he could tell that by my sour expression.

"Right, so wouldn't you say he is basing his opinion off of what has always been? Maybe instead of plotting his death, you should try and convince him there is good in you."

"No way. I see what you're throwing down, but I'm not picking it up. And you better watch that 'good' talk. That could cause a mutiny. What are you trying to do? Get me beheaded? Besides, I currently don't have time to convince someone not to judge me. I have elaborate parties and stuff I'm going to start throwing. Be all social and shirt. I think it would be easier just to let him swim with the fishes. As another great queen said, 'Off with their heads.' I think I'll follow suit."

Tally straightened his bow tie and then crossed his small muscular arms over his suit. "You will not let evil win. You will hold onto what good you have and it will prevail. Mark my words, you better not let your temper get the best of you."

Oh hey. He was annoying the crap out of me. He was like a walking, talking self-help book. I flicked him from my knee, where he hit a nearby couch. His face turned crimson from rage. With quick, angry jerks, he straightened his bow tie, as he dipped into his fae language that I didn't have to understand a word of to know he was cussing me for everything I was worth.

I shook a finger at him. "Now, now, Tally, you need to learn how to control that nasty temper of yours. Also, it's not fair that you can cuss but I can't, and I really miss cussing."

He flew over to the bar. "You could drive a good fairy to drink."

I snickered before I took one more look at Austin's yummy washboard stomach before he hid it with underserving cotton. Mortal enemies or not, I wasn't a nun. The couple was in the midst of arguing, but how Sarah didn't pout or frown when he put on his T-shirt showed more willpower than what I would have given him.

I went into my private chambers to take a quick shower while the lovebirds were still in a heated convo, and the fairy got lit. Fifteen glorious minutes later, I came back out with my hair wet and sweats on. My eyes darted to Austin, who had thrown on some pants as well. Good. I was hoping he would. No one enjoyed staring at a sculpted body that looked celestial. Kidding. Actually, the underworld could use him as a torturing device. Just put him sans shirt in front of naughty soccer moms, and he'd have women running amuck. Not me, though, because I was a queen. I cast one more nonchalant once-over at Austin's chiseled body, which the fabric did nothing to hide. When Tally caught my glimpse, his eyes narrowed in speculation, so I flipped him the bird. Judgmental ash-hole. I groaned as I sat back down in the chair I had earlier vacated to see nothing had changed since I'd left. Sarah still wailed about the injustices of life. Five minutes later, I looked over to find Tally floating face down in a shot glass. Good times.

Finally after another few minutes of arguing, Mr. and Mrs. America decided to call a halt to the bickering. Yay, for the ones who were unfortunately blessed with ears.

Austin and Sarah sat on the couch side by side, both appearing angry at the world. Austin reached out to put a hand on Sarah's knee, and she immediately swatted it off. Uh-oh, trouble in paradise.

Tally dipped and bobbed as he came over to my chair, smelling like a bottle of whiskey.

"Jeez, Tally, how much did you have?"

"Jest a whittle itty bit. Not even"—he hiccupped—"a teaspoon."

Lightweight. He flew around in dizzying circles. One of his wings wasn't beating in synch with the other. I plucked him out of the air and sat him next to me. "Sit down before you get hurt."

He crawled over my hip and sprawled on my thigh, gazing up at me like he would the stars. "See. Told you." Another hiccup. "Evil Demon Queen, my booty."

I grinned down at him. Of course the bowtie-wearing therapist would say, "booty." I glanced over at the too quiet couple. Austin stared at me with a strange expression on his face, and Sarah shot daggers at her boyfriend's profile.

"So," I said, giving Austin a pointed look. "I'm assuming you know where the key is or at least the general vicinity? Or will this be like an ongoing scavenger hunt?"

That got Sarah's attention. Her gaze swiveled to me, as her boyfriend said, "I don't know as of yet." Sarah's shoulders sagged, a look of relief crossing her face. More than just a little bit was off with this couple. "It's been a long day. We'll discuss a plan tomorrow morning."

I watched him as he slowly stood. Interesting. But then again, I'd been saying that a lot about this man. He just lied to me. Surely, he would know no matter how strong his powers were, the Queen of Demons in her true form could sniff out a lie no matter how well delivered.

His whole posture screamed he knew precisely where that key was, but why he didn't want to say was beyond me. I would kill him now, but a vow was a contract. One if broken could forfeit my life. My fingers tapped on the armchair, as I bade them a goodnight. They would sleep in one of my guest bedrooms. Together. My stomach rolled with an emotion I refused to identify as I watched them walk out of the room.

Not wanting to focus on unnecessary emotions, I concentrated on my feet. Yeah, they were tiny little things, and the second toe was freakishly larger than the big toe, but they were my feet. I wiggled my toes with glee. I still couldn't believe I was in my own shell. If I kept a journal like Tally had begged me to do, I would write in really girly handwriting with extra loops that this was the best day ever. Who'd have thought I would ever get my body back? I knew for certain why my father had confiscated it now. The power strumming through me almost made me giddy. He had every right to be terrified one day I would overthrow him. Maybe if he'd given me hugs or words of encouragement instead of nightly beatings, we wouldn't be here right now. Regardless, I would never be weak again. I could protect myself now.

I squeezed my eyes tightly shut. What was I doing? This wasn't how a queen, much less a Demon Queen, acted. We didn't long for affection or pretty words. We were supposed to be all snarls and deadly weapons. Ugh. This was why I needed a therapist. Too bad the one who had shoved his way into my life was now drooling on my thigh, and he wasn't here to try and help me with my weakness, but to exploit it. He wanted me to dig deep and find the good in myself and then put it on display. Ugh. No thanks. I didn't need to think of my feelings, and why I was feeling this way. I needed to bury that shirt. Deep. He was going to be so disappointed in me when I had to kill the Power Eliminator. Maybe I would be disappointed, too, but I would fake it. The warmth from the fire made me yawn. It had been a long day. I was just about to doze off when the sound of someone tip-toeing woke me.

I opened one eye to see Austin heading for the couch. One corner of his lips lifted.

"I'm going to sleep here tonight."

I closed my eye. "I didn't ask."

I could smell his scent from here. The smell of warmth and sunshine made me feel even more relaxed. Turning my face toward the fire, I wondered why anything about my enemy would make me feel safe, especially when there was something not quite adding up about him. From the moment he saw me in my true form, something in the atmosphere changed. My mind turned with possibilities, and just as soon as I latched onto something that could be of importance, sleep dragged me under.

chapter thirteen

The three of us slept all night by the roaring fire. It was the best sleep I'd gotten since I was eight years old. After my body had been stripped from me, it was almost uncomfortable to sleep. Being in someone else's body was like going into someone else's home. You used all the amenities, but it just wasn't the same as sleeping in your own bed or taking a hot shower in your own bathroom, but last night was different. I got a full eight hours of magnificent slumber and might have slept more if it hadn't been for Sarah and her loud screeching.

I awoke when she slapped me across my face. "You nasty, dirty whore!"

Um … what? She reared back a hand to slap me again when I disappeared to reappear right behind her. A trick I could do when I didn't have my shell, but with my shell, I was so much faster. In the blink of an eye, I had her back pressed into my chest and an arm around her throat. Austin jumped to his feet. His hair was tousled from sleep, and his eyes darted back and forth from his precious girlfriend to me.

"If you ever touch me again, I will kill you. I don't know what I ever did to deserve your wrath, nor do I care, but hear me now, the next time you lay a hand on me will be your last. Do you understand?"

When she didn't answer, I tightened my grip until she gurgled, "Yes."

I let her go, and she ran, stumbling to her boyfriend. She threw her arms around his middle. "When you didn't come back to bed last night I thought … I thought you and that demon …"

It took Austin a minute before he wrapped his arms around her stiffly to return the hug. When he patted her back, it seemed like he was just going through the motions. I glanced over at Tally, who must've woken up early this morning because he was looking as fresh as a daisy in his powder-blue suit. He skipped the bow tie today and sipped coffee through a straw, as he studied the couple before us. Obviously, they had issues, but I didn't see him scribbling things on his yellow notepad about them. Which reminded me, he left those in my desk drawer. I needed to get out of this room before I murdered Sarah. I could excuse myself and go see what he wrote about me. It would give me a better understanding of how far I'd come and how far I'd yet to go. Or if I was totally unfixable. Leaving the awkward couple, I headed towards my office. Rifling through the drawers, I came across three legal pads. What. The. Heaven. Was. Going. On?

"Tally! A word please."

The fairy flew into my office. "You know something is really off with those two. I haven't figured it out yet, but when I do—" He stopped talking when he saw what I held. "Hey! Those are confidential."

"Hmm. Sure. Can you tell me why you drew various cartoon characters on these notepads from SpongeBob Square Pants to"—I flipped the pages—"Mickey Mouse and friends?"

He gave a little shrug. "I'm not a real therapist."

"You think?" My voice somehow managed to remain calm. "So, Ariana and the Fae King sent you here to help me work out the kinks, and you're not even legit? Unbelievable."

I was beyond mad. I couldn't believe this little twerp came into my domain and lied to me.

"First of all, I never said I was a therapist." He was right; I just assumed. "I might have compared myself to one, but if you think back, it was you who came to that conclusion." His hands landed on his narrow hips. "And who said I'm not helping you work out the kinks? I might not be certified, but I'm damn good at what I do."

I held up a picture of Goofy. "Yep, you totally missed your calling."

"Is this really necessary right now? We have bigger issues."

"Like how I'm trying not to murder you?"

He landed on my desk, where he began to pace. "No, like those two in there. Something is totally off. It's not just a lover's quarrel, and now we're off to find the key with them?"

A voice cleared from the doorway. Both Tally and I jerked our head towards the intrusion. There stood Austin, leaning in the doorjamb, looking like an ice cream cone. The kind that was so good it had all the kids racing after the ice cream truck just for a lick. He stared at me with a smirk on his face. He knew how good looking he was. Dang him.

"You're right. I say we kill him now."

The smirk dropped. Mission accomplished. He strolled into my office without an invite. "Couldn't help but overhear that last comment. My relationship with Sarah is none of your business." He was looking at me when he said that, which was so unfair because it was the freaking fairy who had been gossiping.

I held up both hands. "Hey, bud, I couldn't give a rip. I could not care less about whatever craziness it is that is going on between the both of you, as long as it doesn't affect me. And as long as your girlfriend remembers to keep her hands to herself, then we shouldn't have a problem."

The Fairy held up a hand. "I'm sorry the queen was concerned about your relationship. I'll have a word with her, and it won't happen again."

Wait. What? I started to flick the pest across the room but he was learning. Dang him, too. He flew over to a bookcase and stuck his tongue out. Real mature that one, and some higher up thought he could help me? That was hilarious.

"Also, none of our business, you say? You know what would help? If you would discuss all of your non-problems somewhere more private. Now, if we're done with this, would you mind if we start discussing the key? Last night, you were raring to go. Let's get back to that kind of motivation. The sooner we find it, the sooner I can get rid of you." I gave him a wink, trying to amplify that last part, just in case he didn't understand my real meaning. He gave me a grin, as his eyes raked over my body. Nope, he understood what I implied, and from the gleam in his eye, I would say he was happy to accept the challenge. Good, the gauntlet had been thrown. The lines drawn. Now, I just had to stay ahead of the eight ball and come up with a plan that would make sure I kept my body.

Austin's arms made a sweep, as he executed a mocking bow. "Your highness, if you would please come back into the living quarters, so we can discuss the key?"

Tally laughed, and I threw his pad with cartoon drawings at him because I can be mature, too. I really should be madder at Tally but I wasn't. I probably did jump to conclusions, and the truth was Tally had helped me more than probably he even realized. My anxiety had lessened since he came into my life. Tally settled down on the edge of my desk and reading my emotions, gave me a salute. Austin walked towards me and extended a hand to help me up from my seat like I had seen him do for Sarah. I stared at his outstretched hand like it was a viper. I stood up without his aid and skirted around him. His laughter followed closely on my heels. That was super weird.

After we all found a seat in the living room, I asked Austin, "So, where do you think this key is?"

Sarah started fidgeting with her sweater sleeves, casting glances at the rest of us. Austin reclined into the couch cushions, where he put an arm around Sarah. His fingers mechanically trailed up and down her arm. "I believe the witch community currently has it."

My eyebrows rose at his statement. That's it? Surely, he had more to go on than this.

"I've got it narrowed down to a couple of covens," he said.

Sarah crossed her legs and then re-crossed them. She scooted back farther into the couch. She was clearly uncomfortable, but Austin's lazy hand motions never stopped caressing her arm. He stroked her like he was petting a cat, never noticing this particular long-tailed cat looked like she was in a room full of rocking chairs. Tally had his typical thinking face on. His forehead was lined with a few wrinkles, as he assessed the situation.

What in the ever-loving hey was going on? Finally, Sarah broke the silence. "I think I might know where the key is."

Austin's face registered shock. "You do?"

I hid my smile as his words rang untrue. I needed a margarita and a bowl of popcorn. I wasn't entirely sure what was happening, but I had a feeling it was going to be entertaining.

Sarah bit her lip, and just the right amount of water filled her eyes. "My sister has been talking about the key recently. More and more. I think her coven has it in their possession." She reached out a hand and placed it across Austin's heart. I knew I should have popped popcorn. "I wanted to tell you, cuddle bear, but she made me swear to secrecy."

Austin nodded in understanding, but his eyes conveyed something completely different. He looked like a hunter stalking his prey. "Can you give me more details?"

She shrugged. "Just that her coven has it. I don't see why it matters, though."

Surely, she couldn't be that stupid. Tally cleared his throat, but before he could say anything, I gave him a subtle shake of my head. I was dying to see where this was going between Barbie and Ken. Could the Dreamhouse be collapsing? What would Skipper do? She'd need therapy from a fake therapist just like me. I folded my legs up underneath me and leaned forward. My eyes darted back and forth between the lovebirds. I felt like I was watching the Titanic right before it hit the iceberg.

She rested her head on his chest. "I mean, who cares?"

Austin's voice was monotone, but he tensed like a tightly coiled spring. "Your sister and her friends, do they plan on opening the portals soon?"

"I think she's already had a trial run. The other day on the phone she had mentioned something about The Battery. She just bought a house close to the portal for the convenience, and she might be having another get-together tonight, but again, who cares?"

Tally huffed. "I can't take it anymore. Sarah, you know your boyfriend is looking for the key. You were in the room when Carmen and Austin made a deal to find the key, so I'm not entirely sure why you keep saying who cares. Obviously, everyone in this room should care."

Sarah cocked her head to the side like a golden retriever.

"Tally, don't bother. You've lost her somewhere in the translation, which seems pretty easy to do." Against my better judgement, I found myself asking Sarah, "Are you saying you don't care if your sister and her little witch friends open portals and simultaneously let hordes of evil supernatural beings over?"

Her eyes flashed to me. "Oh, please, like you have some sort of moral compass. Besides, my sister is one of the smartest witches there is, and she has a plan to bespell everyone she chooses to allow over. They will all be her slaves. She will be the most powerful witch ever to have lived."

Tally rolled his eyes at the stupidity of her words. "And yet she has let you out of her sight."

He had a point. I would never let Sarah know anything I wished to keep a secret. The second she was riled, which seemed to be all the time, she would spew loads of info.

I made eye contact with Austin. As we stared at each other, I realized two things. One, he had chosen Sarah to be his girlfriend for a reason, and love at first sight wasn't it, and two, he was way more conniving than even I realized. What an endearing quality. Good for him. The only one in this room who didn't know this yet was poor Sarah, who was currently drawing little hearts on his chest with her finger. Ugh. Gag city. As she whispered something to her "cuddle bear," I decided I couldn't take it anymore.

"Oh, for crying out loud. What is the point of this? Did you seriously date Mary over there for how long, Mare?"

Sarah's head popped up from Austin's chest. "Three weeks," she snapped, "and we're in love."

"Um. Sure." I looked at Tally. "Three weeks and he was already promoted to cuddle bear. Can you imagine what he'd be called if this sick rendition went on much longer? Snooky ookums or honey cake, perhaps?" I dry heaved a little. "Anyways, wasn't there an easier way to extract information than this ..." I gestured, pointing at both Austin and Sarah. "Maybe a slightly less nauseating way?"

"What are you suggesting?" Austin spat. "I would never beat a woman. I'm not a demon."

"I never suggested that, you son of a bench."

Poor Sarah glanced at us both with confusion. I stood up from my chair, and he stood up from the couch. The tension was thick as we both squared off at one another.

"I would personally rather have a stranger beat me to get information than have someone lie to me, use me, and trick me into falling in love with them."

"Like demons even know what love is!"

"You know I have loved. I loved my mother dearly. You saw it first hand down in that cave, but go ahead spew your hate. You couldn't possibly make yourself look any more judgemental."

Sarah stood up and shouted, "Can someone please tell me what is going on?"

Tally said, "You've been scammed, buttercup. Your cuddle bear used you to get information about the key."

Tally gave me a wink, and I couldn't help but grin. I had to be careful, or I'd get used to having him around.

When Sarah started gasping like a fish out of water, Tally shooed me out of the room. I begrudgingly headed to my office and shut the door. There was so much drama happening, and I was missing out. Things were about to get ugly, and as much as I despised Sarah, I really didn't want to sit in another room while I listened to her wailing. I wanted a front-row seat. Up close and personal. I wanted her tears to hit me. I smiled to myself. Yep, I was definitely evil. An earth-shattering shriek from the other room had me squinting. Three weeks they were together, but she sounded like her world was falling apart. That I didn't understand. Yeah, Austin was out of this world hot, but three weeks? Come on.

I shuddered as a crash sounded in the living room area. If Austin wasn't so high and mighty, he could have asked us for help. We could have figured out a way to get the answers he'd needed from Sarah, and she wouldn't be breaking my personal belongings right now.

Tally lay on my couch. "I haven't seen this much drama since the Fae Prince stole the key right from under his grandfather's nose."

"Hmm." I wasn't really listening. Everything had grown quiet, and that made me even more nervous.

There was a brief knock on the door before Austin let himself in minus Sarah. He had red scratches on his face that healed in front of my eyes. Add that to his bag of tricks. I sat there with my eyebrows arched in question, waiting for him to tell us why Sarah had grown so quiet.

He crossed his arms over his chest. "I teleported Sarah to a Caribbean island. I gave her enough cash for the night and then put a sleeping spell on her, but soon she'll wake up and contact her sister, and then we won't have the element of surprise, so we need to head out now."

"It didn't cross your mind to have her stay here in a dungeon, so her sister wouldn't be privy to our plans?"

He scoffed. "You would have left her here unchaperoned with demons?"

"Whatever you say, cuddle bear."

Tally coughed into his hand to hide his laughter. Austin glared at me. I held up both hands. "Hey, I would think that if retrieving the key is as big of a deal to you as you say it is, then you wouldn't have: one, took the time out to coddle a woman into believing that she can share information with you; and two, let her escape knowing dang well she is going to alert her sister. All I'm saying is that makes no sense."

"I hadn't planned on telling her I was using her. By the way, thanks to both of you, my plan was ruined. I was going to escort us right to her sister."

"Ahh." I nodded in appreciation. "Trojan horse style. Yeah, that would've worked."

"Is that an apology?"

"Eww. Yeah, I'm not really good at those. But I am really good at deflecting and manipulation, so what I can say is this is your fault. You should have shared your plans with us, so we didn't ruin them. But we forgive you."

I thought Austin was about to blow. I snickered as he looked down to the ground, like he was trying out a new meditation pose.

Tally flew over to my shoulder. "She does have a point."

If Tally kept this up, I was going to insist we get matching B.F.F. tattoos.

Austin's blue eyes narrowed. "None of this really matters." He held up his hands and made quotations.

"Oh, but 'the evilest being in the world' vowed to me she would retrieve the key for me. I do not worry about who is alerted."

He was mocking me. Obviously, someone doubted my evil ranking. Ignoring him, I asked Tally, "Did you hear the title he bestowed upon me?" I fanned myself. "Aww. He likes me. Really likes me."

"We leave in ten. I'll be waiting in the living room," Austin said, right before he slammed my door.

"Evilest being in the world?" Tally squinted at me. "There was such shade in that comment, and I'm guessing he doesn't even know you rescued a kitten."

"Shut it, bug."

Ten minutes my perfect little butt. I headed to the bathroom to take a shower. This time a long one, just because I didn't like taking orders. As I climbed into a leather outfit that I thought would suit my new frame better, I made a promise to myself I would find this stupid key soon and be back here reading in front of my fireplace in no time. Austin had looked at me with disgust because I was a demon. I was who I was, and he needed me to retrieve the key. Whatever he assumed me to be, I was going to try my hardest not to disappoint. In fact once the key was found, and he had no more use of me, at that moment, right before he stripped me of my powers, I would look him in the eye while I buried my dagger into him, so he could see how evil I could be up close and personal.

chapter fourteen

"You've got to be kidding me." I looked at the old houses that sat in a row in the historic downtown. They were all painted different colors. Guess that's where the name 'Rainbow Row' came from. I heard and smelled two rivers running on opposite sides of the peninsula. Hooves beat the pavement as a horse and carriage clamored down the street. The weather was excellent, even for a demon. "Charleston, South Carolina, is where the coven is?"

Austin shrugged. "What were you expecting?"

"I don't know. Detroit. Or New Jersey. Definitely not charming Charleston."

Tally snickered from my shoulder. "Remind me to work on you with your judgmental problems."

"Remind me to flick you."

I filled my lungs with the salty air. It helped with the dizziness Austin's teleporting brought. I would ask him if he had a plan, but since his last plan got thwarted, I thought it might be a touchy subject.

"Well, this is the house, but it doesn't seem like anyone is home," Austin said.

I studied the bright, buttery yellow house. He was right; no one was home, but there was a protection spell surrounding the house. I could feel the energy pulsating off it.

"So, I say we hang back. Maybe later tonight, we go to The Battery to see if there is any action."

Austin's face showed frustration. "Fine. I'll rent us a room somewhere close by, and then we will come back around dark."

Now, it was my turn to be disappointed. We were in sunny Charleston. The last thing I wanted to do was be stuck in a hotel for the next several hours. "I say we enjoy ourselves a little."

His blue eyes drilled holes into me. "What do you mean by enjoying ourselves?"

Oh, my gosh. For fifty seconds, you'd think he'd forget to quit hating on my imperfect demon self. "Oh, you know, just the normal, run-of-the-mill demon things, like torturing kindergarteners and only allowing grocery shoppers to have plastic instead of paper." I rolled my eyes. "Seriously? Chill. I was thinking we could hit a swimwear shop. Go jump in the ocean. You know, live a little."

Austin shot me a dumbfounded look. "Why? This isn't a vacation."

"You know as well as I do these witches aren't going to open a portal until way late, if they do it today at all. I mean, hello, civilians and all that. So, you do you, honey, and I'll do me. I'll meet you back here around dark-thirty."

I turned on my heel to walk away when an arm reached out and dragged me roughly to a stop. "No, I'm not letting you out of my sight."

Two emotions rushed through me. Anger that he grabbed my arm, and an emotion I'd rather not think about. There was no way I lusted after the enemy. No way.

"Tally, sweetheart? Can you go wait on the bench? Mommy and Daddy are about to have a domestic dispute."

Tally chuckled as he flew off my shoulder. Austin glared at me, and I innocently batted my eyelashes at him. I refused to be the first to speak. His eyes roamed my face and zeroed in on my lips.

Forgetting my vow of silence, I nervously said, "I'm going. We have time to kill. I've never been to the beach, much less in my own form, and I want to enjoy these next few hours. You know as well as I do these witches aren't going to open a portal in daylight. They'll wait until the city is sleeping, and then they will cast some kind of privacy spell around the park before opening a portal. We can't go storming into their house because they aren't even there, so we have to be patient. Plus, it'd be better to catch them in the act and then take the key. I'm going to the beach."

He nodded. "I didn't say you couldn't go. I just said you weren't leaving my side. I don't trust you."

"I gave you my word."

"Yeah, but how good is the word of a demon?"

"Low blow, ash-hat." I jerked my arm out of his grasp. "Not very good because if you grab me like that again, I'll kill you. There will be no retrieving the key, and for breaking my vow, I'll probably be sentenced to a fate worse than death, but I think it'll be worth it."

I heard his laughter as I strolled away from him. He must think his imminent death was funny, and they called me crazy.

Forty-five minutes later, I smiled from ear to ear. Austin had given me a black credit card and told me to do my worst. Obviously, Austin was making some money. I knew this was going to be a fantastic day when I saw a faux leather bathing suit hanging on the wall. I bought the cutest little cover-up, colorful beach towels, a cooler, and a bag for my crown, not because I was getting the strangest looks ever, but because I didn't want to get sand on it. I also purchased a couple of surprises for Austin. I changed in the waiting room and left what I originally wore in the dressing room. I had no need for leather pants while in sunny Charleston. I slid my new sundress on and took the tags up to the cashier. Twenty minutes later, I headed towards Folly Beach. I hid Tally, who was currently snoring in between bottles of water and a couple of peaches in the cooler.

Handing Austin the bag I had gotten for him, his hand grazed mine, and a wave of heat flicked up my body. His hand tightened on mine, as if he were equally affected by my touch before he asked, "What's this?"

Pretending not to be affected by the merest skin-to-skin contact, I shrugged. "It's for you if you decide you want to have a little fun for a couple of hours, and I used your money, so don't bother thanking me."

Without waiting for a reply, I headed towards the sand to stake a claim on some prime real estate as close to the water as I could get on the crowded beach. I needed some distance from the Power Eliminator. My mind screamed at my body. She was a traitorous bench.

After a few minutes, I noticed Austin had decided to partake in the fun. He sported his new bathing suit and lay on the new towel I got for him not too far from me. Not close enough to look like we came to the beach together, because heaven forbid, but close enough he could keep an eye on me because I was a good-for-nothing, trifling demon. Not that I would admit it to anyone in a million years, but I felt hurt he was so disgusted by who I truly was.

I didn't have time for silly emotions. I was at a beautiful beach with laughter all around me. The ocean rolled in, creating a pretty picture, seagulls flew up above, and children built sandcastles nearby. This was the happiest I'd been in a while. Maybe ever.

I leaned back on my elbows, as I dug my heels into the sand, loving the rough feel on my skin. I only had a few hours of beach time before it was back to securing the key. Then, unfortunately, I would have to kill Austin, or he would have to kill me, because I wasn't letting him take my powers without a fight, but I wasn't going to think about that right now. Not when my super hearing picked up on everything the group of boys down the beach said. They could almost make a girl blush. Almost. From the look on Austin's face, he could hear them as well, and he wasn't pleased by their locker room banter.

How could he possibly take them seriously? Human boys were comical. The pack of college boys threw a Frisbee like it was an Olympic sport. With every wild catch, they would immediately puff out their chest. I rolled my eyes. Silly boys, kill an elite guard of demons, then you can act like a peacock. That thought made me cast another glance at Austin. The human boys started slowly migrating closer and closer to my towel. Every once in a while, there was a bad throw, which was utterly intentional, sending the Frisbee flying towards me. One of the boys in a dramatic, heroic move would throw their frail bodies in front of me, trying to protect me from the flying disc. I could break all their bones with a flick of my wrist, and yet they attempted to protect this damsel from a plastic object. It was cute. Occasionally, they tried to strike up a conversation with me, but I wasn't interested in either of their games.

I studied Austin's profile, as he glared at the rowdy group. His jaw was clenched, and his eyes were narrowed at the young human male closest to me. Austin must have felt my gaze. His eyes held mine for a moment before he reclined back on his towel.

I buried my heels in the sand, as I thought of what emotion had briefly crossed his face. Possession? No, I must be losing my demon touch. Why would he send a possessive look my way? That made no sense. A little boy broke me out of my thoughts when he started crying because his sister jumped on his castle on purpose. In all fairness, his castle screamed underachiever, as it was just a mound of sand with one lone seashell on top. He wailed on and on about the unfairness of it all while his sister skipped back to her parents, who were two sheets to the wind, hiding under an umbrella.

I shot a quick look over to where Austin lay still on his back. He had his arms tucked behind his head, creating a pillow, and his eyes were closed, as he baked in the sun. His abs glistened, and they were on full display. I quietly climbed to my feet and made my way over to the small child. My only intention was to shut the kid up. He was ruining my first beach trip. It was not because his tears hurt something in my heart. That would have been super lame.

His sobs came to a stop as I loomed over him. He was probably having a "stranger, danger" moment, so I waited to see if he was going to kick me in my shins before running to his parents.

He wiped the snot from his nose. "She ruined it on purpose."

I plopped down beside him. "Yeah, siblings can be mean like that." I thought about my own brother who I had never been close with because Father made sure we didn't have a relationship. You'd think siblings would try and have each other's back. Mine tried to stab me in mine. I had more issues than Cosmo. I raked my hand over the squished mound of sand, making it level again. "You know, I've never built a castle. Maybe we could build one together?"

His brown eyes twinkled. "Really? Why have you never built one before?"

I shrugged, as I started packing sand into an empty cup that used to have alcohol in it from the smell of it. His parents must've given it to him to build with. "I don't know, buddy. My childhood was just different. I say we make up for it now, though, and build the best sandcastle ever."

His chubby cheeks squished together with a smile. "Okay. What do you want me to do?"

"Hmm. How about you pack the cups as tight as you can with sand, and I'll work on building us a moat around the castle?"

We had a good system going, and before I knew it, I had created a heck of a moat, if I did say so myself, complete with a sand alligator to guard the castle. Or as Parker said, "From meany sisters." While we built, Parker talked a mile a minute. I noticed his parents had taken in the situation and deemed me harmless. His mother had given me a friendly wave at one point. If she knew her four-year-old, cute-as-a-button son was building the world's best sandcastle with the most powerful demon ever to live, she probably would have had a stroke.

Two hours later and we were done. His parents came over to congratulate us and even asked to take a picture of the two of us in front of our masterpiece. I agreed after Parker begged. His sister pouted off to the side. Whether it was because she didn't help build the castle or if it was because she couldn't pounce on it with an audience, I wasn't sure.

After a few pictures, I reached out and touched one of Parker's cheeks. "You might need some more sunscreen, bud."

"Yes," his mom said, "and some dinner. You ready to go, sweetheart?"

I was completely shocked when Parker threw himself at me, wrapping his little arms around my sandy legs. "Thanks so much. I love you."

My heart swelled with some unidentifiable emotion. "Sure, buddy."

"Maybe I'll see you tomorrow."

"You never know."

He smiled big at me. "Bye, Carmen."

I watched them with remorse as they headed back to their umbrella, where they started to pack up their things. I was not going to miss that kid because that would be weak. The first step was to stop gazing at his little head. I did an about-face and headed towards the ocean to wash the sand off me. This was the first time I had ever been in the ocean. I smiled as the waves rolled over my ankles. I was really starting to enjoy water. I made a mental note not to let demons find out that tidbit. I was already different. What an exciting day this had been. I waded into the cold water. There was a sign warning us it was jellyfish season. Please. Jellyfish didn't want none of this. I dove into the water and started swimming with the current. There was a splash behind me, and I felt someone closing in on me. Great. One of the college boys was an Olympic swimmer. I stopped after a few more strokes to explain to them I wasn't interested, even though I was slightly impressed with their aquatic skills. Austin's head popped up in the water right next to me. Instead of treading water, I sent my wisps of smoke outward to keep me afloat.

Before I could ask what he was doing, he said, "You built a castle."

"Um, yeah. Is that against the law?"

"First, you come out and smile at all the couples holding hands then you built a castle with a kid."

Had I been smiling like a lunatic? "So what?" I snapped.

"So, that's not normal demon behavior."

My blood boiled. I was tired of people telling me I wasn't normal. Looking at me like I wasn't fit to rule. So what if I built a dang castle? My powers were muffled in the water, so very slowly my wisp snaked out and curled around his legs. He registered a moment of shock before they pulled him under. I was going to hold him under until I saw bubbles coming up. Normal demon. I'd show him. First, I couldn't be trusted because I was a disgusting demon, and then he sounded weirded out I wasn't what he constituted as a "normal" demon. There was no winning with this guy.

Strong arms jerked me below the surface. How had he gotten out of my wisps? We both came up sopping wet.

His arms locked around me, and I had hair in my eyes. "I'm sorry if that was rude."

"Why are you apologizing to me?" I asked. "I'm just a lowly demon."

"Are you?" Our wet bodies crushed against one another, and he held me tightly to his chest. His brow wrinkled, like he was trying to figure me out. "Carmen, I came into all of this with a mission. I am supposed to have a clear goal, but you make everything befuddled." Almost pained, he whispered, "What am I to do?"

He wasn't the only one confused. Why did I feel like he was talking about more than just finding the key? And why was he looking at me like he was trying to memorize everything about my face? He wet his lips and my stomach tightened. What was it about this guy that had my head spinning? Yeah, he was undeniably hot, but there was something else. It was a magnetic pull I felt towards him. I was trying to resist, but was losing the battle.

With one arm, he held me close, and the other raked a hand over my face, removing all the hair plastered against my cheek.

I let my head fall forward until my lips touched his, and for a moment I forgot this man had every intention of stealing my powers soon. I forgot he was my enemy. When my lips touched his for that very first second, he stilled, almost like he was afraid he would scare me away, and then his lips moved against mine with fervor. His hands tightened on my hips. The kiss quickly became hard. Demanding. Electricity jumped between us, jarring me enough to bring me to my senses.

The one person who was strong enough to strip me of my powers and leave my helpless, and I enjoyed his kiss. The fire in me dampened. What was I doing? How could I be so attracted to someone who planned on hurting me as bad as my own father had? And why was he kissing a lowly demon?

I pulled back slightly. "Do you usually willingly participate in a kiss by beings you hate so much?"

Triumph flooded through me when he winced at my words. When he didn't say anything and the silence seemed to engulf us both as we floated in the current I decided in that moment that no matter how hot Austin was I couldn't allow myself to fall for him. He could destroy me.

The thing about my natural form was it brimmed with power. Power I hadn't tried out yet, but I knew it was just right there under the surface. Maybe I needed to remind him of what this despicable demon was capable of. I placed both of my hands on either side of his face then I flooded his mind with images of him being trapped in a room while demons tore at his flesh. He jerked back from me. His jaw clenched, and his eyes told me he was fuming mad.

"Thanks for the reminder."

"Any time, cuddle bear."

I watched him as he swam back to shore. My heart did a funny little thing. Was that remorse? I groaned as I swam along the shoreline. I was like a sinking ship. I was taking on water, and it was just a matter of time before the whole thing capsized. I had to be better than this. Stronger than this. I was a queen, for fox's sake.

chapter fifteen

*A*fter my long swim, we had packed up our things quickly. Austin refused to make eye contact with me. Good. Didn't care. Tally was excited to be leaving, as he did not enjoy his time in the cooler. But the half-eaten fruit and bottle of wine told a different story. I was starting to think that my non-therapist was a slush.

I donned the cute little sundress over my bathing suit, and with Austin in a T-shirt and his swimming trunks, we looked like typical tourists strolling the streets. Tally was hidden in my cross-body bag, and was currently foxing benching about it. Apparently, it was undignified he had to hide. Austin was wary of me, but he was back to talking with me. Not that I cared. We killed time by going through the market square and admiring all of the craftsmen's items. I liked this city.

There weren't that many homeless loitering the streets, so the down-on-his-luck, older gentlemen begging for change outside of the market caught my attention. A woman dressed to the nines ignored him, as she walked in front of him with a group of her friends. He held up his hat, and she seemed offended the raggedy article of clothing was so near to her person; she swatted a hand at the man, calling him a few degrading names. He dropped his head in shame, as she carried on with her friends laughing at the audacity of the beggar.

Well, that wasn't very nice. I quickened my pace. In mere seconds, I found myself behind the snooty woman. She was talking about trading in her Tesla for the newer version. Not only was she rich, but she was flaunting it in front of her friends. I bumped into her hard. With one hand, I gripped her arm to steady her.

"Oh, my gosh, are you okay?" I asked. "How clumsy of me."

Her eyes traveled to my cheap sundress before she clucked her tongue in disgust. "Be more careful next time."

I nodded at the slightly older woman. "Yes, of course."

I walked back out of the market to where the beggar sat in the hot sun. I squatted down to his level. "Here you go, friend." I dumped my spoils into his hat. It was a wad of cash I had taken from the nasty woman's pocketbook.

The homeless man sputtered. "You … I don't … Why?"

I covered my hand over his. "Hey, you need this more than anyone I've seen today. Take it. Go get a warm meal and a quiet place to lay your head. Tomorrow is a new day and when the sun rises, remember not all is lost."

His eyes watered, and he quickly wiped a hand over his dirty face. "You're an angel."

"Nah. I'm a demon." I gave him a wink and he laughed.

I could feel Austin's eyes staring a hole into my back, so I didn't dare turn around to meet his gaze. Instead, I straightened and walked back into the market, as I heard Tally mumbling something inside of my purse.

"If I weren't a Demon Queen, I would seriously think about living here," I said. Tally scoffed from inside my purse, causing me to smile. "It's true. Sure, there was that one nasty lady with her group of rich ash-holes, but for the most part, the people are super nice. I can smell the salt from the ocean, and the breeze brings a waft of the beautiful azaleas planted everywhere. There's such a sense of peace here." I could also smell the scent of Austin who was directly behind me, but I didn't point that out.

I picked up a beautiful, handcrafted bracelet. Austin came up beside me and was so close his chest pressed into my shoulder. I did my best to act like his proximity didn't bother me.

He leaned down and whispered into my ear, sending shivers down my spine. "Did you just steal from that woman?" I gave a shrug, as I studied the bracelet. "I want to hear you say why."

I almost ignored him, but when I looked into his eyes, there was no condemnation or condescending on his part; he was truly curious, so I answered him honestly. "That man needed it more than her."

"Nothing is black or white with you other than your soul."

He was right. Even my shell was fifty percent black and fifty percent white.

"I have never met someone like you," Austin admitted.

I wasn't entirely sure he meant that as a compliment, but that was the way I was going to take it. "Thanks, cuddle bear."

I ran my finger over the light blue stone in the middle of the bracelet. The bracelet wasn't even real silver, and the jewels were as fake as the woman's boobs beside me, but something about it made me smile.

Austin looked at what held my attention. "That's nice."

"Yep, it's the color of your eyes." I couldn't believe I just said that out loud. Embarrassment flooded me. I quickly placed the bracelet back down on the merchant's table and headed to a different table away from Austin. Tally snorted, and I gripped my bag until my knuckles turned white. "Whatever your opinions are, bug," I ground out through my teeth, "you better keep them to yourself." I swung my purse violently, causing Tally to curse my name.

I strolled along the vendors, smiling at each one who tried to sell me something. The temperature was perfect, especially when the wind would blow a cool breeze. For the most part, the people were friendly, and the town had lots of history. Normally, I wasn't a fan of the past, but Charleston called to me.

Austin, who was always right on my heels, asked, "Why are you smiling? Thinking of murdering me in my sleep?"

I rolled my eyes. "When I take your life, it will be with you wide awake. I want you to have a front-row seat to the show."

His eyes twinkled with suppressed laughter. Either he wasn't taking me seriously, or he thought his impending doom was foreplay. Regardless, the rest of the day I made sure I kept a reasonable distance away from him, even though my mind often lingered on him, and that was never a good thing. He was the enemy, not a potential boyfriend.

When the sun finally made its retreat, we headed to the historical landmark called The Battery. We arrived a little early, so we staked ourselves out behind two different oak trees. Within two hours, my senses heightened, and power thrummed inside of me. The witches had arrived. Tally flew off my shoulder and settled on a branch above my head.

Being the Demon Queen, I could sense the witches' level of power. To say I was underwhelmed and unimpressed would have been an understatement. Sure, they had power, but please. Taking the key from them would be a piece of cake. Which made me wonder how they got a key in the first place. There was no way witches this weak just stumbled upon a key.

I glanced over at Austin, who must've been thinking the same thing, because he winked at me. I almost smiled until I realized this was it. As soon as he had the key in his hand, the objective would change. We would no longer be on the same team, but on opposing ones. I would not allow him to strip me of my powers. Without them, I was helpless and as good as dead. I didn't want to kill him, but I would do what I must to survive. I just had to keep giving myself encouraging pep talks.

I studied the witches as they fanned out around what was deemed The Battery. There were only twenty-five in the coven. The women varied in age and low-ranges of power, but they all wore long, black robes, as they skirted around the perimeter of the park. One lone witch stood at the end of the rectangular-shaped field. We were watching from our hiding spots as the witches quickly cast a cloaking spell over the park, deterring any late-night visitors. It was also a silencing spell. That worked out well for me because I wasn't known to go into battle quietly.

The leader threw the hood of her robe back. Short, cropped brown hair fell to her chin. With my demon vision, I could tell even at this distance, and at night no less, she had brown eyes and a pale complexion. She looked a tad like Sarah, but her face was more mature and harsher.

One hand snaked to a pocket in her robe, producing the key. She held it over her head, saying, "Sisters, we come tonight to start something beautiful. Are we tired of the Lux telling us how we must behave and commanding us to follow their guidelines or else be deported to a portal?" Many heads bobbed at her question. "Are we tired of the Degenerates telling us how we must listen to their leaders to conquer the Lux? We are our own people. We need neither group. With the spell that we have worked on for the last few years, we will be able to open a portal and control the beasts crossing over. They will do our bidding. While the Lux and Degenerates are busy killing each other off, we will add to the mayhem and blame it on the other group. Then we will rule the world."

I gave Austin a look, as if to say, "Now's the time, buddy."

He mouthed, "Ladies first."

Jerk.

I adjusted the straps of my sundress as I stepped from behind the old tree. I had a fleeting moment of wondering if I should retrieve my crown from my bag, but the truth was it was heavy, and I wasn't feeling it. I made my way across the grass. My flip flops sounded like a gunshot through the night. The witches gasped as I gave a little finger wave.

"Beatrice, we have an intruder," one of the witches said, as she pointed a finger at me. Well, hello, captain obvious, like Beatrice needed someone to point that out. This was going to be a lot easier than I had initially thought.

"So, hi. Is this an anonymous meeting? Or should I introduce myself?" No one made a move. I flipped my long black hair over a shoulder. "All righty then. I'm Carmen. I like long walks on the beach at night, well, considering today was my first day at an actual beach and I loved it, I assume I would like it at night, as well. I have some anger issues, and then there was that thing with the kitten, so I'm seeing a non-legit therapist, but don't worry, he tells me he's qualified, so that should work itself out. And—"

The head witch interrupted me. "What are you doing here?"

"Oh, I'm sorry. I didn't know there was a time limit to my introductory speech. Jeez, you all could stand to be a little bit friendlier, and where are the refreshments? I mean, hello, we are in the South. You know you're cutting down your enrollment by not being very Southern."

"Someone shut her up," the head witch gritted out.

I made eye contact with Tally, who was currently behind the witch. I had given him enough time to get in place to secure the key. I was really starting to like my bug.

Black wisps curled from my body, as I zeroed in on a few witches at a time. I smiled at my new power. Before I'd been limited. When I concentrated, one lone wisp would untwine from my body to do my bidding, but now multiple tendrils unfurled from me with barely any thought. My smoke coated their skin, and I laughed at their shrieks. They fought back with balls of fire and some of the more talented sent lightning bolts towards me, but they were no match. This made no sense. I found it hard to believe someone entrusted them with the key, or they took the key from someone powerful. Power oozed from me easily, and the ground trembled beneath me. I had a small group in my grip. My tendrils squeezed them before I threw the witches against the nearest trees. Austin had appeared in front of witches, closing in on my right. My trusted bug was currently keeping his eye on the prize. The key. I made a steady path towards him and the lead witch.

"Hey," I shouted to Austin. "If you get your rocks off taking others' powers, now would be the time to do it. These ladies need to be taught a lesson."

I had snagged another four witches and threw them a foot in front of him. With one touch of his hand, they were all left crying on the ground. "And by the way, you're not really helping a lot. Can you bring anything to the table?" I told him, as I backhanded a witch with my mind and a few mumbled Latin words. "I mean right now, I've invited you to a picnic—a feast if you will, and you showed up without a side. Not even paper napkins. But you want a seat at my table?"

Austin chuckled as he disabled a witch. "I wanted to see if you knew what you were capable of. You could have taken all these witches down at once."

Hmm. Maybe he knew more about my shell than I did. I looked over at Tally, who had just sprinkled the lead witch with some dust and currently had the key in his tiny hands. He literally looked like he held up a globe, even though the key was about the size of a lemon. My bug was strong. Whoop-whoop.

"Okay," I said. "Stand back." I concentrated on what I wanted to happen, and then once the image was in place, I flicked my wrist, sending out multiple black smoke whips. I looked like a creature formed of smoke. A bad-ash creature. The witches tried to escape their fate, but my wisps were too strong. They entangled the witches in a firm hold, bringing them down like a cowboy roping cattle.

Austin appeared awed as he clapped, but then something changed in him. He shook his head, frowning, as if I was the sole reason he had issues.

"This was super easy," I said. "I mean they barely put up a fight. Something doesn't feel right about this."

He grunted. Was that supposed to be an answer? I watched him as he stole each and every one of their powers. He gritted his teeth, as if it pained him as much as it did them. When he stripped the last one of their powers, the protection spell collapsed. Now, we were out in the open for any tourist or Charleston native to see. There were at least twenty-five witches in robes lying on the ground, moaning. We needed to get out of here quickly. That's where I made my first mistake. I shouldn't have been concerned about fleeing. I should have been gearing up for the real battle.

Tally had just flown onto my open palm with the key in tow as strong arms wrapped around my torso. When the cold biting wind hit my cheeks, I knew it was game over for me. Dang him straight to my homeland! How could I have let my guard down?

chapter sixteen

I sat at a bar in bum freaking Alaska. Totally powerless. Austin was missing, and my Tally had bailed. There was an old jukebox playing in the corner, and I tried not to shiver in my sundress. What kind of person dropped someone off in Alaska in a sundress? He should've just killed me while he had the chance because even without powers, I had decided I would hunt him down and run a dagger through him if it was the last thing I ever did.

I knew he had planned on taking my powers just like dear ol' dad had done, and yet I still felt betrayed. I was a foxing moron. I stared up at the big moose head on the wall. Of all the places, why here? There was nothing but lousy music and men in this bar, and by the way they were gawking; it was apparent Alaska's population was nothing but men. I had been hit on numerous times, and I was pretty sure it wasn't because they found me attractive, but more because they wanted to breed with me. As if. I tried to zap number forty-two, but when nothing happened,

I laughed like a maniac before letting out a sob. I even asked the moose what he thought of all of this. Some of the men scooted closer to me. You'd think my behavior alone would deter them, but with women being a rare commodity, it was obvious they didn't mind a little crazy.

Someone sat next to me on a barstool. A thick thigh brushed mine, and I lost my temper. "No, I don't want to be your baby mama!" I swiveled in my seat to face a smirking Austin.

"Good to know," he said.

"You!" I started poking him in his chest. "How dare you? Do you know what you've done? You are just like my father."

"I am nothing like your father. I can promise you my intentions are completely different." I started to slap him across his face, but as easily as if I was a pesky gnat, he caught my hand. "Easy, sweet cheeks." He turned around and winked at the boys on the other side of the bar. "Let's take our little lover's quarrel outside, shall we?"

"Lovers?" I shrieked. "I would rather become lovers with number thirty-one over there, and he has no teeth and has to be pushing ninety, if he's a day."

Grabbing me by my arm, he hauled me outside of the bar to where a large dumpster sat, and of course with no powers, I was left to just trail behind him, helpless. Helpless! Me, the Demon Queen.

I jerked my arm out of his grasp. "What do you want?"

His hands ran through his short, white-blond hair. His electric blue eyes held mine before he bit his bottom lip and released a string of curse words. "What do I want, she asks? What do you think I want, sweet cheeks?"

I glared back, as I spat, "I don't know, cuddle bear, why don't you enlighten me?"

"I. Want. My. Freaking. Key."

Huh? "What are you talking about?"

"Your fairy took it."

"What?" At his deadly look, I burst out laughing. "Oh, this is great. When I find that bug, I'm going to kiss him."

"This is not funny."

I felt a little bit of my swag returning. "Oh, but it is. You prematurely took the key. You were so worried about taking my power you took your eyes off the one thing you crave the most. The key. And what happened? You succeeded in defeating little ol' me, but you lost the key." I clapped my hands together. "Oh, this is great."

"I brought you here, so I could have some time to think about what I wanted to do with you. Everything is a mess and—"

I patted his chest. "Oh, save it, big guy. I don't need to hear your excuses. The facts are you jumped the gun and now you're screwed."

"Find him," he said through clenched teeth.

"Or what," I snarled. "You'll take my powers?"

A bunch of tall, strapping men in flannel and work boots headed towards the bar. They looked like they were related to the guy from the paper towel commercial. One of them hit his friend in his chest before the group stopped. They stared at me in awe.

Austin grabbed my elbow; I assumed to steer me somewhere more private. I jerked out of his grasp and was about to tell him what I thought of his manhandling when the tallest of the brawny men said, "Hey, little lady, are you in trouble?"

I let my bottom lip wobble a little before I dashed an imaginary tear. "Oh, it's just been a terrible day, and this one," I said, nodding to Austin, "isn't helping."

One of the men looked at my ring finger before he sized up Austin. Then he turned to whisper to his friends. Just because Austin had stripped me of my powers didn't mean I wasn't still immortal with the perks most non-mortals had. I could hear exceptionally well. None of the lumberjacks were as strong as Austin, but they thought they could take him, as long as they stayed in a group. They would be wrong, but it was still cute they would try. Obviously, Austin heard them as well because he snorted. They eyed me up and down before the leader of the group came to a decision. "Wow, you have to be cold. You're not really dressed for Alaskan weather. Would you like to go inside with us?"

Another man piped up, "Drinks are on us."

Austin growled in my ear, "Don't even think about it."

Ignoring him, I let my voice shake. "Well, I haven't eaten all day. I'm not sure if I should drink on an empty stomach."

Now, the men gave Austin the stink eye. The tallest one said, "Oh hon. Come on in, and we will buy you a burger."

I wrung my hands while worrying over my bottom lip. "You know that sounds sort of nice."

"Carmen …" Austin warned.

From the side of my mouth, I said, "Suck a duck."

The men walked towards the door and waited on me to join them.

I turned back and whispered to Austin, "It looks like you got played, playa. I'll be inside deciding my powerless future while you stand out here in the cold, thinking of how your life's mission just went down the drain."

"Carmen, wait—"

"Sorry, can't hear you," I said, as I put a little extra sway in my hips and sashayed to the five lumberjacks waiting to open the door for me.

Three hours later, I had filled my stomach and was smiling from ear to ear from the sheer fact that I had these huge, beastly men eating out of my powerless hand. One of the men had draped his coat over me as I sat there planning, even as I acted like I was intently listening to the cutest of the bunch finishing a story. The freakishly hot Power Eliminator sat in a dark corner of the bar, glaring at me every time I laughed at something one of the men said. Since it seemed to piss him off, I was full of cheer. Out of the corner of my eye, I caught a flash of something. Tally, bless his little fairy self, flew towards the restroom sign. I casually glanced over to Austin. He hadn't taken his eyes off of me, so the chances of him having seen Tally were slim. Austin tilted his head sideways in question, and I rolled my eyes.

Placing the jacket on the back of my chair, I said, "Excuse me, boys. I've got to use the little girl's room." They all stood. Such gentlemen. I walked past Austin's table and gave him a saucy wink.

After heading to the restroom, I opened up every stall until I found my bug. I was beaming as he re-tucked in his shirt and then flicked his suspenders.

"How awesome am I?"

"You are so awesome. I can't believe you stole the key. Ha! Now, we can demand him to give me back my powers."

"Well, that was the plan."

My smile dropped. "What do you mean, was the plan?"

The fairy flew over to the back of the toilet and began to pace on the lid. "Well, see, here's what happened." I let out a loud groan. "I knew what Austin was planning as soon as he appeared behind you, so I made a mad run for it. What we didn't know is that the head witch had shacked up with a rogue werewolf, and him, along with some of his friends, were coming for the opening of the portal. Interesting fact: did you know the Charleston portal contains the most Degenerate werewolves?"

I crossed my arms and tapped my flip flops on the tile floor. "You're stalling, bug. Spit it out."

"Yes, well, I literally flew right into them while leaving the park. They threatened to take off my wings if I didn't give them the key."

I turned my back to him and banged my forehead on the stall door. This wasn't good.

"But listen, after I dropped the key, I flew as fast as my wings would take me, and they didn't try to catch me. They thought I flew away, but without them knowing, I followed them back to where they hang out."

I turned around slowly. "So, you know where the key is."

He crossed his tiny arms over his chest, nodding. "I know where the key is."

"But there's one problem," I said.

He nodded again. "You don't have any powers to take the key back."

About that time, the restroom door swung open, and somehow I knew who it was. Not just because I was the only lady in this whole establishment, but because anytime he was near, my stomach did this funny little floppy thing. It was so annoying. I opened the stall door and came face to face with Austin.

"Are you having fun out there?" he demanded.

I cocked an eyebrow at his tone. I sashayed towards the sink, taking my time washing my hands, as I looked in the mirror and studied the man standing behind me. His jaw was clenched, and he was fuming mad. Then I realized something.

"You're jealous."

He made himself relax, and at that moment, I knew my remark had been correct. Austin was jealous. My brow wrinkled in thought. His first comment should have been over the key, but instead he came in here mad over me flirting with a couple of strangers. Interesting indeed.

He bent to look under the stalls. "No, Carmen, you can flirt with whomever you wish to." He said this as if he didn't care at all, but the tick in his eye was betraying an entirely different story. "What are you doing in here?"

"Um, so you know you're in the girl's restroom, right?"

"Again, what are you doing in here?"

"Thinking of propositioning you."

His head jerked toward mine. "What?"

"Easy, tiger. Not like that. I was wondering if you would like to make a deal."

He rested a hip against the sink basin. "I'm listening."

"If you get your key, then you have to give me my powers back and vow not to take them away again."

"No. You're more dangerous than any Degenerates in the portals put together. A power like yours can't go unchecked."

"Please, I'm harmless."

"Tell that to the five gentlemen at the bar that are ready to take out second mortgages just to make you their 'little woman.'"

"Would this be a bad time to mention that I did that without my powers?" I wouldn't add that I could also disable any of those men without my powers, because maybe I wasn't completely harmless. I turned to face him, as I rested against the sink. "Can I ask you a question?" At his nod, I said, "When you take powers from others, where does their energy go?"

He remained quiet at first, but then I guessed he figured he might get more from me if he didn't ignore my question. "I take it in. It becomes a part of me."

My eyes widened. "That's why I can't get a good read on you. You are everything. How do you handle so much power?"

"Right now, I'm doing okay." His eyes met mine. "Eventually, it will become too much, and I will go insane."

I waited for the punch line and when it didn't come, my mouth dropped open. "But you continue to take others' powers. Why?"

"It's the power I was given. I work with what I got."

"How noble of you." I tried not to spit the word but I failed. "So, here you are, playing judge and jury, and eventually it'll be the death of you. I bet all of my power is about to tip you over the edge." When his eyes narrowed, I smirked. "How many beings' powers reside in your body?"

"Enough to be able to go toe to toe with the most powerful demon in the world and win."

When had the distance closed between us? There was but a scant inch separating us, and my head was fully tilted back, so I could stare up at him.

"So, you will keep taking in powers until it consumes you. Tell me, do you like the surge that it gives you?"

His eyes were riveted on my lips. "Yes."

"You are so worried about controlling me and not wanting my powers to go unchecked, but who will check you? You'll end up just like my father. It's only a matter of time."

"You keep comparing him to me, and I am nothing like that demon." His eyes held so much rage. I was getting under his skin. "And your father's death wasn't painful enough in my opinion."

That was too raw. I had the same amount of anger towards my father, but I had been beaten and tormented for years by him and my uncle. "Austin, did you personally know my father?"

"Someone I knew did."

As in past tense. My heart dropped. What had my father done to this man?

"I'm sorry for whatever it is that my father has done to you or a loved one, but by taking my powers from me, it's put you on his level, in my opinion." His eyes jerked to mine. "I want my powers back, Austin."

"I can't. I just need some time to think."

"Well, then, I guess this is where we part ways."

I started to go past him, but he reached out and snagged my arm, pulling me to a stop.

"No, you will give me the key."

"And if I don't? What will you do? Take away my powers?" I gave a fake shudder before I rolled my eyes. "Excuse me, oh great Power Manipulator, but you really aren't up for negotiations, considering you have no leverage."

"I've found myself in a predicament." He squeezed my arm before he let it go. "I made a vow to someone I would eliminate your powers immediately after I secured the key."

I poked him in his chest, almost breaking my finger. "Why, you double-crossing donkey-eater!"

He grabbed my finger. "Oh, like you haven't been planning to knife me in my sleep for some time."

"That's only after you stole my powers from me the first time. You threw the first punch, buddy."

His jaw clenched in anger. My eyes were like slits as we just stared at each other.

"Who?" I demanded. "Who made you take this vow."

"That I cannot say."

"Oh, of course you can't."

I paced the yucky bathroom floors. Vows were unbreakable. In fact once you made a vow, you had a compelling urge to carry out the promise until it was completed. If he didn't follow through, he would forfeit his immortality.

"Did you promise to strip me of my powers indefinitely?"

His perfectly kissable lips turned up into a smile. "As a matter of fact, I did not."

"Well, there you have it." I cocked a hip out. "Do you think we can call a truce?"

"If you vow to give me the key back, I'll vow to give you your powers back."

"And perhaps vow to never take them again?"

"You're a demon. One that I don't trust, and I might be the only person who can make sure you don't kill innocent people."

His words didn't ring true. He was hiding more, but why? "Do you really believe that?" When he didn't answer, I said, "I have never killed anyone innocent in my life." Anger coated my words. "But for now, I'll settle on you vowing to give me back my powers. After you have your key and I have my powers, then we can discuss your hatred for demons."

"Deal."

We made our vows right then and there in a smelly Alaskan bathroom. If I was one for the sentimental stuff, I might have cried.

"Now that that's done, where have you hidden the key?" Austin asked.

"Um, yeah about that," I said, as Tally flew out from stall number three. "Why don't you do the honors, bug?"

"Have you heard of the rogue werewolves of Charleston?" Tally asked.

"You've got to be kidding me," Austin exclaimed, but I, on the other hand, had questions.

"That's not really what they call themselves is it?" I felt laughter bubbling up. "I wonder if they have that logo embroidered on the back of their leather jackets."

Austin glared at me because, really, how else would he look at me? "This is not funny. I thought that you had the key hidden somewhere safe."

"Oh, but, cuddle bear," I said, giving him a light punch on the arm, "just think of this as another adventure with yours truly, the magnificent queen of the twelve realms."

Tally scrunched up his face. "Yeah, I see what you're trying to do there, but it's just as lame as the Rogue Werewolves of Charleston."

I pretended to pout. "I missed the mark?"

Austin ground out through clenched teeth, "Can you two be serious for one second? Give me the location of this place, so I can get the key and be done with the both of you."

Tally rattled off the exact address while I studied Austin's profile. He was so handsome it almost hurt to look at him. It was a shame I was going to have to make a choice as to whether to kill him or let him live. If I chose to let him live, I was opening myself up to an attack. I had no doubt in my mind he would try steal my strength again. A damn shame. A face like that should be shared with the world, but he'd made his grave, and now he had to lie in it.

chapter seventeen

"Give me my powers back," I said, as we studied the old, white house that had seen better days. It was in the middle of marshland and looked like a strong wind could knock it right off its stilts. There was only one way in. We would have to go up the dock leading to the house, and I wasn't doing it helpless.

"Once we have the key, I'll give you back your powers."

I was so angry I could punch him in his stupidly handsome face. I hissed, "Then I won't be much help to you."

He gave me a sexy grin. "Baby, I don't need help."

Tally flew over to us. "Both of you could stand to be a little quieter. So I've got good news, and I've got bad news. I overheard them talking, and the good news is there's a group of wolves in the house, so the key is probably with them, but the bad news is at some point last night, they opened the portal and have some new friends."

"Did they say what kind of friends?" Austin asked.

"Nope, sorry."

"Once I start to cross the dock, they will be able to hear me. Both of you stay here out of danger, and I'll be back momentarily with the key."

"Ah. Cuddle bear is worried about us, bug. How stinking cute is that?"

Austin stood up from where we had been crouching behind a dune. "It's just simply that I don't need your help, and you both will just get in my way."

I rolled my eyes. "Why don't you just teleport inside their home?"

"Because I'm not sure who will be waiting for me when I get there. Maybe they'll panic and come out of the house. Taking my time strolling up this dock might be the only way I can figure out who they released from the portal."

As soon as Austin started to cross the dock, I saw his whole body tense. His shoulder blades squeezed together, and he made fists by his sides. What the heck? Then I knew what had him so ensnared. Up from the marsh water popped a beautiful girl. Two more broke the surface beside her. Well, at least we now knew what the wolves had brought back. Sirens. Freaking hookers. And it looked like our boy accidentally made eye contact. It didn't matter how powerful you were once a siren set her gaze on her intended target; they were down for the count. His fist clenched and unclenched as he tried to break eye contact.

"What are we going to do?" asked Tally.

I shrugged. "Let them take Austin to the bottom of the marsh?" Tally gave me a disappointed look. "I'm kidding. I have to get my powers back before he dies."

Tally shook his head, and I stood up and made my way to the dock.

Tally flew past me. "I'll go check to see what the werewolves are doing."

I gave a brief nod as I walked to stand directly in front of Austin. I placed both hands on either side of his face, but he could not break eye contact, causing the sirens to giggle. I held up my middle finger to the skanks.

"Baby, I don't need help, my ash," I grumbled, right before I brought his head down to mine and kissed him like our lives depended on it. In reality, it kind of did. After several seconds, he wrapped his arms around my waist and yanked me to him with a growl. His hips grinded against mine, as his teeth caught my bottom lip. One of the sirens hollered and cheered, breaking us out of an entirely different trance. From an outsider's point of view, I was sure that kiss looked like we were hot for each other. We stared at each other in shock. I was the first one to come to my senses. I lightly pushed away from him.

"The big, bad, cocky Power Eliminator had to be saved by a girl without powers. I mean seriously, three hoochies almost took you down. Now, the werewolves are more than aware that we're coming. Give me back my powers." I gave him the stank eye. "Or are you hoping I'll get killed, and then you won't have to honor the vow?"

He gritted his teeth before he once again wrapped me in his arms. I felt a surge of power flow through my body and everything tingled. Because I had my power, not because he had his hands on me again, and he looked like he wanted an encore of our last performance.

A siren sing-songed, "I can love you better than she can."

I gave Austin a wink. "She definitely could because I have no love in the club for you, but if you look at her again, I'll push you into the water myself." I grabbed his hand and dragged him along behind me. "Eyes down, lover boy."

I heard him chuckling as I pulled him across the wooden dock. The sirens swam alongside us while they talked mad trash. They made him several promises; some of them I weren't too sure were anatomically possible, considering the flexibility it would take to achieve such tasks.

Between the Demon Queen and a Power Eliminator, the rogue wolves of Charleston didn't stand a chance. Austin kicked the front door down, and a big, burly guy with coarse hair sprung at him. Austin caught the man by the forearms, and they both fell to the ground, with the wolf on top right before Austin's feet pushed the werewolf in the gut and sent him flying over his head. The werewolf had a momentary look of shock. I understood that expression. Poor wolf had lost his power.

I stood off to the side while Austin fought the wolves. I really should help, but the truth was I didn't feel like it. Besides, there were only fifteen of them. We weren't teammates. We weren't even friends, but that didn't stop me from noticing how hot Austin was while he outmaneuvered the wolves. I was studying my nails when a werewolf stalked up to me, and by the looks of him, he had the intent to do bodily harm.

I wagged a finger at him. "Wolfy, you don't want none of this."

Obviously, he had a hearing problem. One meaty fist reared back to take a swing at my face. Smoke curled from me like tentacles and wrapped around his hand, jerking it behind his back, and within a second I had him wrapped up tighter than a cocoon leaving only his eyes visible. I pointed a finger at a chair, and he went careening into it. He thrashed against my wisps, but it was no use.

I gave him a wink. "Don't fight it. Just sit there and be a good doggie for mommy."

I returned to taking intervals of studying my nails and Austin's fine form. His back muscles bunched as he parried with his opponent. Why did the sexiest man alive have to be my number one enemy? Four werewolves jumped on him at once. It was like a giant haystack before he started knocking them off of him, taking their powers as he went.

Without cutting me a glance, he said, "Thanks for the help."

"Oh, cuddle bear! Don't you remember clearly stating that you didn't need any help?"

Another wolf gunned for me. I held up a hand. "Stop right there." He hesitated for a brief moment. "If you want to end up like your mummified friend over there, then be my guest."

He chose to head towards Austin, where he lost his power within the first twenty seconds of fighting the boy wonder. Talk about a 'danged if you do, danged if you don't' kind of situation.

There was an all-out brawl going on in the middle of the living room, but Austin was pretty close to finishing up. I just needed to come to a decision whether to kill him right away or wait the six months when I was positive he would come for me and then kill him. It would be self-defense. Ugh. Why would a Demon Queen care if the kill was in self-defense? Bad, bad, Carmen. Austin threw a wolf in the air, and he rolled to a stop right in front of me. With the bottom of my flip flop, I pushed him in the face to get him to roll away from me.

To say I was bored would have been putting it lightly until I heard Tally shout. I looked across the room, and there stood a bulky werewolf holding the small fairy in his large hand. I pushed off the wall with intent. No one messed with my bug.

The wolf's eyes swiveled to me. "Stop, or I'll squeeze him until his eyes bulge out of his head."

With one last punch, Austin had disabled the last standing werewolf. They all lay on the floor, writhing in pain, and probably from the loss of their powers.

Austin glared at the werewolf holding Tally. "We just want the key."

"Sorry." The werewolf snickered. "I have plans for the key." He nodded to his friend who was still tied up by smoke before he glanced in my direction. "I've never seen a demon be able to do that before. Release him."

Austin gave me a warning look but I ignored him. The wolf had my bug. With a flick of my wrist, I let the wisps drop. The werewolf gave me a scared look before he almost fell out of his chair, trying to scamper away from me.

"Release the fairy," I commanded.

The werewolf gave a humorless laugh. "Then me and my brother here will be dead. I'm not stupid, girl. We will be leaving with the fairy to make sure you don't follow either of us."

Austin started striding towards the werewolves. "Not with the key, you won't."

Anger flared through me. How could he risk Tally? With barely a thought, I tried to throw him against a wall, but right before he hit, he somehow managed to stop himself an inch away from brick and mortar. He floated quietly back to the ground. The trick must've come from a fairy whose powers he'd stolen. I waited to see what he would do. When he didn't come towards me, I gave my attention back to the brothers.

"You won't leave here alive unless you make a vow to let him go unharmed within the hour."

The werewolf holding Tally asked, "What are you?"

"The Demon Queen."

The brothers glanced at each other momentarily before the one I had previously wrapped in my wisps spoke up. "Agreed. We will vow it now. Give us time to get away, and then we will release the fairy."

As soon as they said their vows, I stepped to the side and let them pass. After they ran through the front door, I knew what was coming, but I couldn't help but sigh when he opened his mouth to scold me.

"What were you thinking?" Austin said quietly.

That was interesting. I assumed he would be screeching by now. "Oh, I don't know. Maybe I was thinking they had my friend, and I wasn't going to let him die because of my actions."

"You made a vow to me to get that key."

"I'll get you your stupid key."

He shook his head before he put his hands on his narrow hips. "No, what I'm saying is that a demon was willing to break a vow that could actually cause them death in order to save a friend. Which brings me to demons can have friends?"

"Why are you butt hurt? I said I would get you your stupid key and I will."

He gave me a smile as he took several strides towards me. "I'm not butt hurt, Carmen. I'm impressed. Maybe I have misjudged you. I would have saved my friend, too." He stepped over a moaning werewolf then stopped right in front of me. "Do me a favor? Remember this moment. That you were willing to do anything to rescue your friend."

I couldn't even nod because he made me nervous with the way he gazed at me. He studied my face for several seconds like he was trying to decipher if I was real or not. Why was he leaning into me? I couldn't make myself move, even though his lips were inches away from mine. Was he going to kiss me? Excitement and wariness crept through me as I waited in anticipation.

Austin jumped back from me, a curse word shouting from the same lips I'd just been watching. He leaned down and punched a werewolf in the face, knocking the man out.

"He bit me on the ankle!"

I couldn't help the laughter bubbling out of me.

He turned back to me with a sexy grin. "You think that's funny?"

"Hilarious."

"Yeah, probably wouldn't have been so funny if it would have been your ankles."

"But it wasn't."

He brushed my hair behind my shoulder. Back came the wariness. "What do you want to do for the next hour?" he asked.

I looked around at all the powerless werewolves who still hadn't made it to their feet. It sucked being human. "I don't know about you, but I'm not sure how I feel leaving those sirens in the marsh and who knows how many are out there." At his shocked look, I asked, "What? You want to leave them there to take down any fisherman that comes this way?"

A slow smile spread across his handsome features. "No, of course not. I just didn't think we would be on the same page."

I stomped to the front door, kicking powerless wolves out of my way. Was wanting to save unforeseen humans from the sirens' grasp a weakness? Yes, it was. As I crossed the dock, I just hoped the Power Eliminator on my heels didn't take advantage of it. When I got back to ruling, I was going to have a hard time with my underlings if boy wonder ran his mouth about me building sandcastles and saving future fisherman. I took off my sundress with little finesse and a lot of aggravation and kicked off my flip flops.

"I'll hunt the sirens down and then throw them up on the dock. Try not to make eye contact with them when you strip them of their powers." I stood there while his gaze raked over my bikini-clad body. My hands were on my hips when a thought came to me. "Austin, when you take their powers, you won't use their seduction powers on, um, you know …"

He took a step towards me. "On you? No, Carmen, when I seduce you, you will willingly fall into my arms, not because I tricked you, but because that's where you will crave to be."

My heart thumped in my chest. For the first time in my life, I took the cowardly way out. I pretended like I didn't hear him, as I dove into the murky water. It wasn't until I had wrangled the seventh siren when I realized he had said "when I seduce you" not "if." My heart raced with unexpected emotions. Was I hoping he would seduce me? No, those thoughts could be suicidal. Besides if I was nothing but a lowly demon, why would anyone want to seduce me? There was no denying he had looked at me like he wanted me, and he thought it was just a matter of time before he had me. I couldn't allow lust to get involved, or I could lose the one thing that mattered the most to me: my powers. I never wanted to feel helpless again.

chapter eighteen

We were back in a bar. If we weren't careful, we would get a reputation and be forced to attend meetings. At least this time, my sundress fit the atmosphere. When an hour had passed, we decided to head back to downtown Charleston to see if we could find the wolves who had disappeared. I knew Tally would find me, but after the third hour of looking for the wolves and Tally not showing up, I was a bundle of nerves. They took a vow to release him after an hour, so where was he?

Austin reached over and placed a hand on my leg. Butterflies flew in my stomach, and I tried to act like he had no effect on me when he said, "He's fine. He'll probably track you down any second."

"Yeah." But where was he? "Sure."

Tingles zipped up and down my spine as his thumb rubbed the inside of my knee. He was trying to be comforting, but his touch was nothing but distracting. The shrill sound of a telephone rang behind the bar, breaking me out of the lust zone I was readily leaning into. I crossed my legs to avoid further contact. It was definitely safer that way. A couple of rowdy college kids made some loud jokes as I began to rub my temples. I needed to get out of this bar to somewhere quiet where I could think.

The bartender shouted, "Is there an Austin here?"

Austin gave me a confused look, standing up to take the call. What was that about? I studied his profile as he talked on the phone. His brow was furrowed, and his jaw was clenched. I heard a couple of "Why's" and a "You've got to be kidding me" but for the most part, he was just listening intently to whatever the caller said. A couple of young girls leaned in their seats to get closer to him. They were annoyingly distracting as they giggled, and one even dared to make squeezing motions with her hands as she ogled his butt. He completely ignored them as he focused on the caller, and his hand continued to clench the phone. He obviously wasn't a fan of whatever was being said to him. Without a goodbye, he hung up and made his way back to me. Both girls sighed, and I almost stuck my tongue out at them. Geez, what was wrong with me? He placed a warm hand under my elbow, guiding me to the door. Oh no, please don't let it be bad news. If something had happened to Tally, I didn't know what I would do.

He pulled me in between two buildings, and my eyes immediately adjusted to the darkness. My back was against the brick, as Austin leaned into me, almost crowding my space. He waited for two tourists to walk past the darkened alleyway before he began to talk.

"That was the soothsayer, Ariana. I know where Tally is and—"

"Where?" I demanded.

He lightly gripped my elbow he'd never taken his hand off of. "The werewolves kept their word, and they did let Tally go, but your friend decided to spy on them to see where they were headed. You know the saying, 'fool me once shame on you?' Well, Tally didn't fool them twice. They have him at the portal, and this time it's going to be a little harder to get him back."

I gazed up into his face, trying to understand what he wasn't saying. "They took him into the portal?" I didn't give him a chance to confirm. "Why would they do that?"

"The werewolves know the Queen of Demons is after the key. They also know you'll be coming after your friend, so they need to go in the portal to retrieve the one being they think will vow to bring you down, if they allow him out."

"Oh, puh-lease. Who might this creature be?"

"Being born of fire, your weakness is naturally water, even though you've taken a liking to it, so they seek the bastard son of the King of the Sea, who can control water. They obviously don't know how much you actually like water."

I had heard of this king before, but never his son. It didn't matter. Tally was counting on me to come rescue him. I gnawed on my bottom lip, as I thought up a plan. If they were already in the portal and had the key, how would we enter?

Austin put a finger under my chin. "We will get the key back, along with your friend. You don't need to worry."

I patted his chest, rolling my eyes. "I'm not worried about defeating this so-called king's son. I'm worried about how we're going to get in the portal."

"Easy. We teleport there ahead of the wolves and then use the key they have in their possession." I raised an eyebrow. "Oh, did I forget to mention they are headed to portal thirty-two in Ohio? By the time they get there, we will be waiting for them."

What in the fifty shades of crazy was he talking about? Perhaps he had already swooped up too much power, and had tilted over into crazy land, because he sure as hades wasn't making sense.

"You're giving me a migraine. Why did you tell me all about this son of the king if we will be at the portal before the werewolves even go into the portal? We can snatch the key and Tally and never set foot in the portal." Duh.

"Sorry, I also forgot to mention the part where Ariana said we had to go in the portal." Forget? He didn't forget. He chose not to lead with that. I could tell by the effortless way he apologized. "She wants us to actually be the ones to release the king's bastard son, Malakian."

I straightened the bunched fabric under my fingers, and that's when I realized my hand was still on his chest—his remarkably wide, muscular chest. I removed it quickly. "And is this the part where you tell me why we would agree to that?"

"I'd prefer not to."

I pushed him away from me. "The longer I'm gone from the underworld, the harder it will be for me when I return. Do you understand? And yet you will not tell me the reasoning behind this adventure that doesn't need to take place?"

He briefly looked like he was at war with himself. Decision made, he said, "No, I won't tell you."

Jutting my chin out, I said, "Then count me out."

He invaded my space. "Sorry, that's not part of the deal, but I will tell you what part of the deal was. You. Getting. Me. The. Key. I hate to be such a stickler, but you did let it out of our grasp and technically did break a vow. What's to stop me from taking your power now?"

I glared at him. "You dare to threaten me with that again?"

"Yeah, I dare. I've got a lot laying on the line."

"More than just the key? Tell me Austin, what or who did you see back in the enchanted maze because I don't think it was the key and I know that I'm no Nancy Drew but why do I have the feeling that you are in a tangled mess?"

He leaned into me again. "None of that is your business."

His words conveyed he was pissed, but the way his eyes kept darting to my lips sent a whole different message. Maybe not admiration but definitely lust. I licked my lips just to test the theory, and sure enough he let out a small growl, tightly closing his eyes. He wanted me but was upset with himself for wanting me. How ironic. Somewhere along the way, I wondered what it would be like to have a willing recipient send me those kinds of looks. Obviously, he would never admire me because I was still a demon, and nothing more to him than a chess piece.

Austin returned to regarding me scornfully, and all traces of lust were wiped from his face. It dawned on me that if I ever did go down the rabbit hole of intimacy with Austin, once I got him the object he desired, he would still cast me to the side like a toy he was done playing with until it was time to recycle that toy. For the first time, I felt a little sympathy for Sarah, and then I remembered I really didn't like her and just like that it was quickly gone. That girl was a disaster. I stared up into Austin's handsome, waiting face with one thought: I had to end him. Before he ended me. We were not friends. Not even close. But unlike him, I would not broadcast it so loud. A good queen knew how to judge her opponents. I would find his weaknesses and bring him to his proud knees, and the glory of it would be he would never see it coming.

With that thought, I plastered a smile on my face. "You're right, a deal is a deal." I placed my hand on his arm. "Are we traveling through your airlines or mine?"

He gave me a wary look. "I know the exact location, so I'll take us. First, we will drop off your bag."

I hefted the bag up on my shoulder. Leaving my crown in my chambers didn't sit well with me, but who knew where we would end up? I couldn't just walk around with a huge crown on my head. The stares would be relentless. I released a heavy sigh as I closed the distance between us.

His voice was thick and deep as my body molded into his. "Just hold onto me."

He bent and … smelled my hair? What in the gob smacker was he doing?

Wrapped in his arms, I tilted my head up. "Did you just smell my hair?"

He gave me a boyish grin, like he had been caught doing something he wasn't supposed to. "You smell nice."

Um. Weird. And yet heat flooded my belly. I clenched my eyes at my weakness. I was supposed to be getting him to warm up to me and lower his defenses, so I could land a sneak attack. He wasn't supposed to be doing that to me. I let my forehead hit his chest, as I gave myself a silent pep talk. I was fierce and strong. I would not allow anyone to strip me of my powers again, no matter how hot they were, or how gently they cradled me in their arms. I was a black mamba biding her time, waiting for the perfect time to strike, and when that time arose, I wouldn't hesitate.

chapter nineteen

We were literally in the middle of freaking nowhere. A rusty, old metal building that had a Pepsi logo on the side stood in the middle of a potato field. There were various types of farm equipment parked in the building, but not a soul was to be seen. Knowing we were enemies, and it would eventually come to a showdown, I refused to talk with Austin, but it was hard to ignore his presence. We had both changed as soon as we'd arrived at my chambers. At the time, I was thankful he had changed out of the tight T-shirt and his swimming trunks that showed off his muscular legs. But I didn't know if his current attire was much better. Those faded jeans molded to him like they were made for him, and his plain faded T-shirt was pulled even more taut over his muscular chest than the previous one.

Why couldn't my mortal enemy be hideous or at least not so mouthwateringly hot? His white-blond hair was such a contrast to his tan skin that, that in itself would make one take a second look. Then when you noticed how truly handsome he was, it was hard for one's eyes not to roam over to him occasionally. At the moment, I felt him staring at my profile, so I refused to let any roaming of my eyes happen. I would pluck those babies out first.

"Is this how it's going to go? You ignoring me?" I pretended like I didn't hear him. "Carmen, what do you want me to do? Apologize for holding you to a vow that you took?"

Seriously? I could take that key away from those wolves the moment they landed here and complete my vow, but that wasn't what he was asking. Forgetting my promise to myself to be silent, my eyes swiveled to him.

"That's not what you need to apologize for. You want the key? I'll have it in your hands shortly. But no, you're listening to that old hag, and you want me to go along with her plan. I'll be away from my realm where chaos is probably ensuing right now because while the cat is away, the mouse will play, and not only that, but you threatened me again."

He came to stand in front of me. Bending his large frame and tilting his neck so he could study my face better, he put one long finger under my chin, forcing me to look at him. "Are your … your feelings hurt?"

"Bahahaha! You are hilarious. Of course not. I'm a Demon Queen."

"I know." His hand dropped from my face, as he stood up straight. "I know."

No doubt disappointment colored his words. He resented me. Resented everything I was and stood for, but yet there was a constant hunger in his gaze. It must be hell to hate someone and want them at the same time.

He was at war with himself, and that made me smile. Whether we wanted to admit it or not, we were on a level playing field. We both were attracted to each other and neither of us wanted to be.

Austin reached into his pocket. "I got you a little something, and I wanted to give it to you before we went into the portal." He pulled out the beautiful bracelet I had been admiring at the Charleston market. He handed it to me, and my fingers shook as I reached for it. In all my life, I couldn't remember anyone besides my mother giving me anything other than punishment.

I just stared at it when he took it back from me and put it on my wrist.

I ran a finger over the jewels that reminded me of his eyes. "It's beautiful."

"Not nearly as beautiful as its keeper."

Words escaped me, and I was completely shocked he'd thought to get me something. The air grew thick, and the silence became awkward. He started to turn away from me. I reached out for his arm, stopping him. He glanced down at my pale hand on his tan arm, but didn't pull out of my grasp.

"Maybe it does hurt a little. The fact that you are probably planning in the near future to take away my powers upsets me. Even now you taunt me with stripping away the very thing that I've longed for."

"It's a two-way street, you know. Can you look me in the eye and tell me you aren't planning on stabbing me in the back with those pretty little claws when the perfect moment arises?"

I released his arm. "We could be friends. Call a permanent truce. Vow not to destroy each other."

"Isn't that a demons goal? To destroy the world or least to snuff out the good in the world?"

I felt my blood boiling. With biting words, I said, "I don't plan on destroying the world, so that shouldn't be an issue. I just want my throne and peace. Is that too much to ask for?"

"Maybe it is," he said with remorse.

"And maybe your hatred for demons will ruin us both."

For a few moments, he didn't say anything. We just continued to stare at one another for answers we probably wouldn't find.

"Maybe," he said. "Maybe we're both damaged beyond repair."

Before I could agree with him, I saw the wolves from the corner of my eye. I grabbed hold of Austin's arm and traced him behind the steel building. I put a finger to his lips, telling him to be quiet. He gave me a nod before I turned to peer around the building. As his warm scent engulfed me, his hands settled on my hips, making my heart race. I ignored it as we both leaned together to look and see exactly where the wolves were.

They marched through the flat land laughing and telling crude jokes all the while, unaware they were being watched. Idiots. There was no Tally. What had they done with him? If they had harmed him, I would eviscerate them where they stood. I started to trace to them, but Austin, sensing my emotions, pulled me closer to his body, wrapping his arms around my chest. My blood turned to molten lava at his touch.

He whispered in my ear, causing me to barely suppress a shiver. "Wait."

Still trapped in his embrace, my fists clenched by my sides, I watched the two wolves shove each other playfully, as they continued to cross the plains. They neared the shimmery air signifying they were closing in on the portal humans couldn't see, but immortals could find just by the energy the portal pulsed with.

I tilted my head back. My eyebrows rose in question. It seemed like now was our chance. Austin's gaze roamed my face, so many emotions crossed his face. The lust didn't surprise me, but the regret I saw had me silently questioning what he knew that I didn't. His arms slid down my body and rested again on my hips. He shook his head and grimaced, as if he was in pain. He dropped his hands from me, taking a deep breath. He wanted me. It was in his hungry eyes, but there was something stopping him. Was it because I was a demon? Fury once again flooded me.

The wolves' laughter carried over to us, shaking me out of my anger. He took my hand in his, and right before he teleported us to the entrance of the portal, I decided that it was more than okay he wanted me. In fact that was great news. Using his desire might not be that bad of a plan. First things first, though: take the key back, find Tally, go rescue some King's son, and then slay the hot beefcake currently teleporting me. I could do all of the above and be back in hell reigning over a horde of demons in less than a week. Because I had ambition, and I was a boss like that. When we landed in front of the wolves, I had a stupid grin on my face, even though my stomach rolled from Austin's teleportation.

Catching sight of us, they stopped in their tracks, as I gave the taller one a wink. "Why, hello, boys. So we meet again. I do believe you have something of mine."

The tall one crossed his arms over his barrel chest. "You're not getting the key."

"Yeah, I was talking about the fairy." I tilted my head towards Austin. "This big boy right here is the one lusting after the key."

The shorter, less stout of the two, must have had more brains because he knew a dead end when he saw one. He took off sprinting through the fields like he could escape me. I teleported five feet in front of him.

"Was it something I said?" He shook his head, as he backed away from me. "Oh, I hope this doesn't hurt my yelp reviews." I crooked one finger at him, giving him a smile. "Come, love, it doesn't have to hurt unless you want it to."

The taller of the two wolves started towards me. "Leave my brother alone."

Austin grabbed him by the shirt. "Whoa, not so fast. Let the lady work."

The wolf snarled, "What are you going to do? Take my powers from me, so you can beat my ass?"

Austin smiled without humor. "I don't have to take away your powers to beat your ass. Would you like a demonstration?" Austin's fist was so fast it was almost hard to track. The bone-crunching wasn't as hard to hear. It almost made me wince. The wolf called his true nature to him, as he morphed in front of our eyes. His bones enlarged, his shoulders widened, and he just became … more. Taller, stouter, and aggressive. Austin seemed to grow bored, as he waited for the wolf to settle into his new frame. Another difference between golden boy Austin and me. I would have struck while the iron was hot. There was no honor in killing, so I say get it done and over with fast. The smaller wolf tried to make another escape attempt while he thought my attention was divided. My smoke shot from my body, tangling the smaller wolf around his feet. With an unforgiving thud, he fell hard on the ground, my wisps slowly dragging his body through the dirt back towards me.

Without looking at him, I said, "Isn't this the second time I've done this to you? You'd think you would learn by now that you can't run. Now, be a good boy and stay."

He called me a slew of dirty names, and in return I sent him an image that would be sure to haunt his dreams for nights to come. His mind was easy to project to, unlike Austin's. He absorbed everything I sent him. When he screamed, I backed out of his mind nice and slow. I didn't want his mind to crack because I needed him to know why he was in this situation in the first place. He should have never messed with an ally of the Demon Queen's.

I gave my attention to the other wolf circling around Austin. Right before he decided to attack, Austin anticipated the move and teleported behind the wolf, kicking him behind the knee, causing the wolf to stumble. Before the wolf could turn around, he teleported in front of the wolf. Austin threw an elbow and slammed it into the wolf's already bloody face.

I stage whispered to the smaller wolf writhing on the ground, whimpering at my feet. "Ugh. You know that had to hurt. Should we take bets on how long your brother will last? I'm going to say another fifteen seconds, but only because it looks as if Austin is growing bored."

Austin ignored me, as one leg swept out, knocking both the legs of the wolf right out from underneath him. The wolf barely hit the ground before Austin pounced on him, squeezing him by the jugular. "I could make it pop, you know? Do you concede?"

The wolf made some sort of gurgling noise. Austin said, "I'll take that as a yes. Now, I'll strip you of your powers."

The wolf immediately rolled into a ball when Austin was through. I knew the feeling, bud. It totally sucked.

I gave a slow clap. "Are you done showing off?"

The power he just confiscated rolled off him in waves. His hands rested on his hips. His chest rose with adrenalin. "Admit it. You thought that was hot."

My stomach tightened, and I did have a sudden urge to fan myself. Wait! I was seducing him. He was supposed to yield to me, not the other way around. I made myself do an eye roll. "Well, if you're ready to move on, I'd like to question the wolves about where Tally is."

Austin bent over and rifled through the now sobbing wolf's pants and jacket until he found the key.

"I can't believe you made him cry," I said.

Austin pointed to the wolf lying at my feet. "Yeah, well, you made that one piss himself."

I gave a dainty shrug, because what could I say? I was freaking awesome. I knelt down next to the terrified wolf. "So where is my friend?"

"He—he's—he."

"Use your words like a big boy."

He swallowed hard before saying, "He's in a dumpster. You know the gas station right before this exit? That's where he is."

Austin gave me a look. "I'll go retrieve him. Keep this one tied up."

Rage rocketed through my body. A dumpster? They threw my friend into a dumpster? Like trash?

Austin was back in less than sixty seconds, cradling a worn-out looking Tally. I noticed two things at once: his body was bloody, and his wings were bent. A fairy's wings were their most sensitive body part. The fact that they were folded like an accordion meant he was in severe pain.

Through clenched teeth, I asked, "How bad is it?"

Austin cupped Tally in his palm. "Pretty bad but I think he'll live.

"That's more than I can say for this one," I said, as I kicked the wolf groveling at my feet.

"You could kill him," Austin said, "or you could let me strip him of his powers, and we can take both of them through the portal. I can't think of a worse fate."

I wanted this wolf's head, but when the wolf started crying, "I can't go over there with no way to return," I decided he had just sealed his fate.

Tally moaned. "My wings."

I scooped him up from Austin's hand. "Tally, will you recognize me as your queen?"

His words were barely audible. "I'm a fairy," he croaked out.

My voice boomed. "Will you recognize me as your queen?"

"Yes, Carmen. I will pledge my allegiance with you."

"Then I command you to heal." I made tiny circles with my hand over his broken body. "Sana, amicus meus." He began to heal right before our eyes. I held onto him until his body was unbroken.

Several moments later, he gazed up into my eyes with embarrassment. "I can't believe I was foolish enough to get caught."

I shrugged.

"Is this a bad time to point out that most demons would've let me rot?"

I gently flicked his now healed body off the palm of my hand. "Shoo, bug."

He laughed as he flew over our heads in a circle, testing out his now healed wings. "So, what are we to do with these two?"

"You've missed a lot," I said. "We have to go into the portal to find someone the soothsayer wants. Then it seems everyone's vows and promises will be complete, and this one," I said, jerking my head towards Austin, "won't try to steal my powers for a spell."

Tally glared at Austin. "You need therapy. I can help with that."

"Careful fairy," Austin said, as he grabbed up a wolf by his shirt collar. "I don't have an attachment to you like the Demon Queen does."

I crossed my arms over my chest. "First off, don't threaten my friend …" Both of the guys' eyebrows rose, either at the word "friend," or my admittance of one. "Oh please. Evil reigning queens can have friends. That does not make me weak."

Austin looked confused. "You're right, but does that make you evil?" His eyes lingered on me before he walked past, dragging a wolf towards the portal.

I gave a smile. Yep, that boy wanted me.

Tally flew over to my shoulder. "I'm not sure I like the devious look on your face."

"Oh, stuff it." Turning to Austin, I said, "We won't be able to use our powers once we go through."

"I won't need to use my powers. I'm strong enough without them." Cocky much? "But you will be able to use yours."

"Yeah, I'm pretty sure I read the community newsletter on the bulletin board of freaking nowhere that said no powers in portals."

Austin shifted the bulky weight of the limp wolf from one hand to the other, like he weighed no more than a carton of milk. "I said the same thing, although a little less witty, to the soothsayer, in which she replied that a select few can retain most of their powers in a portal. She went on to mention you were one of the few."

"Humph." I ran my tongue over my teeth. "Let's go see if the creepy old hag told the truth, and don't worry, boys. I'll protect you lesser beings with my powerful self."

Tally groaned. "Who else knew that was coming?"

"I actually think you need to stay here, Tally," Austin said. "Now that you've healed, you will need to recoup before you're a hundred percent, and without the usage of powers in the portal, it might be—"

"He's right, Tally," I said, and Tally flipped me the bird. "Now, Tally, that's no way for a shrink to act. Jeez, where is the professionalism nowadays?"

"So, you two are just going to go without me? I pledge my loyalty to you, and in the next five minutes, you dump me."

"Tally," I said, "no one is commanding you to stay here, but …" I looked over my shoulder to see Austin listening to me intently, so I lowered my voice. "You're my first friend I've had in a long time. I don't want to lose you. Would you please ease my fears by staying here, where it's remotely safe?"

To no avail, Tally tried to straighten his tattered clothes, as his chest puffed out. "I'm honored to be called your friend. I will stay here, my queen."

He flew off my shoulder, his head held high, as he headed towards the metal building. Someone honored to be my friend? I rubbed the palm of my hand over my chest. My emotions were a tad all over the place. Shirt. I did love the bug. What was going on with me? Throwing my shoulders back, I gathered up the other wolf off the ground and waited while Austin inserted the key into the portal. Instantly, the portal opened, and we stepped through into a land of—what in the Tomfrickery was this shirt?

chapter twenty

ortal thirty-two looked like a bad Disney movie. The sky was a light purple and bushy pink shrubs, rocks, and water made up the landscape. We chunked both of the wolves over to the side, so we could study the scene in front of us better. Mermaids lay on various rocks with nothing but seashells covering their breasts. One, in particular, basked on a flat rock all by herself while other mermaids were stretched out in lazy patterns at the base of the rock. Her auburn hair flowed down her back, and round blue eyes studied us. When we walked past her, she hissed at me. Who would have thought mermaids could be evil?

"You better chill, Ariel. I will make you sushi because whooping your slippery behind is not beneath me."

Austin grabbed my elbow. "We've barely made it through the portal, and you're already making threats."

"Hey, Flipper started it." As he dragged me along, I glared at Ariel over my shoulder. "And just so you know, your movie sucked."

Austin laughed before saying, "Try to remember you're a queen."

"Yeah, a Demon Queen, as you keep reminding me."

"Maybe I'm reminding me," he said so quietly I almost didn't hear him.

Two bodies of water lapped on either side of the narrow pathway, forcing us to either walk on slippery stones or swim. Stepping from one rock to another, we walked along the path with no destination in mind. Austin never removed his hand from my elbow. Obviously, I didn't need his help, so one would think it was because he liked having contact with me.

"Do we have a plan on how to find this Malakian?" I asked.

"We will walk to the heart of this plane and see if someone can point us in the right direction."

"I thought mermaids were supposed to be sweet and friendly." I looked at all of the mermaids glaring at us as we passed. "Obviously, I was wrong."

"You do realize they can hear you, right?"

I clapped a hand to my mouth in fake shock before letting him see my smirk. "You do realize I don't care?"

"You will be the death of me."

You have no idea, big boy.

Every once in a blue moon, Austin would stop and ask someone if they knew of the whereabouts of Malakian. Most told us to sod off, some ignored us, and a few begrudgingly pointed towards the mountains. With no other helpful hints, we headed in the direction of the peaks that seemed farther away with every step we took. Must be an illusion. When night came, and we weren't any closer to the range we desired, Austin let out a string of curses that made me smile with fond memories. Oh, how I missed dropping a properly, well planned f-bomb. Those were the days.

"We should just make camp here unless demons require no sleep."

I plopped down on a rock. "Oh, wow. Another snide remark about my demon heritage. Color me shocked."

Austin ran a hand through his hair in frustration before he took off through the woods. Ugh, and where did he think he was going? I lay back on the flat, smooth rock, wondering as I gazed upon the stars, how an awesome queen such as myself ended up here? Willingly in a portal. There was a part of me that should be concerned. No. I sat up with jerky movements. What was wrong with me? I should be really concerned. Yes, he just strolled off. Yes, he had the key. Yes, this could have all been some trick. Maybe he hadn't talked with the soothsayer. Maybe this was his plan. Take the Demon Queen to a portal. Leave her there and never think about her again. It was a brilliant plan, actually. So brilliant that I'd be impressed if I wasn't the poor smuck who now found herself deserted on a plane with a bunch of fish. I paced and thought. Would Tally figure out a way to come for me? My mind spun.

"What are you doing?"

My mouth dropped open at Austin's approach. He stood there with a bundle of wood in his arms. His gaze raked over me before a smile lit his face. "Did you think I deserted you?"

"What? No." Yeah, kind of.

"You did," he said, as he dropped the wood between us. Dusting the bark off his shirt, he kept smiling that infuriating grin, as he got to work building us a fire.

Plopping back down on the rock, I said, "Okay, so maybe I thought you had jilted me. So why haven't you?"

"We haven't found Malakian yet."

I leaned back on the rock, studying him. I wasn't buying it. Could it be he didn't want to leave me behind? "No, you could have gone off on your own to find Malakian and left me here."

After the last stick was piled on, he gave me a calculating look. "Maybe that's still the plan."

Was it? Facing the pile of wood, I placed my hands to my lips and blew a fiery kiss. The flames landed on the kindling, making an instant fire. "Here, let me warm your icy heart with a little flame." The fire took on a life of its own, creating an image of a crown. A simple trick but it was enough to have Austin taking a step away from the building flames. A hand rubbed over his shoulder blade where his tattoo was; his eyes never left mine. He looked troubled.

"What is it with you and that tattoo?"

His eyes met mine over the fire. "Did you read it that night?"

"Not from the angle I was at."

"It is something I have in remembrance of my mother." The flames cast a glow onto his face. "She was run off the road when I was little. Her injuries were pretty bad but considering she was a healer, she could have healed herself. But she was pregnant with my sister, and she decided to save the baby instead of her own life."

"That's horrible, but it sounds like she was a terrific mother. What does the tattoo say?"

He just stared at me. His eyes turned to narrow slits, shadows dancing on his face in the light of the flame. Why was he mad at me?

"Whatever. I don't care." Or at least I shouldn't. "Back to what you said earlier, regardless of whatever your plan is considering me, be aware, I'll be on my guard."

He cast a glance to the fire before his eyes connected with mine again. "No, my queen, it is I who will be on my guard."

It wasn't until sometime that night, right before I fell asleep, I realized Austin had called me his queen and without malice in his voice. Nothing made sense anymore, especially when it came to the slightly above smoldering male companion I traveled with.

Sleep came to me fast, and what was more shocking was the ease in which I slept. When the sun started peeking its head over the mountains, I snuggled in closer to the warmth surrounding me. A hand tightened. My eyes flew open as I studied the arm draped over me. The forearm was golden and covered with curly hair the color of wheat. Definitely male. Austin. He was the reason I had the best sleep of my life. I tried to ease away from him, but his arm flexed, pulling me tighter into the warmth.

"Trying to escape?"

I rolled over, facing him. "You're awake?"

He laughed. "I've been patiently waiting for you to wake up. I wanted to see what emotions I would get out of you this morning. Shock, denial, determination were just a few, and then there is the current emotion, anger."

I slapped his chest. "Let go of me, you douche."

His head tilted back with laughter. "You make it too easy."

He thought he could read me? I would give him something even I didn't see coming, just to watch that smirk fall right off his face. Grabbing two fistfuls of hair, I pulled his lips to mine. He didn't even have time to register shock before our lips touched. At first it was like hitting a wall of resistance, but within seconds I quickly realized why Sarah had fallen in love with Austin if he kissed her with half of the enthusiasm he bestowed upon me. His tongue met mine in an epic battle. Moments could have passed by or centuries, and I wouldn't have known. I flipped him over on his back. Within a millisecond, he had tossed us in the air, so he was now in the dominant position. My heart raced as his hand lightly squeezed my throat while he deepened the kiss. My whole body burned, aching with a need that was foreign to me. Just as I felt like I was going to explode, he broke off the kiss to lightly trail his lips along my throat.

In a raspy voice I didn't recognize, I said, "See, you can't guess everything I'm about to do."

He chuckled before he rested his forehead on mine with a sweet innocence I'd never known. "Be careful of what games you play; you might just find out how bad of a loser you are."

"I don't lose."

His lips lifted into a smile, as he stared down at me. "You didn't send me a horrific image this time, so I consider that a win on my part, not to mention this is the third time you have kissed me. Another win."

"You know for someone who professes his hatred for demons, you sure didn't mind making out with one."

I shoved at his chest. His steely blue eyes met mine, and not for the first time I saw the warrior behind his pretty-boy charm. He was deadly, and whatever his reasons for not leaving me yet on this plane were, it didn't mean it was because he was soft, or he didn't plan to do just that. He stood with a lethal grace. I ignored his hand, as I made my own way to my feet.

"I'm conflicted. You're nothing like your father. I've realized that early on but I didn't want to admit that you could be different. I needed to hate you." My eyes turned to slits. I needed to get away. He grabbed my arm in a light grip, stopping me from retreating. "You're angry. Why?"

"Really? I'll tell you why I'm mad. You're more like my father than I have ever been. After all it's you who has stripped me of my powers twice now. And now I'm just thinking of how you might be trying to screw me over, again. Oh, and you needed to hate me? Why because I'm a demon or is it because of one of the millions of secrets that I know you're holding on to? Do you want to talk about it?" Great. Now I sounded like Tally. "Do you want to tell me why you have such a strong hatred for demons?"

His hand dropped from my arm and I let out a frustrated sigh. Austin looked at me once before he stared into the embers of the dying fire. "I don't want to discuss those things but how about I tell you what I'm thinking right now? I think you're like a drug. I know I shouldn't inhale you, but my body craves you. The more I'm around you, the more I want you. This arrangement started out like your soul. Black and white. Now everything is complicated. You're right in the fact that I do have secrets and they are weighing on me heavily. One thing I never thought I would fear is disappointing you, and now it's one of my biggest fears."

I was shocked. I didn't know what I expected from this warrior standing in front of me, but his feelings, however confusing they were, were a surprise. He was messing with my head more than I had ever planned on messing with his. My lips still felt swollen from his kisses, and I still smelled his scent mixed with mine. The worst part was I took comfort in all of that. I needed space and quickly.

"There was a small pond not too far from here. We passed it along the way. I think I'll go back to it and rinse the dirt from me," I said.

Without waiting for a reply, I started back down the path in which we had come from. If he were going to try to ditch me, now would be the time for him to do it. Also, if he really wanted to leave me here, could I stop him? Maybe. But there was a part of me that really wanted him to make that choice of not leaving me behind. Technically I still have my powers. I could overpower him, take the key and leave him here, but that thought left me feeling sick. I would rather be dead than stuck in a portal without powers and I knew the strong Power Manipulator would feel the same way. I said I was nothing like my father and I meant it. What kind of Demon Queen was I? I sounded like a hopeless romantic, instead of a ball-busting, man-eating, crown-wearing queen. Maybe I needed a legit therapist.

I continued down the rocky path until I reached a vast pond. Shedding my boots, I grabbed the hem of my Rolling Stones T-shirt and started to inch it above my torso. I looked out over the water and noticed it was translucent and beautiful. Almost as beautiful as the male sitting in the water at the far end. My hands dropped my shirt back into place as I studied the male. His tree-trunk arms rested on the bank, and his head was tilted back as he laughed. There was a bevy of pretty women sitting around him, just as mesmerized as I was by his musical laugh. Sandy blond hair was pulled back and tied away from his face while the sides were shaved. I'd never been a fan of men wearing ponytails until this very moment. He was smoking hot in a David Beckham kind of way. Not as hot as the man I was currently avoiding, but then again, could anyone truly beat Austin in a beefcake contest? What did they say about speaking of the devil and he shall appear? Without turning around, I sensed Austin behind me. He could have left me, yet here he was, seeking me out, and here I was wondering why that made me so happy. When the man in the pond's laughter died, I realized he had caught sight of us.

His gaze perused my body before he licked his lips. "Looks like there is new fish in the sea, and who do I have the pleasure of seeing in my dreams later tonight?"

Austin bit out, "Are you Malakian?"

The man's eyes narrowed. "Who's asking?"

"I'll take that as a yes. I've come with an offer for you," Austin said.

The man snorted. "Sorry, I don't roll that way. Now for her," he said, pointing at me, "I will willingly listen to any offers."

"Cute. But she's not interested," Austin said, halfway stepping in front of me. I hid my smile. Austin, whether he knew it or not, was acting jealous. "We're here to talk business with you. Ariana, the greatest soothsayer to ever live, has sent us."

The man gave us a calculating look before he stood. Whoa. Boy. There was no fin for this guy. There he was, in all his naked glory. Austin shoved me fully behind him. "In order to impress the Demon Queen, you'd have to sport more than that."

The man wrapped a towel around his waist. "Demon Queen, huh? That's impressive as hell. Pun intended."

I poked Austin in the back. "See? Some people think I'm impressive."

Austin craned his neck to look at me. "I never said you weren't impressive. Can we not do this right now?"

Malakian interrupted us. "Apologies. I didn't realize you two were a couple."

"We're not," we both said in unison.

I glared at the bane of my existence. "Austin, here, has a problem with my demonic lineage."

Malakian grinned. "I don't. I guess his loss is my gain."

"Enough." Austin grabbed the bridge of his nose. Obviously, he had run out of patience. "Do you have a place more private to talk?"

After studying both of us and trying to figure out our game—good luck with that, buddy—he whispered something to the girls. After they giggled, they swam under the water, coming out on the other side of a bridge where they climbed up to bask in the new rays of the day.

I looked at the pretty scenery. "This doesn't seem like a horrible place."

Malakian shrugged. "It's not. Except for the fact that everyone here is hungry. There is food and water, but if we try to eat or drink, we become violently ill. Also, there is no sleep. If our eyes close even momentarily, we are hit with an onslaught of visions we wouldn't even wish on our worst enemies."

I glanced at Austin. We were able to sleep last night. Peacefully even.

Austin shook his head. "I couldn't sleep last night."

"So yeah," Malakian said, "it's only paradise if you don't miss food and sleep." He gave a wave at us both. "So, you have privacy. Now talk."

We walked over the round stones paving the way to where he stood. I watched where I stepped, but my head snapped up at the anger in Austin's voice. "Stop staring at her."

Malakian gave me another once over. "Or what? You said you're not together. Besides, she is beautiful. It's hard not to stare."

Austin took three long strides, putting him nose to nose with Malakian. "Keep undressing her with your eyes, and I'll fillet you where you stand, fish boy."

Malakian smirked. "Yes, you're right. Definitely not a couple." He put his hands up in surrender. "Tell me why you are here."

I grabbed Austin by the elbow, gently pulling him back beside me. "We're here to free you of this plane."

"No shit?"

Austin lifted one shoulder. "Why would we lie?"

Malakian studied us both for a moment. "Are there conditions to my freedom?"

I snorted. "The soothsayer always has conditions. We are nothing but pawns in her game, but does it matter? Do you honestly want to stay here?"

Malakian shook his head. "No, I miss my powers."

"So, let's get out of here." Before I could see if my teleporting skills worked in the portal, the ground quaked. Small rocks and pebbles jumped and rolled along the bank.

"This isn't good," Malakian said.

I stared in horror and mild fascination as the water in the pond churned like a small tornado. Waves hit the bank and came crashing over my boots.

Austin asked, "What is going on?"

Malakian rolled his eyes. "It's Herman, and he's the only being here who retained his powers. Talk about life being unfair."

Herman? That name sounded harmless. The water rushed in the direction of the bridge, causing the mermaids to scream, clinging onto one another. Since my boots were already soaked, I walked ankle-deep into the water, ignoring Austin's warning. I wanted to get a closer look at this Herman. Whatever was in the pond stopped so fast, water splashed up and over the girls on the bridge. The current changed directions, and whoever Herman was, he headed for me.

Malakian mumbled something and Austin shouted, "Back out of the water. Now!"

I took several steps back towards dry land. "Who is Herman?"

Malakian sounded bored. "Oh, just a sadistic prick who has been on the search for his wife since we got to this hellhole, so far he hasn't found a mate he deems acceptable."

A man who I assumed was Herman broke the surface of the water. His hair was red and spiky. The rings in his eyebrows, nose, and lower lip glinted in the sun. Water dripped down his pale skin and scrawny chest. He had no legs, but he made up for it with numerous tentacles.

"You," he said, pointing a finger at me. "You are the one I've been waiting for."

Dumbfounded, I pointed my thumb at my chest. "Me?"

"Yes, you are meant to rule beside me."

"Oh yeah, that's not really going to work for me. I'm already a ruler in my own dimension, and to be honest, I'm not really a team player. More of a riding solo kind of girl, but thanks for the offer."

His fingers urged me to come forward as he came closer to the bank. "Come to me, my bride, so we can consummate our marriage."

Eww. Gross. My gag reflexes were in full throttle mode.

"Carmen," Austin said, "come toward me, now."

"Well, it's not every day you meet someone as crazy as you, so thank you for the experience, but if you don't mind, we have to be someplace, so swim on, little dude." I looked over my shoulder at Austin, as the water splashed behind me. "Can you believe the nerve of some people? I mean—"

I stopped speaking as Austin's eyes grew wide. He grabbed me by the wrist just as a long tentacle lashed out of the water and wrapped around my legs, and since Austin refused to let me go, both of us went flying into the water. One tentacle surged from the pond and slammed us both on a rock jutting up out of the water. Austin's hold on my wrist broke, but Herman's grip didn't falter. Oh goodie. He was pulling me down to the bottom of the pond.

Underwater, he said, "I will love you forever."

I tried to voice my opinion, but I was a demon, not a mermaid. Water filled my lungs. This wasn't good. In fact since I was born of fire, technically water was my Achilles heel. Just because I was different and enjoyed water didn't mean I was as powerful as I was while on land. Not Herman, though. Not only was he able to talk underwater, but he had unimaginable speed. As he kept trying to woo me with pretty love words, we continued to shoot to the bottom like a bullet. Since I couldn't speak when he told me how extraordinary I was, I replied the only way I knew how: I gave him the bird. My lungs ached as he threw me down on a makeshift altar. Being immortal, I couldn't die, but the intense feeling of taking on water and drowning over and over again was not pleasurable. Four of his tentacles rested over the top of me, stretching me to the table. He picked up a golden dagger.

"You will take a blood oath to me," he wheezed.

Maybe I needed to convey my message better? That's when I reached out and grabbed him by the nose ring, tugging hard. He cursed. While he held his nose with one hand, I snatched the dagger from him. With a quick slice, I cut a tentacle from my body. He released me. His roar was enough to cause the water to shift and move, making my departure harder, as I swam against the current. Out of the corner of my eye, I saw Austin swimming towards me. Holding onto the dagger, I pushed off the altar. Austin stretched a hand out to me, and I almost touched his fingertips before Herman caught me by my leg. Frognog monkeysucker. He jerked me back towards him. I landed hard on the altar once more, letting out a scream underwater when I saw he had a long blade in his hand, and he was swinging. My Latin couldn't work if I couldn't talk. My smoke curled out of me, but through the liquid, the tendrils were slow as a snail, and Herman didn't have that problem.

"If you won't be my bride, then you shall be no one's,' he said.

I watched in horror as the blade started coming down, and it was headed for my throat. The whacko planned on killing me. This was the most intense relationship I'd never been in. I flinched as a body tackled Herman a second before the steel had a chance to deliver a final blow to me. The momentum shot the blade forward, and it sliced my leg. Blood swirled around me, as dizziness swept over me. I was in shock as I watched my leg detach from my body. Austin ripped Herman's head off, and the remaining tentacles released me from the altar once more. Blood floated around me as I drifted up to the surface. A strong arm wrapped around my waist. I was so dizzy and out of air, and the surface seemed miles away. I was immortal, so it didn't make sense I felt like death would be knocking on my door soon. Austin grabbed my face. Slanting his mouth over mine, he pumped oxygen into me. My lungs filled as he kicked us to the surface. The moment our heads broke above water, I passed out.

When I woke, a gentle hand stroked my back. The smell of blood had my nostrils flaring. My body throbbed as I looked down at the source of my pain; I remembered I was missing a leg. There were strings of tendons lying on the rock I was on. I gagged. The smell was about to be my undoing. Strong arms wrapped around me. I whimpered.

"Shh, it's okay. You're going to be okay."

A few inches above the knee and down, everything was just … gone. "Am I?"

"Of course you are. Don't look at it anymore. Look at me."

I gazed up at Austin. The pain was unbelievable, but I would not cry. The soft look he gave me pushed me over the edge. I felt one lone tear streak down my face.

His jaw clenched, as if he were the one in pain. "Listen to me. You are fierce. You are a queen. Not just any queen, but Queen of Demons. We will be laughing over this in no time."

I sniffled. "Yeah, well, it isn't funny right now. His name was Herman! How was I supposed to know he was going to try and chop me up?"

Malakian stood off to the side. "I did warn you he was sadistic."

Austin stroked my face tenderly. "It doesn't matter. You're okay. That's all that matters." He looked at my leg before he let out multiple curse words. "Why is it not healing?"

I tried to peer at my foot, but he palmed my face and shoved it into his chest.

"You were supposed to be able to obtain your powers here, and yet you're not healing."

I took a couple of deep breaths, focusing on his spicy scent and not the pain. "Maybe I can use my powers, just not to their full extent. Or maybe I'm just too—" A sob escaped me. I couldn't even say the word weakened without crying.

"Then we've got to get you out of this plane and quick, so you can heal."

The frantic sound in his voice confirmed my suspicions. He didn't sound like a man who had planned on leaving me here in this plane. He scooped me up in his arms. "We're leaving now."

He jostled me, and I let out a hiss. He made a cooing sound that was as comforting as it was disconcerting.

"Austin, you never planned on leaving me here, did you?"

"No, Carmen. I'm finding it harder and harder to believe that I could—" He cleared his throat. "I won't leave you here because you don't deserve it. Just like I wouldn't have left you in Alaska."

Malakian came to stand closer to Austin to get a better look at the mangled leg. "I hate to break up whatever this is, but she is still losing blood. A lot. Immortal or not, if we don't get her out of here soon, she will die here, and it's a good day's walk back to the portal. Do you have a plan?"

"We run. If you can't keep up, you get left. The hell with what the soothsayer wants."

"I'll keep up," Malakian said.

Austin took off at a brisk pace. There was no way he could run this fast the entire time. Each time his foot struck the earth, I wanted to scream. The pain was so sharp black dots rimmed my vision. I buried my head into Austin's chest and fought a wave of nausea hitting me full force. I was losing my fight to stay awake, and I was grateful for it.

Austin picked up the pace, if that was even possible. "Faster, fish boy, or you'll be left."

There was something in Austin's voice that rang so true. If Malakian didn't keep up, he would leave him here. What did that say about the Power Eliminator? I would think about it when I woke up. If I woke up.

chapter twenty one

I awoke the moment we crossed through the portal. Pain radiated through me, and I had sweat beads gathered on my brow. Austin laid me gently in the field. His hand pushed the hair back from my face. I peeled my eyes open to see his look of worry. His shirt was thoroughly drenched. Both him and Malakian looked utterly exhausted. I realized this had nothing do with lust, power, or vows. Austin truly cared for me. Something in my heart expanded. His blue eyes quickly took in my body, and I couldn't miss the look of relief when he glanced at my leg.

Behind him, Malakian stood with his arms outstretched. "Ah, it feels good to have my powers back."

How in the world he kept his towel on, I'd never know.

I winced as my leg began the slow process of regenerating. Tally came flying in like a crazed mama bear. "What happened to her? I knew I should have gone with you."

I held up a hand, staving off his slew of questions. "I'm okay."

Tally flew over to my good leg. He carefully inspected my wound before he shook his head. "I can't let you out of my sight." He glanced over his shoulder at me. "And who is the weird guy in the dirty towel?"

Malakian pounded his chest like a caveman. "Freedom, baby." He gazed around the field. "Water, I need water."

Austin pointed to a water pump not too far away.

Malakian saluted me. "Bombshell, it's been nice knowing you. Sorry about the leg. I'll come to visit you."

Austin never took his eyes off of me. "And I'll kill you."

Malakian shrugged. "Territorial for someone who's not in a relationship."

Austin growled, causing Malakian to back away with barely suppressed laughter. We watched as he turned the old pump on, and after a few seconds, water began to flow onto the dirt. Malakian smiled with delight as the water pooled at his feet. What did he think he was doing? And in a towel no less. I watched in fascination. The moment the water touched his toes, Malakian started to morph. His body turned transparent as he merged with the water. There was now a big puddle at the base of the pump. The water sloshed together before it started to flow towards the creek I assumed was used for irrigation. We watched as it, or I guess technically Malakian, rolled right into the creek. I was truly impressed.

Tally flew over and turned the pump off, mumbling something about wasting water before he said, "Well, that was an odd bird."

"Fish," I murmured, causing Austin to laugh.

"See, that's another thing," Tally said with disgust. "I obviously missed out on all of the action. Now, you both will have all of these nauseating inside jokes I won't be privy to."

Feeling drained, I yawned. "I'll catch you up. I promise."

Austin gathered me in his arms once again. "I'm taking you back to your world. You will be more comfortable there." Would I? His arms tightened around me as he commanded, "Sleep, and you will heal faster."

"Yes," Tally said, "heal, so you can put your best foot forward."

Hardy har har.

I snuggled into Austin's warmth, already drifting back to sleep when Tally settled on Austin's shoulder. I was going home to rule on the throne I deserved in my shell. Why did I feel so lost when I should be happy?

I woke up in a massive bed with not one, but two legs. The only problem was it wasn't my bed. I looked around at the room I was in. Generic curtains, artwork, and a staged room. I was in a hotel, but why? I sat up slowly in confusion. On the dresser was a bag full of clothes I assumed would fit me. I was also assuming something was off in the underworld. That could be the only explanation as to why I ended up waking in a four-star hotel instead of my own bed. Today was going to be a clusterduck day. I could feel it. First things first, I was in a desperate need of a shower, so before I dived into the why's of my surroundings, I was going to enjoy a hot shower. I peeled off the dirty, tattered clothes and left them in a pile as I hopped into the small, tiled shower. After I was done, I took my time getting dressed in a red, off-the-shoulder sweater and tight, black leather pants. I silently thanked whoever picked out my attire. If today needed to be a butt-whooping day, not only did I look the part, but I felt good in leather. I leaned an ear against the adjoining door and listened. I could hear the rustling of papers, but more importantly, I could smell the familiar warm scent I had grown accustomed to. The door separating our rooms was locked, so I gave it a quick knock. A few seconds later, Austin opened the door sans T-shirt. His jeans hung low on his hips, and the first button was undone. He was holding a white box in his hands.

I cleared my throat, and his blue eyes met mine before they traveled the length of me. My stomach tightened as heat swirled in my belly. From the moment I laid eyes on Austin, he had been intriguing, but now I felt a connection and a need. It was a want that scared me and also made me feel things that I had thought I was surely incapable of feeling.

After several moments of us staring at each other, he finally broke eye contact. He looked back down at the box he was holding.

The mighty Demon Queen was nervous. Unbelievable. I just went with the first thing that came to my mind. "Thank you for saving my life in that portal. I can't believe I almost got killed by an overgrown octopus. That's super embarrassing."

He didn't laugh or even smile. Instead, he walked into my room and sat on my unmade bed and stared at that box he clutched in his hands. For whatever reason, I became a little nervous.

"I'm assuming you picked out my clothes?" He gave a nod but wouldn't look at me. "Well, thanks for that, too. So, we got the key. You're going to help save the world." I walked around the desk and sat on the edge, facing him. "I bet you will have girls falling at your feet. You might even get your own fan page." Still nothing. "Not really sure why we're in a hotel. I'm sure there is a great explanation for that." He gave another nod. "What's in the box?"

That got his attention. He leaned back against the headboard, and I noticed how drained he looked. "An insurance policy to make sure that I'm motivated. I was trying to figure a way to get myself out of this mess before I found this in your chamber address to me."

"The box?" I asked. He nodded. "So this insurance policy I presume is the reason we're here instead of in my own chambers?"

"I just needed time to think. Weigh my options. There is no way out of this mess without hurting someone."

"What mess? Maybe I can help."

He ran a hand over his stubble. "You would help me? I thought you would be kicking me out of your life and planning my death by now."

"Austin, I only planned your death because you were planning mine."

"I never once threatened your life."

"You threatened my powers, and to me, that is the same thing. I've lived almost my whole life without my shell … without my powers. It was stifling. Like I couldn't breathe. I was existing, but I wasn't really living, and now that I know what it feels like to truly live, I would rather die than go back to just existing."

He stood up to pace, leaving the white box on the bed unattended. His long legs ate up the distance on the standardized carpet.

"Where is Tally, by the way?" I asked.

"Fool's errand."

"Uh, why?"

"We need to talk," he said, but then he was quiet. Instead, he just paced. I sat there watching him as I tried to figure out what inner demons the Power Eliminator battled. He stopped several times like he was about to share something with me, but then he would just resume pacing again.

"Austin," I said, but he continued to ignore me. Finally, I got up and blocked his path. "What has got you so bent out of shape?"

"You." My heart sped up. "You're not what I thought you were going to be. You're kind and have a gentle heart, whether you want to admit it or not."

"Shh, be quiet, will you?" He was going to give me a bad reputation if he kept that up.

He ignored me. "She knew. This entire time she knew. Are we all but pawns to be manipulated?"

If I could stop noticing how insanely hot he was, I think I would be a tad freaked out by his erratic behavior. If the powerful Power Eliminator was extremely upset about something, it couldn't bode well for me. "Who knew?"

"Now, looking back, she was the one who told Dansby to go to that club."

"Dansby, I've heard of that before. You said that when I got my shell."

Now that I was thinking about it, he'd lost control that day, just like he was doing now. Part of me wondered if he had taken on too much power over the years. Was he on the brink of insanity?

"That's when I started to realize perhaps I was being played. The day you got your true form." He reared back and punched the metal door frame going into the bathroom. I flinched as I heard the bones in his hand break. "She knew how this was all going to unfold, but she didn't tell me."

"Look at me. Austin, please," I begged. His blue eyes met mine, and for the first time since I'd walked into the room, some of the fog clouding his vision started to clear. "Talk to me. Explain things."

"You calm me," he said, as he took two giant strides towards me. His startling blue eyes roamed my face, asking me for some answer I wasn't privy to, because I didn't know the question. I barely recognized this Austin. The one who was silently out of control. Where had the arrogant, over-confident Austin gone?

His hand reached out to tuck a wayward strand of hair behind my ear. I grabbed his wrist, holding his hand to my face. "I shouldn't care but I do. What's going on with you?"

He gave a laugh without any mirth. "You care?" At my nod, he said, "Well, then my fears have come true and I'm about to majorly disappoint you." He closed his eyes before he said, "I've lied to you this entire time. I've said things. Horrible things to try and keep a distance between us when it was just a losing battle. The truth is I'm the evil one."

I could tell by his body language he thought he told the truth, but the demon in me knew evil when I saw it, and Austin was far from it. I stood there, waiting patiently. Whatever had caused him this much stress couldn't be good. My stomach tightened in knots. When he didn't resume speaking, I said, "Austin, I've done some pretty bad things I would consider evil, but I can promise you that each time I did those despicable acts, it was because I was backed in a corner. A lot of us would do anything it took to survive. Why don't you unload what's on your mind?"

"You will hate me afterward."

My lips tugged up in a smile. "Would you care if a demon hated you?"

"I'd care if you hated me, yes."

He pulled away from me and went over to the mini-fridge to pour himself a drink. I sat on the edge of the bed and quietly scooted the box over to me while I impatiently waited for him to explain what was going on.

"In the enchanted maze I saw my friend." His deep voice was strained. "Dansby is my best friend. He has been since second grade. His powers aren't phenomenal—in fact they aren't even mediocre. He can tell when someone is lying. That is his power. His only power. Because he isn't powerful, most supernaturals can't recognize him as one of their own, allowing him to slide under the radar. Dansby has always thought he was a lot slicker than what he really was. I've recently found out that Ariana had a run-in with Dansby. She gave him an idea, and within a week he had started playing in underground casinos where supernaturals were known to frequent and party. The casino is layered with heavy magic to create a safe zone. All factions from the Lux and Degenerates can play in the casino without fear of losing their life. There are two rules: no fighting and no cheating. Break either of those, and you forfeit your life to the one you accosted. Dansby would play several hands of poker, sometimes purposefully losing just to come back and win a big hand. He had an advantage. He knew when someone lied about their hand. He made a lot of money that first month. Drew a lot of attention to himself. So much in fact that he earned himself a nickname, they called him lucky. One night he was playing against a group of Degenerates. Long story short, they caught him cheating. They have him now."

My heart dropped. "Ariana set him up?"

"I believe so, yes. I wouldn't be shocked at this point if she tipped the other players off."

"Why would she do that?"

He swished the whiskey around in his glass. "Exactly."

"He's still alive?" At his nod, I asked, "If he's not powerful, why are they keeping him alive?"

"Because I am powerful, and these Degenerates have a need for my talent." He nodded at the box at my fingertips. "That box you've very coyly tried to get close to, flip the lid."

And I thought I was in stealth mode. I flipped the lid off the box and winced. "Is that what I think it is?" He nodded. "And it belongs to Dansby?"

"Unfortunately."

I looked at the bloody pinky finger resting in the box. Someone was sending Austin a message. "Okay, well," I said, reclining on my elbows. This was a super easy fix. I didn't know why he was wigging out so bad. "Why are we sitting here? Let's go get him back."

He laughed without humor. "An evil queen would never say that but I'm not surprised. See, here lies the problem. Demons have him." Dread pooled in my stomach. Of course they did if he found the box earlier in my chambers. I was slowly connecting the dots. "They have offered him to me for an exchange."

I sat up and eyed the door, ready to flee. I had a sinking feeling I knew what the exchange was. "Let me guess. These Degenerates are under lords?" When he wouldn't meet my eyes, I said, "You've offered me up on a platter, huh? Let me take another stab in the dark here. The under lords were also the ones who made you take the vow of stripping my powers."

Everything was quiet. We both just stared at each other. He knocked back the whiskey and then slammed his empty glass down on the bar.

"How long have you known about this little exchange?"

"From the beginning. As soon as Dansby went missing four weeks ago, I got a phone call. Ariana told me I would need to find the key in order to rescue my friend. She said just by looking for the key, it would bring the Demon

Queen into my life, and you were the only thing the under lords were willing to barter Dansby for."

"Let me guess, the demons didn't tell you this, but the soothsayer relayed the info?"

He nodded. That dang soothsayer probably told the demons to kidnap Dansby, and how they could use him as a pawn.

"Yeah, she set me up," he said, as he drained his glass again. "It gets worse. You see, I didn't need the key to track you down. Without your shell, I could have easily found you and handed you over to the under lords. I was told that when I crossed paths with you, you would ask something of me, and if I didn't find what you were looking for, I would forfeit my friend's life. Also, I could not make the exchange until after I had the key in my hands."

He took out the small black ball and sat it on the counter. We both stared at the object.

"But you don't believe any of that to be true?" I asked.

"No, I don't. I also don't believe we needed to go into a portal to rescue that overgrown fish. And yet Ariana said if I didn't rescue Malakian, I would never know the location of Dansby. That day at the bar when she called me, it was as if she kept adding on and changing the rules. Every time I'd get close to the key, something would change. She told me I wasn't to attempt his rescue until her or her protégée contacted me. She played me, and I let her because Dansby is like a brother to me."

My voice tight, I said, "Yeah, that part I wouldn't understand. After all, my only sibling tried to kill me. Here's another thing I don't understand. You belittled me from the beginning. You even reprimanded me for not caring about the key, and you were never truly interested in it. You also acted like you had to be talked into working with me."

"If I would have immediately taken your help, wouldn't it have been suspicious?"

I frowned. I'd give him that.

"And don't get me wrong. I think it's important that someone retrieves the key from the Degenerates. I just never thought I was that guy."

I was so freaking hurt, but I wouldn't show him that. I tilted my chin up. "When you didn't leave me on the plane or when you saved my life, it wasn't because you cared. It was because I was your bargaining chip, and you couldn't ruin that." He made a motion to reach for me. "Don't you dare touch me. Ever again."

"Carmen, that wasn't the reason."

"Yeah?" I snarled. "Well, enlighten me. What was the reason then?"

"I figured out why she gave me—us—the runaround." He reached out and grabbed my wrist, pulling me off the bed. My whole body stiffened. Was this where he stripped me of my powers? "Because I needed the time to fall in love with you."

"What?" I gasped.

"Because you see, you're my mate."

Everything in me shifted. I felt sucker-punched. Air was no longer circulating through my lungs. I could hear the ancient clock on the bedside table ticking. I had a fleeting moment where I felt hope … the thought of being someone's mate. It was the rarest form of love; could I possibly have that? Then sanity came crashing back Not only could I not have that, but this man was willing for his mate to be the sacrificial lamb. Talk about shitty luck.

I jerked my wrist out of his grasp. "That makes it worse, doesn't it? So tell me, why did you share this info with me? Why not just let it all be a surprise?" At his silence, I tilted my head sideways. "So what now? Is this the part where you drag me kicking and screaming to wherever the tradeoff place is?"

Without waiting for an answer, I went on the offense. With all the power I owned, I threw a combination of punches to his face while sending terrifying images to his brain. I hoped he wouldn't be able to discern what was real or not and allow me the time I needed to kill him. After I spun around, the heel of my foot careened into his throat. A split second before it connected, I realized I had pulled the hit to soften the blow. I could have easily broken his windpipe but I didn't. He deflected my next hits, but it was clear he wasn't trying to spar with me. He was trying to lessen the damage I was doing to him. He had betrayed me, and yet I didn't want to kill this man because I cared for him. I wasn't fit to be a queen. Just as I had decided to retreat, teleport myself far away from him, he grabbed me around the waist, and we both toppled over on the floor. Ropes of smoke flew out of me, wrapping around him and squeezing.

He gritted his teeth in pain, but he didn't let me go. "I told you because I needed you to understand. Remember when you were willing to do anything including breaking a vow to save Tally? I made vows before I even knew you. I have to honor them but I vow to you I will fix this." There was such finality in those words. I wasn't shocked when I felt the power being drained from my body. Betrayed, hurt, pissed, but shocked? No.

He climbed to his feet as I lay there on the carpet embarrassed as a lone tear trailed down my face. I quickly dashed it away. I watched him as he ambled over to the bar and poured another drink. He drained it in less than a second then threw the empty glass at the wall. I winced as it shattered into a million pieces.

I could hear the pounding of footsteps outside of my door. Before my uncle and the other under lords busted into the room, I heard the man that I had fallen in love with whisper, "I'm sorry."

As I came face to face with my uncle and reality sunk in, I knew what utter betrayal felt like.

chapter twenty two

Twenty hours later, I sat chained to a wall completely powerless. The chains were overkill, but I guess they made a statement to every demon who decided to come to the dungeon area. I was like a freak show act. The demons would come point at me, make jokes, and then walk away. I gave another vicious tug on my chain. If I could get loose even powerless, I'd make them pay. Somehow, I'd make them pay.

A demon shuffled toward my cell. I knew who it was before I even looked up. "So what's the plan, uncle? Keep me chained up for eternity?"

His black eyes leered at me. "Don't be silly, niece. I'm only keeping you chained up long enough for every demon here to realize you aren't as powerful as what was foretold."

I blew a piece of hair out of my eye. "Foretold?"

"Ah, yes. The reason you were tortured so violently. We couldn't kill you outright, but you deserved punishment for the false prophecy. The records have been destroyed, but there are still a few that are loyal to the crown who remember that night. You see, niece, a long time ago a soothsayer predicted you would come along, and you would make the demon nation more powerful than it ever has been before by changing us for the better. Then you would bring us to our knees in submission. I have a problem with that. Several, actually. We don't need change. We don't accept change, and we don't bow before anyone. So you are chained for those who remember the old telling. I want them to see how wrong that soothsayer was. When I rule, no one will doubt I am the true intended ruler."

I refused to act interested in anything he had to say. I faked yawn. "Sorry, I might have taken a power nap. When's lunch?"

His fist hit the bars that separated us. "Your death will be a public one. It's within the hour. Prepare for it."

"Prepare for it? How does one prepare for a public execution? Like should I meditate or do some yoga and shirt?" I rolled my eyes. It would be nice to be able to cuss on my death bed. "You're a joke, and that's what you'll still be when you're officially named King of the Demons. A joke. Just like your sorry ash brother."

He bared his teeth at me and I just laughed. He could kill me, but he would never have my respect or my fear again.

I waited until I could no longer hear his footsteps before I let out a sigh. So, this is how I would go out? I imagined something a little more dramatic. Instead, I would be led like a goat to be slaughtered in front of a bunch of morons.

I heard a giggle and then a deep southern accent. I banged my head against the wall. What had I ever done to deserve to be tortured like this? Seeing her again? Ugh. The next hour couldn't pass soon enough.

"Why hello. So we meet again."

"What's up, buttercup? Heard about what cuddle bear did to you. So unfortunate. Men, right?"

Her eyes narrowed as she licked her pink lips. She started to grab the filthy bars between us but then thought better of it. She probably didn't want to ruin her manicure. Sarah tossed her brown hair behind her in an exaggerated motion.

"I hear he was the one to actually put you here." I gave her my most bored expression. "Oh dear, did you think he wouldn't betray you?" She laughed like a dolphin.

"I guess the real question is, why are you here?"

"Oh hon, I never left."

What? Austin had said he took her far away. "Is that right, Mary?"

She glared at me. "You know my name. But what you don't know is that I overheard some of the conversation Ariana had with Austin. I'm not as stupid as I seem."

"That's terrific news because there for a while even I felt sorry for you."

"Funny. So after I threatened Austin that I would tell you everything."

"Why didn't he just kill you and save us all the trouble of ever having to listen to your voice again?"

"He thought I was vindictive but harmless. Plus, I had a fail-safe plan. I had contacted my friends and let them know that if I didn't check in once a day they were to contact you with what I had learned."

"You have friends?"

She glared at me. "I've been trying to escape this stupid place but it's impossible with all of its mazes. Good news is I found your uncle. He's taking me right now to meet the other under lords. He is going to let me be a part of a ceremony. It will make me a more powerful witch. Then he is personally going to escort me out of this horrible place."

I shook my head. "Nope. He's going to kill you. The under lords have a thing for witches. Especially ones that are found where they don't belong. You need to run and hide. You need to—"

"Stop your lies. I just wanted you to know Austin never loved you, just like he never loved me. The only difference between our stories is that I will walk away one of the most powerful witches to ever have lived, and you will die here tonight in this sad place."

She'd be dead before I would. There was no reasoning with her, though. I would actually be one of the last faces she saw before the under lords killed her.

"I just wanted to come down here," she said, "to tell you why he betrayed you so easily."

I knew why. For his friend. "I'm not interested in conversing with you."

"But surely you want to know the reason he hates you so much is because your father killed his mother when he was a toddler."

My throat was dry. "What?" She knew she had me. She smirked. I had so many questions, but it bugged me she felt so great about bringing me so much pain. "Tell me, Mary, how did your sister end up with the key? I mean, that was a real shirt show if I've ever seen one. There wasn't one witch there even remotely powerful."

She was so taken aback by my question she answered honestly. "A soothsayer gave them the key." Dang Ariana. "But … but Austin, he—"

"Meh. I'm done talking about him. I'm over it."

That was not the answer she wanted. She wanted to break me, but you couldn't break something that already felt broken. I might die tonight, but I wouldn't let her try to hurt me for her enjoyment. She stormed off and to her retreating back, I yelled, "They really will hurt you. You should run."

I could hear her dolphin laugh as she walked past the cells and up the stairs. It was a shame she wouldn't listen to me.

Twenty minutes later, I heard drums. They would beat for the next thirty minutes letting everyone know to meet on level twelve. There would be a very important execution. Mine. I gave my chains another tug. This was not how I wanted to go out, being betrayed by the man I had fallen in love with. He had used me from day one. My father had killed his mother. No wonder he hated demons so much. The only reason he didn't open up to me and tell me about his past was because he had planned all along to end my future. I felt my eyes fill. I clutched my teeth and willed the tears away. I would not cry.

Quiet footsteps approached. I threw my head back and straightened my shoulders for whatever onslaught of words and taunts were about to be thrown my way. Was this it? Would they walk me to the execution platform now?

I wasn't prepared for what or who I saw.

"You. What the fudge do you think you're doing here? Come to pay your last respects?"

Austin stood in front of the cell with a finger across his lips. I watched as he pulled a key out of his jeans.

"I stole this from the demon guarding you, but unfortunately I had to knock him out. It's only a matter of time before someone realizes he is not sleeping." He kneeled in front of me as he began to undo my chains. I started to speak, but he shook his head. "Not now. Tally is creating a distraction. We want everyone to think it was him who let you out. Without your powers, they will be searching here for you."

As soon as the chains dropped from my wrist, I reared back and slapped him across his face.

"I deserved that and much more. Now, can I continue on with this rescue plan, or would you like for me to take another hit?" I could hear footprints coming our way. He scooped me up in his arms and teleported us to my chamber.

"Um, yeah, so I was thinking you were going to teleport me somewhere relatively safe. Like, I don't know, somewhere that demons weren't searching for me," I snarled.

"Easy. This is safe. No one who means you harm can come in. I have put my best magic around your chambers. We need to discuss a plan."

"How about this for a plan? You give me back my powers, so I can go destroy some demons, and you disappear to somewhere. Don't care where as long as I never have to see your face again."

His blue eyes narrowed at me. "I get why you're upset—"

"Upset? No, I'm foxing livid." I picked up a book lying on my desk and threw it at his head. "You betrayed me. Thirty more minutes and I would have been executed."

"No you wouldn't have. We've been there the whole time. Tally and I just had to wait until the moment was right and fortunately Sarah provided us with an opportunity to free you without being seen."

"I needed to be freed because you betrayed me."

"I understand but hear me out. I took a vow to strip you of your powers and then to hand you over to your uncle. I also took a vow to not tell anyone. If I broke my vows, I forfeited my life, and then I couldn't save Dansby. Yes, I kept my secrets and ended up betraying you but I vow to you I wouldn't have let your uncle kill you."

"When were you going to tell me about my father killing your mother?"

His eyes flashed to mine. "Who told you that?"

"Sarah. You know the distraction that you needed. The one that is probably being tortured right now. You should probably go save her before it's too late. Just give me back my powers before you leave."

"I can't save her while protecting you. I was told that—"

"Ariana created this whole mess, so I could not care less what that woman has told you regarding my future. Zero foxes when it comes to that old bat. Why didn't you tell me the reason you hated demons so much was because one had taken your mother from you?"

"When is it a good time to tell the girl you have fallen in love with that her father, who she clearly hates just as much, took someone important away from you? From your family. How would that conversation go?"

I balled my fists up. So many things were going through my head. He betrayed me just to rescue me. All of his secrets have finally caught up to him. My eyes filled with unshed tears, but I refused to let him know how much he'd hurt me. "What did you mean when you said you need to save Dansby? I thought you did that."

"No," he growled. "I kept my vows. Did everything I could to save him and in the end it still wasn't enough. When I turned you over I told your uncle it was time for him to honor his vows. He said he would give him back to me after your death."

"Why didn't you let me die?"

"Because everything has changed." He started pacing in front of the fireplace. "I don't know when everything changed but it has. Maybe it was when you saved your friend, or maybe it was when you built a castle with that little boy. Or the numerous other things you've said or done to show me who you really are. I don't know, Carmen. All I do know is, I don't just love you. I can't live without you. I can't sacrifice you for Dansby. I tried not to care, but all I see when I close my eyes at night is your face. You haunt my dreams, and God help me, I can't sacrifice you." He tugged at his hair. "Not even for Dansby. So somewhere along the way I started planning and thinking of how could I get out of my vows? The answer was I couldn't. I tried to keep my distance because so many times I felt myself wanting to tell you but I couldn't."

"You hurt me."

He took one step toward me. "I know and I'm sorry." He took another step and another. "It's all coming together." His blue eyes searched my face. "Don't you see? I was the only magical being who could retrieve your shell, and when you finally got it, I immediately recognized you were my mate. The search for the key was so we could build a connection, and I could see you were not who you wanted everyone to think you are, but so much more. The trip into the portal was so I could fall in love with you and realize what I would be sacrificing if I traded you for Dansby. She wanted us together."

I couldn't believe the soothsayer would use Dansby like that. She wasn't evil. Meddling yes, but not evil. But an innocent man was now going to die because of her.

His words rang true. His eyes pleaded with me to understand, but I wasn't overly confident with my emotions right now. I needed time to sort out everything he had just laid on my doorstep.

He reached a hand out to me and I flinched. "I'm just returning your powers, but before I give them back, I want to say I vow to never take your powers from you again." His eyes darted to mine, frantic. "Please don't leave me."

Power once again flowed into my body. I tensed as my chamber door opened. A disheveled Tally flew right before me.

"I made a huge ruckus, but it's only a matter of time before Maligno figures out it was Austin who set you free. We need to come up with a plan, quick." His eyes darted to Austin, "And I'm sorry but I couldn't find Dansby anywhere." Obviously while I was in the dungeon they had been talking.

I grabbed Tally, and as my eyes met Austin's, I realized he knew what I was going to do before I did. Holding Tally to my chest, I avoided Austin's outstretched arm as I teleported us away. Away from the underworld and away from Austin.

chapter twenty-three

It was night time in Punta Cana and the beach was completely deserted, so I headed towards the ocean. Tally flew beside me, thankfully not saying a word. I discarded my shoes and kept walking. I sat down where the tide brushed up against my toes and finally allowed myself to cry. Tally sat on my shoulder, his little hand gently stroking my hair and not knowing, just by that simple touch, he made the tears flow faster. That act of kindness pushed me over the limit.

After several minutes of crying, my voice was raw. "I think I'm better now."

Tally sighed. "Do you want to talk about why you're crying?"

"You know why."

"But I'd like to hear you say it."

I wiped the last remaining tears from my face. "Fine. I fell for Austin somewhere along the way. From the moment I saw him, I felt a pull, which makes sense considering I'm his mate. I let myself care about him. I let my guard down, and he stripped me of my powers, just like my father had done. Then he went above and beyond by handing me over to my uncle to be executed. If that's not enough reason to cry, I finally found out why he hates demons so much and to top it off, he said he loves me. Loves me! Can you believe that?"

"Yes, Carmen, I can. You're pretty easy to love. That man never had any intention of letting you be executed. I can promise my wings on that one. In fact I'm not entirely sure that your uncle had completed teleporting you before Austin had found me and had us hidden in a crevice in the dungeons." Tally flew over to my drawn-up knees, so he could look me in my face. "I get why you're upset. You have every reason to feel the way you feel, but I would like for you to see things from his perspective. I like Ariana, in fact I would count her as a friend, but she played Austin. Because of this mess she created, his friend's life is on the line. Now in her defense, there are certain parameters she has to work within. If she was to tell someone the how's, what's, and why's, it could change the fate of that person, and she really does want the best for the ones she wants to succeed. Austin was desperate to save his friend and made vows that were unbreakable. He figured out a way to not break his vows which by the way would have killed him and he also figured out a way to save you. His mate. Now, he has lost you, and once your uncle figures out Austin was behind your rescue, Austin's friend Dansby will be killed, too. Yes, Austin took your powers like your father, but that is where the similarities end. This whole mission began because of his love for another human, and it's turned into a disaster because of his love for a certain Demon Queen."

"This is a mess."

"Yes, life usually is. We all make mistakes, Carmen. He made his before he even knew you. You just have to figure out what you're willing to forgive and move on."

He was right. I opened my palm, and he flew right to it. He gave me a smile and nod like he knew my decision and was proud of me. Within seconds, I had us teleported back to my chambers. I was ready to flee just in case my uncle had infiltrated. Magic was all around me. I could feel the energy pulsating.

Austin sat in a chair, his head in his hands. The moment he realized I was back he jumped to his feet. "You came back."

Tally asked, "Does the magic I feel belong to you?"

"I put an intricate spell around Carmen's chambers. Anyone wishing her harm won't be able to enter. I started to just leave, but I was hoping …"

"Hoping I'd come back?" I asked. "Are you done with the secrets and manipulation?"

"As long as Ariana is steering this vessel, I'm sure there will be more manipulation involved, but from here on out, I'll tell you everything. I vow it."

My shoulders relaxed, as I did something I'd heard about, but had never partaken in. Forgiveness.

"So by me not getting executed, your friend dies?" His chin dropped to his chest. "I refuse to accept that as an outcome. We need to come up with a plan to get him back."

"If only it were that easy. I plan on making a rescue attempt, but I have to go at it alone, because he'd be dead the moment they realized we were working together."

He wasn't going in solo, so I ignored that comment. "You haven't received a go-ahead from Ariana?"

His blue eyes turned to steel. "Like I would trust her, anyways."

He had a point. Who knew what Ariana's motivations were at this point? My bones felt tired as I sat on the edge of the bed. "Do you know where uncle Maligno has your friend?"

"No or I would have already rescued him." He ran a hand over his face. "This is all my fault."

"No, Ariana is responsible for Dansby's demise. We are just pawns for her amusement."

Everyone should be able to agree upon that.

Tally flew over to the couch. "What do you want to do, my queen?"

"Do I even still possess that title?"

"Your uncle is not the official king until he kills you in front of witnesses," Austin said. "I did hear a couple of guards talking. Your uncle had them search your chambers and found the crown you left here. He currently has it."

Tally said, "It's just a crown. A great symbol but it doesn't make you a ruler just by wearing it."

"But I want it back. You just wait until I get my hands around his thick neck. I'm going to squeeze so hard that crown pops right off. Dang it to hay, I bet it fits him better, too."

We had to think of a plan to save Dansby and snag my crown. I started pacing the floor.

Finally, Austin snagged me around the waist, bringing me flush up against him. "I'll get your throne back if it's the last thing I do."

I slapped his chest. "Dang right you will." I started to pull away from him but stopped myself. This felt right, and I enjoyed being in his arms. When was the last time I did something out of pure enjoyment instead of things that were expected of me?

When I didn't break out of his hold, he gave me a mouthwatering grin. "If one were deserving of you, you'd be a formidable mate."

"You can bet your ash."

"I'm sorry, Carmen. Turning you over to your uncle was the hardest thing I have ever had to do because I knew that you had no clue that I wouldn't let you die in those dungeons. I knew what you would think of me and the disappointment on your face was about my undoing. Even after all of this I don't know how long I have until they figure out it was me that freed you and they kill Dansby for it."

"We'll figure it out. I am not a fan of Ariana but I can't believe that she would allow Dansby to die."

He swallowed back his emotions and then kissed me tenderly on my forehead. He did that not so weird thing where he smelled my hair. I relaxed in his arms and felt his warmth before I finally broke the contact. Then I thought of a plan to save his friend that he cared so much for and a way that wouldn't get me killed. My strategy was risky, but definitely doable.

chapter twenty four

We had stayed up most of the night going over our plan. So far Austin's magic held, and no demons were able to bust down my door or storm my chambers. Right before dawn, Tally inserted his opinion on the whole thing, which was we were all screwed, before he went into the guest bedroom to get some much needed rest.

I talked with Austin over every possible outcome and when daylight finally came, we were as ready as we could be. I dressed quickly in leather pants and a soft tee. I did a simple French braid with my long hair and completed the look with various daggers strapped to my body. One could never be too prepared when facing twelve under lords, and especially if it was my uncle who led the pack.

Austin gathered me in his arms and kissed me softly. His hands slid up and down my ribs. Our connection was getting stronger now that both of us weren't fighting it.

We were about to walk out the door when a girl who looked vaguely familiar materialized in front of us, shrieking, just to disappear again. She kept popping up all over the place like gophers popping out of a hole until she finally stopped about a foot from me. She had her hands way out to the side and knees bent like she was a surfer riding a wave.

"Who the hay are you?" I shouted.

The girl took a couple of deep breaths. Her jet-black hair was cut to her chin, and the ends were dyed cobalt blue, matching her eyes. She was very slender and had a gothic look to her that I begrudgingly admired. "Dude, I can't master this shiznit. I swear, Ariana makes it look so easy peasy. Every time I try to pop up somewhere, my bowels loosen in the process, and I never know if I'm going to stick the landing."

My brow wrinkled. "Yeah, way too much info. Who are you? Why are you here? And why are you still crouched?"

She straightened up. "Just making sure that I'm done … you know, with the landing."

I looked at Austin, and he had a huge grin on his face. "Jo? What are you doing here?"

The girl smiled at Austin. "Whatzup dude?"

Austin opened his arms, and the girl went into his embrace. As they hugged each other, I tapped a finger on my chin, trying to understand this feeling going through me. Jealousy? No, of course not. I was sure wanting to rip a stranger's pretty little head from their shoulders was a normal reaction to seeing the guy you had the hots for and potential mate giving a brotherly hug. Yeah, totally normal.

Austin pushed Jo back to get a good look at her. "Jo, I thought you were training. I'm sure you have an explanation?"

"Yeah, but I don't know how long I'll be here, so you'll have to take the condensed version." She took a couple of steps and then stumbled. "Can we sit for a sec? I always feel so yucky after traveling. Too bad I couldn't take an uber here like a normal person."

Austin raised his eyebrows in question, causing me to roll my eyes. "Sure, have a seat, why not?" I pointed for her to sit on the couch while I took a seat at the desk chair.

Austin sat next to Jo and then made the introductions. "This is Jolene, my sister's best friend."

"Whatzup," Jolene said. "We've met before, but at the time, you didn't have that banging body. By the way, heard you get to keep that one, so congrats on your hotness."

Now, I recognized her. "Ah, you're the soothsayer that's training under Ariana."

"Yep. It's been epic." She leaned back in the couch and propped one of her military boots on her knee. "So, I'm here because Ariana is like old as dirt, and she needs a break, but if we're being honest, what a crappy time to take a break, you know? I mean, we have mini wars popping up all over the place, and she decides she needs to go off to talk to the Fae King for a week. What-evs. Not passing judgment but if I were, I'd totally tell her that her timing really blows."

I felt a headache coming on. "We have pressing matters, so if you wouldn't mind telling us why you're here, that would be great."

"Oh, she used her ruling tone with me." She made her hands into claws. "Meow."

I gave Austin a look. "Is she a close family friend? Like one everyone would really miss or …"

Austin laughed. "Jo, get to the point."

"I feel like the news I'm about to deliver needs a theatrical presentation and a good build-up, but just go ahead and kill my vibe." She held up a hand. "Wait a minute. Something is coming through the switchboard. Ugh. Has anyone else noticed how freaking hot Death is? I mean, the things he can do with that scythe. Honest to God, he is the only one I don't mind getting flashes of during the night. Wowzer."

"You get a lot of flashes of other supernaturals?"

"Naw, just the key players. Ariana has helped me zone in on what's important. I accidentally got a couple of visions of you when you were in that dude's body. My condolences on that."

I was confused. "Why were you getting visions of me?"

Jo looked around the room like we were all dense. "Um, because you have always been flagged as a key player. You were meant to rule and find the key to guard."

I thumped my chest too hard like I was a caveman. "Me?"

"Yeah, I know, crazy. You're like hot, but evil, and yet not evil, and yet fate has marked you as a key player. Tots weird."

"Fate must be a crazy bench."

"Yeah, I know, right? Not sure she's totally lucid. Ah, and you still can't cuss. Dude, blows for you." She snapped her fingers, "Okay, so I'm here because you all are about to make a huge mistake. Huge. If you go to the underworld with the plan you have, Dansby dies." She looked over at Austin. "Dude, by the way, sorry about Dansby. He was always nice to me and your sister at school."

Austin was all business. "Tell me you have a suggestion."

"Duh."

Austin and I stared at her for a minute while she just blinked.

I threw my hands up in the air. "Oh, for fox's sake. Will we be here all night?"

Jo beamed. "Oh-em-gee. I love her." She elbowed Austin. "You did so good."

We must've woken Tally because he flew into the room, momentarily coming to a halt when he saw Jo sitting on the couch. He asked, "What's Ariana's lackey doing here?"

Jo laughed. "Cute. Okay, so you've got to go to portal two. Spoiler alert: It's a crazy portal. The inhabitants are like a bad mix of contestants from Survivor, The Bachelor, and The Voice. Yikes. I know. But homegirl should be well equipped with crazy by now, so go and sort them bad boys out. You will quickly figure out who will be a team player and who sucks."

I looked at the blank expressions on both Austin and Tally's face, glad to see I wasn't alone. "Um, you want us to go to this portal for what?"

Jo rolled her eyes before she slapped her fist several times, pretending like it was a microphone. "Hello, is this thing on? Yes, you three. Portal, now. Find the good little followers. Bring them back here. Kill the bad ones. Yada-yada-yada."

Tally flew over to me. "She's insane." I nodded. "Are we going to listen to her?"

"Probably," I said. "So tell me, Jo—"

Jo squealed. "Did you hear that, Austin? She used my nickname. Me and the Demon Queen are going to be besties! I just knew it." She made a continue on gesture. "Sorry, go ahead. Oh but wait, I've seen this, so really, I know what you're going to ask. So to answer the question you haven't asked, the Lux did a shitty job of who they sent over to the portals. Currently, my BFF, also known as his sister—" she pointed to Austin—"the Werewolf Queen, is working with a couple of other queens, and they are combing through the portals to make sure that non-deserving supernaturals aren't left to rot there. Contrary to belief, not all demons are bad, and you will find that out in portal two. Also, Carmen, you're not even at full potential yet." She cupped her hands around her mouth and staged whispered, "You're at half-mast, and it's a little embarrassing. You need to let go of stuff. Relax, babe." She closed her eyes. "Austin, you have to help her. Your power will help her come to full potential because, without it, she won't win against the under lords. Also, not sure if you noticed, but boy, you're tilting into the danger zone with all that power you have been consuming, you macho man, but no worries. Your mate can anchor you." Her head cocked to the side. "So many damn things are coming in at once. I'm away from the keyboard right now, people." Her head swiveled back to Austin. "Oh, did I mention that you both will be unstoppable, kick-ass immortals? You need to align the souls, bro." She didn't seem to notice his blank stare. He wasn't the only one having a hard time following her. "Yep, you need her, and she needs you. It's like a stalemate love story. I'm just hoping it doesn't end like Romeo and Juliet because one of the scenarios I saw of you both was a real tear-jerker. I tots ruined my mascara that day."

"Umm …" Tally raised his hand. "I've got questions. Loads."

Jo winced. "Eww. Yeah, I'd like to help but …" She tapped her empty wrist, where I assumed the scatterbrained girl was supposed to of had a watch. "I've got things to do. Fortnite is calling my name. Just kidding. I don't just lay around in men's boxers while playing video games." She glared at Tally. "Why did someone tell you that?"

I snapped my fingers. "Stay with us, scary chick."

"My bad," she said, winking. "So Austin, I'll report back to your sister that you're doing good." She gave me a nod. "Austin's mate, if you do a real wedding, I would be a helluva commentator. I could do a play by play before the actual play by play. Just call me." She faced Tally. "And fairy, stay to the left of Carmen when you go in the portal. You'll thank me later. Sayonara peeps."

She closed her eyes and disappeared just to reappear behind the couch. "Mother trucker." She tried again, ending up next to the fireplace. "Come on you sad stack of—" Then she disappeared again.

I waited for a few minutes. "Is she gone?"

Austin nodded. "I think so."

"That was as mildly entertaining as it was depressing. Hope she gets it together a little better before she officially takes over for Ariana," Tally said, as he sat on my armchair. "If Ariana plans on Jo taking over as head soothsayer sooner rather than later, we all might be in a bad situation before long."

I shrugged. "I liked her."

Tally grinned. "You said that without wincing."

Austin's eyes bored into mine with such heat. "Our Demon Queen is becoming okay with who she really is."

"So, we're to go to a portal and find demons that will follow the queen?" Tally asked.

My breath caught as I realized Austin wasn't listening to Tally; instead, his hungry gaze locked on me. He looked at me like he was barely able to keep himself from stalking towards me. I couldn't take my eyes off him, either. I licked my lips nervously, as he continued to stare at me with blazing eyes.

"Gross guys." Tally flew off the armchair in disgust. "You don't have to be a soothsayer to see what's coming next. I'll be in the other room preparing to leave for portal two. When you are both ready, let me know."

Neither one of us acknowledged him as Austin stood and made his way over to me like a panther stalking his prey. My heartbeat felt like a trapped bird inside of my chest. My palms grew sweaty as I waited for him to speak.

"Come with me," he said.

"Where to?" I asked, but I was already putting my hand into his.

"You'll see."

I held onto him as he teleported us. Before I opened my eyes, I knew where we were, and a smile lifted the corner of my lips. The breeze blew my hair as I took in the salty air. I looked around at the deserted beach.

"Where exactly are we?"

"Daufuskie Island in South Carolina. You liked Charleston so much I thought I would show you another beach around the same area."

"I love it," I said, and I did, but I didn't understand why we were here. I asked him while I took off my shoes, so I could feel the sand between my toes.

"We're here because you are happy in this environment, and I think I understand what Jo was rambling about. If I'm to help you unleash your powers, I need you to relax."

"Are you sure about helping me? So far, you've done everything you can to make sure I can't keep my powers, and now you want to help me claim more?"

He took off his shirt and placed it on the sand before pointing for me to sit down on it. He sat crossed legged in front of me. Our knees were touching each other. "I really didn't want to like you. Liking you meant sacrificing my best friend. I did my best to try and keep you at a distance, but the pull was too strong. Truth is I believe no amount of power could tip you into the evil column."

My face scrunched up. "How will I ever rule the underworld if they don't fear me?"

"The way the underworld is right now, do you want to rule it? I know your goals, but when you conquer them, will you be happy?"

Happy wasn't a feeling that went hand in hand with ruling, was it? He lightly stroked the insides of my arms while he gathered his thoughts.

"I know demons operate on fear, but I don't think you will ever be capable of the evilness that will get their attention. I don't have the answer to your question, but if you allow me, we will find out together."

No one had ever looked at me with such tenderness. I felt myself trying to swallow down my emotions. I needed to change the subject, so he didn't see how vulnerable his words made me feel. "How are we supposed to be able to help one another?"

"The first time I drained someone, it was a powerful sorceress. At the time, I didn't know how to handle the surge, and it left me crawling on my hands and knees for a week. There were a ton of ramifications, and I often regretted that encounter until today. That sorceress's power is going to save us both. I've never used it in this manner, so this will be a bit of trial and error." He grabbed my hands, intertwining our fingers together. "I'll need to remain in contact, so try not to pull away."

The heat of his hands made warmth pool in my belly and my breath quicken. I closed my eyes and concentrated on evening out my breathing. Being this close to him, with him touching me, was proving difficult.

My eyes flew open, as I felt a warm caress inside my body. "I'm assuming you don't have a handbook?"

He smiled at me. "I'm hoping this will come to me naturally, and hopefully we won't need a learning curve. You'll have to be patient with me."

I scooted back a little. Being his guinea pig didn't sound like it was going to be fun in the least.

His voice was calm and soothing. "Just let me in. Don't block me. If you try to put up walls, it'll hurt us both. I want you to relax. Think of the sound and smell of the ocean. Feel the dying sun casting its last rays onto your face and just let me lead."

I gave a tiny nod. That was the best he was going to get from me. After a few deep breaths, I felt myself relax. His power knocked to come inside me, causing me to tense up.

"Relax, or it won't work."

My instincts told me to pull away, so I had to force myself to take a couple of deep breaths, and open up to him. A steady stream of warmth entered my body. It felt like it pinged around inside of my rib cage before settling down.

His voice was steady, as he said, "I want you to think about what is holding you back. What is it that you fear so much you're unwilling to embrace your powers wholeheartedly."

I started to shrug, but his power felt like it was squeezing my lungs, so I answered honestly. "I'm scared that I will be like him, and I'm scared that if I'm not, then I will never rule."

His power turned into a soothing stroke, like it was trying to comfort me. I dropped my chin to my chest.

"Carmen, you will never be like him, but you were born to rule. I'm sorry it took me so long to understand that. Please, open up. I promise I will not leave your side."

I felt deep inside myself, where I had an untouched supply of power. Once I opened what I considered Pandora's box, I could never reel it back in.

chapter twenty-five

With one deep inhale, I let the remainder of my power bubble up to the surface. It chased Austin's powers like two butterflies circling each other before my power completely mingled with his. I felt his and mine combining. His hands tightened on mine.

"Pull back," he said. "Release my power."

But it felt so good … so right. "Why?"

"If you let our powers merge completely, we will become mated. When we become mated, I don't want it to be on a whim. I want you to think long and hard about it because once you commit to being mine, I'll never let you go."

Would it be horrible to be committed to this man for the rest of our immortal lives? No, in fact, I couldn't think of anything that would make me happier, but with regret I heeded his warning, and with one last little rub against his power, I gently retracted, only for his power to chase mine. He obviously loved the feeling of our powers being as one as much as I did. I smiled as his power swirled and rubbed against mine like a purring cat. It was clear his power was the pursuer, and at any time he could have broken the tether connecting our souls together, but he didn't. And by doing so, he also made a choice, sitting there on that sandy beach. Before coming here, I was his mate, but now we would both be leaving with an unbreakable bond. I held no regrets, and judging by his emotions pouring into me, Austin had no regrets, either. We sat there in silence, as I felt the newfound power thrumming through my body. It was almost too much. I needed to release some of it.

He tilted my chin up. Concern was written all over his face, but I physically felt his anxiety.

"How am I feeling your emotions?"

His brow furrowed. "We might have held on too long. I'm not sure if it's a permanent thing, but if so I'd imagine that from here on out, one of the perks will be that we can read each other's emotions."

Perks? I frowned. "You have got to be kidding me." I almost groaned. Now, he would know when I was thinking about how hot his ridiculous body was, or when his touch flustered me.

He laughed. "I personally think this is going to be very beneficial. I can feel your lust from here." I pushed his hand away, causing him to laugh harder. "Apart from each other, we are the strongest of our kind, but together, our powers are unstoppable."

My body felt like a current of electricity jolted it. I grimaced in pain, my head throbbing.

Deft hands grabbed me up, sitting me in his lap. Austin rubbed my back. Tears gathered in my eyes. With every stroke, the urge to cry out from pain lessened. Within a couple of minutes, my power was under control.

I tilted my head up to study the man who gently rocked me.

"Better?" he asked.

"Yes, what did you do?"

"I took a little of your power from you. You have a well of power that will be hard to control for years. Think of your power as electricity in your body. Our powers combined are like an electric current in a circuit. Together, we make up a negative and a positive. If you allow me to help you, then it won't be so bad when you're at full throttle, and somehow you managed to ease the powers inside of me. I'm still as powerful, but it's almost like you tidied up my powers, organizing them into files that are easier to obtain. I feel clearheaded and energized for the first time in a long time."

My lips curved at the excitement in his voice. The pain had dissipated entirely, so I let myself have this moment. I rested my head against his hard chest, breathing in the warm scent of him. The sound of the ocean relaxed me, and I just wanted to live in this moment forever.

"What will I do with all of that power when you're not around? Will it consume me?" I hadn't meant to ask that out loud. Embarrassed, I went to scramble off of his lap, but he held me, still not letting me up.

He kissed the top of my head, as his hands tightened around me. "Carmen, I don't plan on not being around. Wherever you go, I will follow."

Doubt colored my words. "So, you'd camp out in the underworld, never seeing the sun again, just to stay by me?"

"If that's where you choose to reign, then yes. You're worth a thousand suns."

Choose to reign? Like the location didn't matter? I didn't exactly know what that meant, and honestly, I didn't want to think about it too much. Hope could be a crappy thing.

"Carmen?"

"Yes."

"Look at me." I tilted my head back up once again. His electric blue eyes roamed over my face before they settled on my lips.

I touched the sides of his cheeks as his lips crushed mine. This kiss was different. Kissing someone and knowing they had feelings for you was a giddy experience. He craved me with every second, but more than that, he adored me. As he deepened the kiss, I committed this to my memory. If we perished in the fight against my uncle, I would die knowing I knew happiness, if only for a moment in time.

After we watched the sun go down, I took us both back to my chamber, where we would prepare for tonight. I took one last glance in the mirror. I looked completely badass, if I did say so myself. I had decided to change into tight pants and a corset to match. It was sexy and powerful, at the same time. Austin had changed into his standard apparel: a pair of well-worn jeans that were more than likely going to break my concentration and a tight-fitting T-shirt. He gave me a knowing look that made me roll my eyes, but before I could tell him where to go, a wave of his lust struck me. I almost staggered. His soft laugh died on his lips. Was this what it felt like to be totally enraptured by someone? The air thickened right before Tally ruined the moment by flying in between us.

"Whoa, whoa, whoa. Where have you both been?"

"Hey, Mom," I said, "did I miss curfew?"

"Cute. Real cute. Are we ready to start a war or what?" Austin asked, "Have you heard anything from Ariana?"

Tally looked confused. "No, why?"

Austin shrugged. "Just making sure she didn't have any final instructions." His worry carried through our connection.

"Do you think she cares about us?" I scoffed. "I'm not a huge fan of the soothsayer, but it's obvious to even the simplest minded she has her own agenda. Besides, you don't need to worry about me. I'll be fine."

Tally flew over to my shoulder. "We will protect you."

"Boys, I think I can take care of myself."

Austin pushed off the desk. "You must've already forgotten about the octopus."

"In fairness," Tally said, "I would have let that slip my mind, too." At my glare, he laughed. "I mean seriously, how embarrassing."

We all froze as the phone on my desk started ringing. It could be my uncle or it could be Ariana, and in that case I had a few choice words for that meddling crack head.

I looked at the phone like it was a deadly snake before jerking it from its cradle. Austin's shoulder was pressed into mine, as we waited to see what doom hurtled our way. I denied the caller a greeting, but that didn't deter them.

"Whatzup?"

I recognized that voice. Austin sighed, as I said, "Jo?"

"Yeah, I'm just sitting here painting my toenails thinking about life and shit." I started to hand the phone to Austin, but Jo said, "Dude, are you seriously about to pass me off? And I thought we had a connection."

I sat on the bed and thumped my head against the headboard. "What is it that you want, Jo? I'm sure you didn't call me to talk about the weather. What bad news are you prepping me for this time?"

"It's not my fault that my job sucks. I'm a queen maker. I have to make sure that all key players get their crowns and keep their crowns, so they can keep the keys. Do you have any idea how stressed I am? Like right up there with someone who ate the last thin mint, and the girl scouts are greedy little hoes who won't sell you anymore, stressed." She popped her gum a couple of times. "Look, I'd come to you right now, but my nails are drying, and I get motion sickness, so here's the thing, dude, you're so outnumbered. I'm talking about Gettysburg outnumbered. You're going to lose so many lives. I've seen every possible scenario and let me tell you, none of them are fantastic."

Austin jerked the phone from me. "Damn it, Jo, you should've led with that? What do we do to prevent the loss of lives?"

"Top of the morning to you, too, bud, and thanks for asking how I'm doing. So the bad news is it looks like your girl will get to keep the crown, but a lot of blood has got to flow. But there is one more option that should work."

"Should?" he roared into the phone. I put a hand on his harm, trying to get him to relax.

"Well, yeah, it sucks because I don't have a clear plan and Arianna is missing, and you know what they say about good help? Seriously, you know, right? Because I've totally forgotten."

Austin was about to crush the phone in his hand, so I took it back from him.

"Jo, I'm sure you didn't just call us to tell us that lots of people putting their lives in our hands were going to die because of it."

"I didn't?" She giggled. "You're right. I didn't. So here's the thing. Your powers are crazy wicked. When you go to battle, you can go hard, but don't let all your power go at once. When you do that, you're as weak as a newborn kitten. I had one of those once, you know."

"What?"

"A kitten. Anyways when asked to kneel, do it, and when your eyes become riveted on the blood flow, know that help's on the way. Just hang tight. Anyways, the pizza delivery guy is pulling up. I gotta run. Chat soon."

Austin jerked the phone from me again. "Wait! Whose blood flow?"

She hung up the phone with him still screaming her name. He ripped the phone from the wall and threw it across the room. I had a feeling the hotel would be sending us a bill. His emotions swarmed me, and it was enough to make me choke. I quickly built a wall inside of my mind to keep his emotions from crushing me.

His electric blue eyes swiveled to me. "Did you just cut me off?"

"Yep."

"Let me back in."

"Not until you control your emotions better. You're suffocating me."

Tally flew over to the bed. "I feel like I've missed something. What's going on?"

I was about to tell the fairy about Austin and my powers mingling, but it still felt raw and new. I didn't want to lose that feeling by sharing.

"After we go to the portal, you will need to go check in with Ariana. If you can, try to be back before we enter the underworld." Tally started to argue. "Tally, please. It could help me secure the crown without losing lives."

After a couple of seconds, he nodded. "Consider it done, my queen."

Relief flooded through me. This way at least Tally would be out of the fight and somewhere relatively safe. I couldn't stomach the thought of losing him.

I stood up. "Now, if you two princesses are done chit-chatting, I think we should go get my crown back."

Tally was still complaining as we teleported to the portal located in a dirty town in California. There were homeless people scattered about on the sidewalks and every corner. The buildings looked neglected and had graffiti all over them. Trash blew in the wind, and the smell was about to be my undoing. Our boots hit the pavement with a thud, as we walked towards the portal between two dark buildings. The alley smelled strongly of urine and something a little harsher. I tried not to gag as Austin took the key out of his pocket.

"Demons might try to rush at us, so as soon as we open this door, we need to be prepared," Austin said.

"Make sure you close the portal behind us. I don't want anyone escaping." I grabbed Tally and put him to the left of me. "Stay on this side of me."

As soon as Austin held the key to the portal, the air thickened. We stepped in and immediately a spear was thrown to the right of me right where Tally had been.

Tally sighed. "Ah, so that's why I needed to be to the left of you. Maybe that Jo is a work in progress, but still she's pretty good. That spear could have killed me."

I grunted. If I weren't a dethroned Demon Queen, I'd send the scattered girl a gift basket. This plane was eerie with its crimson sky and dead trees. Lava ran like a lazy river through the black rock. When I took stock of what beings we would be working with, I almost laughed. This had to be some kind of joke. We were screwed, and there was nothing any of us could do about it.

chapter twenty-six

"**D**id she say demon portal, or did we just assume?" I asked.

Austin ran a hand over his face. "Shit."

"Yeah, I second that," Tally said, as he flew to my shoulder.

Werewolves strutted around shirtless like they owned the place. Witches lounged around the lava like it was a pool to sunbathe around, and they were on vacation. Fae creatures looked at us with pure disinterest. There were a couple of smoke demons who seemed to be in the midst of an intense workout program, but they stopped midway to stare at us. A troll hiked up his pants on his squat little body before he gave us the bird.

There had to have been a mistake. These creatures were not what I envisioned when I thought of who I'd rule. "Are we sure she said portal two?"

"Yep," Austin said.

Thirty red demons stalked towards us. Their black horns grew ramrod straight in aggression.

Austin whispered to me, "I'm here if you need me, but if you want true followers, it is you who needs to make them kneel before you. This is not the time to hold back."

One of the witches sounded bored, as she said, "Oh great. The demons are going to terrorize the new chick."

Another one piped up. "Ugh. At least we get a break."

"Yeah, but it's not going to help our reviews on Travelocity."

All the witches giggled, as the demons continued to stride towards me. Not being used to my full power, smoke ropes flew out of me lightning fast, snaking around the demon's ankles and rooting them to the spot. One demon howled in pain as my wisp amputated his foot.

Whoops. I tilted my chin up, pretending like I did that on purpose. Tally shook his head, and Austin released a deep sigh. Like they could seriously judge me. At least now I had everyone's attention. I heard some complaints it was unfair I retained my powers in the portal, and the smarter ones knew my powers were superior. Those were the ones who gave me their full attention. The smoke demons, appearing like ordinary humans, smirked as the red demons struggled to get out of my grasp. Shadow demons the size of Tally and a couple of fairies intermingled as they marched like ants to get a front-row seat. They clapped with joy over the red demons' demise. It was apparent the red demons weren't a crowd favorite. One tiny shadow demon jumped up and down as he chirped how beautiful I was. I gave him a saucy wink in return.

Without loosening my grip on the red demons, I asked a nearby werewolf, "How big is your plane?"

He shook his head. "Not big. I've heard other planes have blue skies and water, but what you see is what you get here. I can walk the whole plane in thirty minutes. Most of the beings are usually found at the bar."

It was obvious they weren't as evil as some of supes I'd seen, and yet their plane had no food, water, or space. I looked at two shadow demons playing with each other. I sensed no evil in them. Mischief, yes, but evil? No. It made no sense how someone like my father was allowed to walk around free, but those two harmless shadow demons were sent to this plane, even if it wasn't one of the worst. Actually, the portals were numbered from least evil to most evil, so portal two wasn't the worst by far but still. I was sure being trapped here was not on any of their agendas. Not for the first time, I thought some Lux had screwed up big time. The Degenerates were supposed to be the bad guys, yet it wasn't a Degenerate who made the many mistakes of unfair sentencing to portals that I'd witnessed and heard about.

"Wait." Tally's face scrunched up. "You're allowed a bar?"

If the wolf took offense to that, he didn't show it. "Yeah, the witches can make a brew. They won't tell us the ingredients, but since a lot of things don't grow here other than a few herbs, we pretty much know what they're making the drinks with, but pretend it's all top secret."

"I'll be calling a meeting in thirty minutes. Please, have a couple of people split up and scout the area. Find any stragglers and tell them to meet us at the bar."

A handsome smoke demon pushed off a dead tree he had been leaning on. He shook out his shaggy brown hair. "And whom shall we tell them requested all of our presence?"

I jerked on my smoke ropes, gaining the attention of the struggling red demons. "You tell them the Demon Queen is here, and I bring a message of hope."

The smoke demon's smile dropped, as a look of awe washed over his face. "Yes, your highness."

A fae boy who was prettier than he was handsome came strutting forward. Hands in his pocket, he purred, "Queen, may I be of service to you?"

Austin took one step forward and inserted himself between me and the fae. His words were low and harsh. "Nope, she's good."

Possessiveness leaked from his every pore, and even though I tried to hide my smile, I knew he easily read my emotions. He wanted everyone to know I belonged to him, and though we hadn't discussed our relationship or thoroughly worked out all the kinks, his urge to claim me as his made me happy.

I whispered to Austin, "Thought you were going to let me handle all of this."

He shrugged, and I bit the inside of my cheek so as not to laugh out loud.

Tally's eyes swiveled back and forth between Austin and me. He knew something of significance was going on; he just couldn't quite figure it out.

I could tell Tally was about to ask us when Austin nodded towards the demons I had in my clutches. "Those don't look like followers to me."

"We'll see." I tapped my foot on the black rock impatiently. I let the full weight of Austin's words settle around me. Would I have any followers? Doubt crept over me before I banished the thoughts. I didn't want Austin to know my misgivings. One thing was for certain: when I left this portal and if I had any followers, I wanted to make sure I had an army of people following me because they chose to do so, not because they were forced. I sighed as I looked around at the beings still gaping at me. If someone had told me a month ago that as a new queen, I would try to trade out the bad demons for a band of misfits, I would have told them they were crazy. But here I was.

I released the red demons. The one who snarled at me I sent flying into a tree, causing the witches to clap with glee. We made our way down the black path until we came across the bar that was built with dead trees. Someone had carved "Welcome to the Lava Pit" above the bar.

The three of us sat at a wobbly table where I tried to pretend I wasn't nervous I would be leaving this plane empty handed. Austin continued to glare at anyone who tried to come too close to me. It was apparent that even though Jo sent us to this plane, he trusted no one here. However, I was trying to get recruits for a war that wasn't theirs to fight, so his moody looks weren't helping the situation. He felt my aggravation because he gave me a small smile before he attempted to relax back in a poorly made chair. He still looked lethal, but I appreciated the attempt. Twenty minutes had passed when the wolf and smoke demon finally reappeared. "All who wished to be here are accounted for."

"Oh, goodie." I went to straighten my crooked crown when I remembered my uncle was wearing it. Ash-hat. I walked over to the bar and stood on it, so I could see all the faces crammed into the space. Some were outside standing, so I spoke loud, making sure my voice carried to the three hundred bodies who had heeded my call.

"I'll cut right to the chase. I'm Carmen Salvador, the Demon Queen." I pointed to a brunette witch at the front. "Are you happy here?"

She rolled her eyes. "Um, no. There's no food or water. Our plane is so tiny we practically sleep on top of one another, and the worst part is we have lost our power. It's like I can't even remember who I once was."

I nodded. "I know how that feels, so my sympathy is with you on that one. I'm looking for warriors who will pledge their allegiance to me. If you can obey me, I will offer you your freedom. You will have a place in the twelve realms of the underworld, and those who are most trusted will have free days on earth, as long as you vow not to hurt humans."

One of the witches raised her hand. "Um, isn't the underworld kind of like this here?" Yeah, except we didn't have a bar. "No offense, but would it be an upgrade?"

She was right. Could I ask these beings not only to fight for me, but trade in one hell for another? I didn't even want to return to the dank place. I had to stop myself from pacing.

"You're right, uh …"

"Mary."

Tally busted out laughing. "Oh, this is great."

I said, "Your name is for real Mary?" At her nod, I winced. I hoped this didn't get confusing. "Mary, I'm going to be honest with you— all of you—there are things going on in the underworld that I'm not proud of, but I assumed that was the way it had to be done. What if I told you that after everything is sorted out, I would be ruling from Charleston, South Carolina?" I glanced over at Austin, who smiled from ear to ear. "I would require all of you to find residency within a forty-mile radius. You would have normal lives, as long as you followed the rules."

Someone from the back asked what this so-called Charleston looked like. With barely a thought, I sent each potential subject before me, minus Austin and Tally, an image of the small Southern town. There were mumbles after that, as they all concurred how powerful I must be to directly send so many of them images simultaneously.

A witch slowly started clapping. I gave her a wink. "That's just chump change."

One wolf regarded me with skepticism. His big, bulky arms covered his barrel chest, as he widened his stance. "What are some of these rules that you speak of?"

"I've already stated two. You'd need to live close by in case I request your assistance. You have to take a vow to serve me as your queen, and last but not least, if I allow you your freedom, you have to make sure you earn it by not harming humans or doing anything that would warrant my scrutiny."

One fae creature whispered to another. "She doesn't sound like a demon."

I smiled. "I'm a different kind of demon. I'm one with a conscience. Not sure how long all of you have been here, but let me catch you up. Some keys are missing. Some beings are wanting those keys for nefarious reasons. Some are wanting those keys to keep them safe and hidden. Thrones keep changing owners, and crowns are getting misplaced." Freaking uncle. "I plan on keeping my throne. I also plan on a life of peace, but sometimes to acquire that, one must go to war. As you all have noticed, I have a key, which I will guard with my life. If war comes to my doorstep, then I will fight along with all of those under my reign. You do not have to join my army. In fact you don't even have to stay here. From what I've heard, there is a group of queens who are making their rounds through the portals. They have a way of telling who is deserving to be there and who isn't. The ones who were misjudged get a second chance at freedom, so some of you could very well be out of this place in no time with or without me."

The wolf who had asked me the question earlier smiled. "You didn't have to tell us that. I've never had a pack, but I think I would be honored to be a part of your tribe." He took a knee in the middle of that crowded bar. "I pledge myself to you, my queen, and vow to be loyal to you and you alone."

Tears gathered in my eyes as one of the tiny demons said, "I pledge, I pledge."

I couldn't help but smile. "I understand all of you know nothing of me, and yet I'm asking quite a bit from each and every one of you. Talk amongst yourselves and make your decision. I'll be at the portal waiting for any that choose to come with me. I leave upon the hour."

As I made my way out of the bar, the group of red demons I had previously tied up formed a semi-circle in front of me. Austin made his way to my side. We stood side by side, waiting for them to either move, let us pass, or throw the first punch. The leader of the group spoke in my demonic language, but I replied in English for all of the witnesses to hear.

"I am fit to be queen. I'm more powerful than any who have come before me, and I will lead without having others fear me because I won't need to. They will follow me because they respect me. And yes, you can try to take my key, but trust me when I say none of you are strong enough. Now, get out of my way."

They would let me pass, or I'd skewer them on the spot. It was one of those kinds of days. They didn't budge so with a wave of my hand I sent all seven of the demons careening into the rocks to the right of me.

I waited for an agonizing fifty minutes, wondering who would show up and who wouldn't. Finally, almost three hundred new subjects appeared before me and the portal opening. Before I could speak, they all dropped to their knees. Trying to reign in my shock, I looked over at Tally and Austin, who had also taken a knee. My heart flipped in my chest. My sinuses acted up as they made a vow to protect and serve me as their queen, and for the first time, I truly felt like a queen. I cleared my throat and told everyone to rise. Austin opened the portal, and we exited as a group full of hope for a better reign and a better tomorrow. Our first mission was to go to the underworld and fight for what was ours. There couldn't be two self-proclaimed rulers. Besides, the crown was mine.

chapter twenty seven

It took us time and energy to teleport that many beings into the underworld. No one seemed pissed that their first mission was about to begin. So far, everyone was all smiles because they had their powers back.

A smoke demon who seemed to be the leader of his kind came to a stop beside me. "Queen, can I say that I love it here."

My eyebrows rose. "In the underworld?"

"Yeah, totally. It's got a creepy vibe, but I'm feeling it."

"Huh. What's your name, soldier?"

He tipped an imaginary hat. "Thane, my queen."

"Nice to formally meet you, Thane." I gave my attention to the demons, who gazed at me with adoration, which was a total one-eighty of my standard treatment. "You guys like it here, too?" They gave me a nod. Interesting.

I addressed my new army. We were all crowded in the center ring of level one. Demons who had been milling about stared at us in shock. If the under lords didn't know we were here yet, they would soon.

"I want you to divide yourselves into teams. If you feel like you work well with someone, or you know your power might not be incredibly strong but it can help someone else be more powerful, buddy up with them. No one is to go solo. Level twelve is where my uncle Maligno will be. So, that's where we will go. I'd like for the witches to seal off the exits. I understand it's not going to hold the under lords out for long, but it'll slow them down, and honestly we don't want them to not enter. We would just prefer not everyone enter at once."

I looked at all of the eyes staring back at me. "Going into battle is never easy, and I wish I could give each of you a clear plan, but the truth is I can't. A soothsayer has brought us to this path. Any plan I come up with would be totally useless. Our goal is to go in, defeat the under lords, kill anyone that refuses to kneel, rescue a man named Dansby, and do all of this without dying."

They all nodded. I looked around for my bug before I remembered I had sent Tally on a wild goose chase. I told him I needed him to report to Ariana and the Fae King, just to make sure we were on the right path. He hesitated, but in the end, he'd decided to do my bidding. It was for the best. Worrying for him would distract me in the fight. Fairy dust didn't work on fire demons. He would be outmatched, and I had grown way too attached to my bug to let anything happen to him.

Austin and I made our way to the front of the tunnel, so we could be the first ones to enter level twelve. We were side by side, as we readied ourselves for the final showdown. We both had dropped our walls, letting our powers dance together. He reached out and grabbed my hand.

"When this is over, and we get your crown back, I want you to marry me."

We were forty seconds from the door that would lead us to our battle ground. "Dude, are you asking? Because that sounded more like a demand."

His blue eyes twinkled. "I'm sorry. Would you do me the honor of becoming my wife?"

I patted his chest while continuing to walk. "I know we're mates, but I think we have already mated. You know when our powers rubbed together for too long? Yeah, well, I think it's already a done deal, but if you need a fancy wedding to make yourself feel better, then I guess I could wear something non-leather and white for a short period."

He laughed as his hand squeezed mine. "So, you've known this whole time we were mated?" At my grin, he laughed again. "And this whole time, I was worried you were going to bail on me when you figured it out."

"Nah. I'm kind of liking you around."

He tugged me into his side where he crushed me in a half embrace.

"Not that I don't love this PDA, because I do, which I'm sure you can tell, but we're kind of in the middle of a battle, so rain check, Romeo."

He chuckled, giving me a bow. "Yes, my queen."

Both of us were consumed with emotions as we opened up the steel door leading us to the top level of the underworld. I felt his apprehension through the new bond we had created. Our end goal was to rescue his friend and not get killed. He thought at some point he would have to decide between helping me fight the under lords and saving his friend. He already knew the decision he would make, and his guilt poured through our link. I knew Austin would have a hard time living with the weight of that decision, so it was up to me to make sure he didn't have to make it.

The truth was I was more powerful than the twelve under lords, but my anxiety rose when I thought about how they could use Dansby against us. With Austin by my side, it wouldn't be that hard of a challenge, but what if the thousands of demons residing under each under lord attacked us at the same time? No matter how powerful we were at the end of the day, we were vastly outnumbered.

What awaited us on level twelve had my palms sweating. All twelve under lords stood facing us with at least a thousand fire demons behind them. My uncle, who wore my crown, held up a hand to stop the idle chatter behind him. He looked at the group standing behind me and roared with laughter.

"What is this, niece? Have you found a group of has-beens that might follow you?"

A werewolf somewhere to my right growled.

"What I've found, Uncle, is that people follow me because I offer them hope of a better tomorrow, not because I hold a blade to their throat."

A look of disgust crossed his face. His eyes swiveled to Austin. "You made a vow to me."

"One that I honored," Austin said. "I delivered her to you without her powers. Then I rescued her and gave her powers back."

My uncle's voice shook with rage. "I thought we had an understanding."

Austin shrugged, as if he was bored with my uncle. "That was before I recognized her as my queen."

"You," my uncle snarled, "a Power Eliminator, would stoop as low to call her your queen?"

Austin's eyes turned to glaciers. "I cannot think of a better person than Carmen to rule, and I think you know that as well. She is everything you will never be."

My uncle seethed. "I will kill your friend after I'm done killing this ragtag group of misfits."

"You can try," Austin said.

I was glad one of us was sure of ourselves. I had a group of three hundred or more behind me, and I couldn't fail them.

My uncle shouted, "Fight 'til the death," and then mayhem exploded.

Shouts and cries rang through the underworld. As I roped in an under lord about to take down a smoke demon, I saw witches gathering their powers to lash out at any demons who made it past where I stood. Other witches were sealing the exits. Tiny demons ran through the crowd, tripping up the larger fire demons. They might not have been significant or powerful, but wherever they went, they created chaos and enough confusion to allow a larger force to make a kill. The werewolves had transformed. A true wolf, contrary to what Hollywood studios portrayed, didn't take on the shape of a wolf but just became larger. Even their faces widened.

There was such a raw, brute force in their movements. It was completely different than watching Austin. He had two blades in his hands, and with an athletic grace that surpassed anything I'd ever witnessed, he moved through the fire demons with deadly accuracy. The under lord that I currently had hooked with my wisps was screaming. I unsheathed the blade from my back, and with quick work, there were eleven under lords now. A sea of red washed towards me. I was quickly surrounded by fire demons. My smoky tendrils held all those I wished at bay; the rest I let slip through, so I could dispatch them quickly. No matter where I went, Austin kept an eye on me.

Witches were now fully engaged with the demons, and I always kept swiveling around, making sure no one needed my help. There were a couple close calls, but through the crowd, my ropes would find the demon who was about to take one of my soldier's life, and I would bind him until someone decapitated the trapped demon. If Austin was tiring, he didn't show it. Every thirty seconds, he brought down two demons. The werewolves hunted in a pack. Their backs were to each other as they fought in a tight circle. It seemed to be working for them. I snatched another under lord up and then another. The bold ones cursed me as life left their bodies.

My blade was covered in demon blood, as it made a figure-eight through the air. A wave of demons crashed through the witches. My wisps spiraled from me in different directions, creating a barrier between the witches and the demons. I sent them images that would break even the hardiest supes. While they were stunned, Austin and I made short work of taking the head of each one. With a few Latin words, I pushed a third of the remaining demons against the wall. A look of fear showed upon their faces.

Austin shouted above the clanging of metal. "That's it. And there is so much more. Now's the time to let loose. Just make sure you don't expel all your power. Save some."

I had a brief moment of fear. What if I liked the feeling of being all-powerful? Would I become addicted to that amount of power? No. No, I wouldn't let myself. I wasn't evil, and for the first time in my life, I was more than okay with that. While swinging my blade, I fully committed, as I concentrated on letting my walls down. I immediately felt Austin's powers meeting with mine. They danced around each other, like long lost lovers. My whole body hummed, as I looked at the demons pinned up against the wall. Ropes of smoke flew out of me yet again, but this time they braided together before circling the demons, bringing them to their knees. They thrashed against my hold, but it was pointless.

The wolves shouted with triumph as they descended upon the group. The witches made catcalls as they watched with fascination. The remainder of the demons stormed us, but we were ready. Austin had a fine bead of sweat on his upper lip, as he wielded his blade. As our powers still danced with one another, his sword became untraceable. Heads would hit the ground, and I just assumed it was because they had met his blade. Within minutes, a task that had seemed daunting came to a close. Together, we really were unstoppable.

There was only one under lord left to finish, but I couldn't be the one to end him. I had made a vow to Tally. Austin would have to be the one to send him to the underbelly of the underworld. I searched everywhere for my uncle, but he was nowhere in sight. Witches, wolves, tiny demons, smoke demons, and a few fire demons were celebrating without knowing the predicament we were in.

"Someone blew through my protection ward," a witch shouted. "I'm drained. Someone find Raquel. Tell her to hurry."

It was too late for Raquel to help. I felt power closing in on us. Austin's eyes met mine, and his grief came through our connection. I knew what he was thinking. What if my uncle didn't just go for reinforcements; what if he had gone for Dansby? The witches had done their part by making it harder for the demons to enter, but the truth was we were vastly outnumbered. Demons from levels one through eleven were coming in fast. Knowing my weakness for humanity, my uncle could use Dansby to get what he wanted. The crown. And he knew I would give it to him. Everything we had done would be for nothing. My uncle teleported in front of me. I heard his laugh before I could see him, and I knew deep in my bones what he had brought with him.

chapter twenty eight

Whether the dread pooling in my belly was from Austin's emotions or mine, I couldn't decipher. I only knew in the next few moments, I was going to let someone down. Whether it was Austin, the army behind me, or Dansby, who was currently being held in my uncle's arms, was beyond me. A league of demons surrounded us, waiting for my uncle's command. With one nod from my father's brother, the enemy separated the witches from the rest of us and then forcibly moved the wolves to the center of the level to make sure they didn't try to escape. The demons in my army stared at their fellow faction with pure hatred. We were surrounded. I couldn't begin to help them out without risking Dansby.

Could I listen to Jo? Trust her? What if she was wrong? Could I sacrifice so many for one? Was it even my call to decide who lived and who died? I stared at the boy who was going to be our downfall. Dansby was everything Austin wasn't. He was of average height, a little pudgy, and was so scared I was shocked he wasn't trembling. He looked at his friend with almost hero worship. However strong the bond was between Austin and Dansby, one thing was for certain: Dansby put all his faith in Austin to get him out of this mess. Dang Arianna to hay.

My newly acquired army showed no fear as they waited for what I was about to do. They just saw us annihilate a group where the odds were twenty to one, so they were unsure as to why I just stood, unmoving and staring at my uncle.

My uncle's smile showed me he wasn't confused at all. "Do you wish to save this pathetic being?"

I cocked my head to the side, unwilling to play his game. His smile grew wider.

"Kneel," he commanded.

Austin shoved himself in front of me. "This has nothing to do with the queen—this is between you and me."

My uncle, Maligno, procured a small dagger and pressed it into Dansby's skin. Blood trickled down his throat. "I said kneel."

Wordlessly, and to the shock of everyone behind me, the cold marble ground met my knees.

My uncle laughed. "This is hilarious. I can't believe you found a group that would follow someone like you. Someone who would so easily give up everything and for what? For some sorry excuse of wasted space to live?" I eyed the blade cutting deeper into Dansby's flesh. My gaze followed the slow trickle, realizing that this moment was what Jo had spoken of. Dansby's faded blue eyes darted between his friend and me. Austin's fist clenched. I wondered if he was going to be able to control his rage long enough to see if Jo told the truth. One lone wolf slowly started making his way over to my uncle while everyone's attention was on us. What was he doing? He was going to get himself killed.

"I'll have your vow now. Vow to give me the crown. If you do this, I will vow to let your band of misfits leave here unharmed, along with your new friend, and the back-stabbing Power Eliminator," he said, as he gripped Dansby tighter.

He didn't mention my freedom because we both knew as soon as I took that vow I would be dead. I'd knelt and seen blood flow as Jo suggested, and yet no help came. There was nothing left to do but make the vow. At least none of my army would die here today, and Austin and Dansby would leave in one piece.

The knife's tip was pressed so hard into Dansby that his skin folded around the tip. Blood poured down his skin in a steady stream.

I opened my mouth to make the vow when Austin cut me off. "Carmen, you can't trade your life."

I gave him a ghost of a smile. How far we had both come. In the beginning, he had one goal. Save his friend. That was it. No matter the fallout. He was more than willing to trade my life for his friend, and now he was unwilling to let me sacrifice myself for the greater good, and not too long ago, I would have only thought about the crown and nothing else.

The only way to avoid bloodshed was to take the vow. Before my mouth could open, I felt a familiar presence. A slight figured appeared to the right just to disappear again. At first I thought it was my imagination, but when

Jo reappeared behind my uncle again wielding a blade, I smiled. With one whack, a part of my uncle's spinal cord was severed. His head was still attached as he hit the ground. No one moved.

"Ahh hell," Jo said. "I need to work out more. Hold a plank or something. My muscular system is complete shit." She tossed the blade to the werewolf, who had been easing towards us. He stood gaping at her. "You, kind sir, with the bulging muscles, be gentlemanly and finish him off for me, will you?"

The werewolf blinked at her for several seconds before he swung the blade, finishing the job Jo had started. The crown had rolled in between a couple of gaping fire demons. It was clear no one knew what to do without their leader.

Jo shoved Dansby towards Austin then made a heart symbol towards me with her hands. "There you go, bestie. Like a wise man once said, 'if you have a problem, yo' I'll solve it.'"

I stood. "Vanilla Ice?"

She nodded. "Dude's right up there with Shakespeare."

She made a little gesture with her hand. "So, I assume you got the rest of this."

"Yep."

"Cool then. See you at the wedding."

She went to disappear only to reappear four more times. No one moved. They were all riveted to the gothic beauty. "For the love of Pete. Really? Get your shit together, Jo. Everyone's staring. Talk about performance anxiety," she said. Finally, she disappeared for good.

The remainder of the fire demons no longer knew whether they were to continue to fight or not without my uncle leading them. After a few moments, they started swinging their blades in a hurry. I sent them images of what was to come. With the protection spell down, more demons from the different levels entered rapidly. Before we knew it, my army was pressed up against the wall.

"Now's the time to unleash all your power," Austin said.

"I'll be weak afterwards."

His electric blue eyes met mine. "I'll protect you."

I didn't hear as much as I felt the truth in his words from our bond. I gave a quick shout to my army, "Stay behind me."

I let my power simmer before letting it boil. Extending my arms towards the thousands of demons, I forced their greatest fears to play out in their minds. This had them stopping in their tracks. I was tired of fighting. I needed to end this sooner rather than later. I let my wisps snake to the outsides of the level. The black smoke uncurled from me as it hung to the edges of the plane. The demons were in my snare. I continued to bombard them with visions of pain. I closed my eyes, and as a steady burst of power flowed out of me like a volcanic rush, I tilted my head back and screamed. My army became deadly quiet as everyone turned to watch the power uncurling from me. Energy streamed from me in intense waves, even as my knees hit the ground. My face was drenched with sweat. I dug from my core and with one last push, I sent out a wave that had my thick braid flying in the air. I opened my eyes to find the fire demons lying on the marble floor, dead. Their eyes were open and unblinking. I had killed them. I slowly made my way up to my feet, as everyone stared at me in shock. I had figured out the third way to kill a demon. To crush their soul.

Demons who hadn't rushed into level twelve when the battle was raging came walking in slowly. I had a feeling they were late to the game because they didn't want to fight. They took a second to take in the scene before they decided to kneel. I made my way to my uncle's body. I had a moment of deja vu as I took the crown off his detached head. I dusted it off before I placed it where it belonged. It sat crooked on my brow. I realized what it took and what it truly meant to be queen. The burden was so heavy I didn't feel triumphant over this battle. I felt tired.

I cleared my throat and shouted above the fighting, "It is finished."

We had zero casualties, although some of our group had injuries. Thanks to their fast healing, though, they should be back to normal after some rest.

A witch doctored Dansby, making cooing sounds. I smiled as Austin clapped him on the back.

I walked over to the two. "So you are the infamous Dansby?"

He shyly looked up at me. "I am. This is not how I wanted to meet Austin's mate."

Austin's brows drew together. "How did you know Carmen was my mate?"

Dansby groaned. "That old woman, Ariana, came and woke me up at my house." His brown hair fell into his eyes. He quickly shoved a hand though his hair. "She said that Carmen was your mate. She also said that if the both of your powers didn't align, Carmen would be dead within a couple of months, and you would be dead within a year. Then she told me I could be of help. I asked her how, and the rest is history."

I stared in horror at his right hand with the missing pinky and the bruises covering his body. At first glance Dansby didn't look very strong in fact he looked weak, but in reality he was a warrior at heart.

Austin shook his head. "I'm sorry that you had to go through all of that to save me, but I will be forever grateful that you saved my mate."

I knelt down in front of him. "Yes, Dansby, thank you for all that you have sacrificed."

He gave me a cheeky smile. "No worries. Ariana was completely up front, and she did tell me that in your new army there was a shy, but cute, girl named Tiff that could regenerate my finger for me. She said it would take her multiple tries, but eventually she'd figure it out. Besides I can say I had a hand in not only bringing you two lovebirds together, but in securing the key."

I rolled my eyes at Austin. "A key that Ariana turned over to the witches. That's how those low-level witches got the key in the first place."

Austin said, "Really?" the same time that Dansby said, "Semantics."

We all laughed. I stood up and excused myself to give them a little time to talk. I made the rounds and spoke with every single person that was in my army, congratulating them on a job well done. For the first time in my life, a sense of peace washed over me. Everything might not be perfect, but it was pretty dang close. Crooked crown and all.

chapter twenty nine

An hour later and everyone's adrenaline was still pumping. They reenacted the fight but this time with laughter instead of fear. After talking amongst the demons in our group, I decided to put Thane in charge of the underworld. Anyone who wanted to stay could. Even though the witches offered to make potions to hide the fire demons' true identity, the fire demons felt more at ease in the underworld. Thane would be in charge of a good chunk of fire, smoke, and shadow demons. I would check in with him bi-weekly, just to make sure everything was still running smoothly.

Austin had made a couple of quick phone calls and had rented out some houses for the witches, wolves, and other supernaturals close to downtown Charleston. The witches were jumping up and down. They acted as if they were moving into a sorority house. Poor downtown Charleston would never be the same again. We went over the rules once more, and then we sent everyone on their way.

Tally flew in, halting when he took in the carnage. "Whoa. Looks like you were busy." At my nod, he said, "Ariana was nowhere to be found."

"Oh well. Looks like we didn't need her input, anyhow."

His eyes narrowed in speculation. "You didn't need her advice, did you? You just didn't want me here."

I knew he was about to start yelling at me, so calmly I said, "Tally if you would—"

His tiny hands squeezed my face, stopping me from talking. "You love me. That's why you sent me away because you were scared you would lose me."

I rolled my eyes. "Maybe."

He laughed before he kissed my cheek. "I love you, too." Before I could flick him, he flew out of range. "It's okay. I know your true feelings."

I groaned. "Go away."

"Speaking of away, would you mind if I helped Whitney move into her new place? I stopped to talk to her on the way in. You see she had a thing for Steve, the sensitive, yet slightly intimidating werewolf, but then he dumped her for Bethany, and she hasn't been handling the break-up very well."

I tried to hide my smile. "Absolutely. In fact you might want to travel around to each group to make sure they are settling well."

He gave a fierce nod. "Yeah, that's what I was thinking. Some of the witches and wolves are really young. They might need someone to talk to."

"And who'd be a better listener than you?"

"Plus, it'll give you some alone time to maybe go on a honeymoon? Hey, did you know all the witches were out there by the exit gossiping about how hot it was that you and Austin pulled from each other's power?"

"Yeah, it was cool."

"Officially mated, huh?" Embarrassment flooded me. "I'm proud of you, kiddo."

That was the first time I ever remembered hearing those words. "Thank you, friend."

He saluted me. "I'll check back in with you."

I didn't like the fact that he wouldn't see me every day, but I was glad he'd be helping others. Besides, it wasn't like he'd disappear from my life. He had found himself a full-time job amongst my army, and as long as Tally felt like he was useful, I had a feeling he'd hang around.

Austin came up behind me, wrapping his arms around me. "You ready?"

"For what?" I asked.

"I have a surprise for you."

I looked around for Dansby; the last time I'd seen him he was laughing with a busty redhead.

"Where's your friend?"

"We found Tiff, and she has convinced him to come with her to whatever house she was assigned. She's actually really excited to be working on some spell to regenerate Dansby's finger. He was so nervous when she talked about an accident she had with a toad, but he couldn't get out of her snare. His feet were dragging, but she acted like she didn't notice as she pulled him along."

"Poor Dansby."

"Poor me. I'm ready to go."

"But look at this place." We both gazed at all of the fallen demons and the blood coating everything. I grimaced, as I stepped on something squishy. "We can't leave like this."

"Oh, I'm already way ahead of you." Austin whistled and at least fifty tiny shadow demons rushed towards us. All of them were hopping up and down, causing me to smile.

"Majesty, Majesty, we clean up mess, yes?"

"If you're sure?" At their nod, I grinned. "Thank you."

They all cheered with glee as they went about cleaning up the dead bodies. Like tiny ants, they started to carry the fallen demons.

I shook my head in amazement. "Oh, before I forget, the key—"

"It's in my pocket."

"Yes, well, how easy would it be for you to put half the key back in the enchanted maze? Make everything exactly the way it was minus the elite guard?"

"It's doable. And what would we do with the other half?"

"I'll put it somewhere safe. Maybe under my pillow." I gave him a wink. "I mean, who would want to wake a demon?"

Austin laughed as he gathered me in an embrace. "I love you."

My face burned, as I felt something whoosh inside of me, constant and steady. This was the second time he had thrown around the L-word, and it made my heartbeat erratic. The worst part was because of our connection, he knew it, too.

Cheers erupted around us. I tried to pull back from him. I felt like I had gotten caught with my hand in the cookie jar.

Austin twirled me around before he teleported me. I had no clue where we were going and it didn't matter. I was free and in love; what more could I ask for?

chapter thirty

The white beach house sat on almost an acre of land. A long dock stretched from the backyard to the ocean. Seagulls flew above us as the wind blew the seagrass.

"It's yours, ours, if you want it. Do you like it?"

"The house is ours?"

He nodded, and I flung myself into his arms. "Oh, I love it. Where are we? Not that it matters, but I feel like I should know the name of the place I call home."

"Isle of Palms. It neighbors Sullivan's Island, the entrance to Charleston Harbor. We're right on the beach, and the queen is close to her subordinates." He said the last part with a wink.

"I love it. It's perfect."

He swooped me into his arms as carried me over the threshold. "I can tell you love me." At my disgruntled look, he laughed. "You don't have to say it, mate, I can feel it. But what I really want to know is, do you trust me?"

I had never trusted anyone before, but I really thought about his words. If you genuinely cared for someone, then without love, there could be no trust, and no trust without love.

"Yes," I said, as he sat me on our new kitchen countertop. I wanted to take a look at our magnificent house, but whatever he was about to say, I knew it was important I gave him all of my attention.

"My mother knew that her time was limited. You see, she was best friends with Jo's mom, who also saw the future, and she had told my mom that her time here on earth would be short-lived, so my mom wrote my sister and I a letter. I had mine tattooed onto my back. At the time, I didn't exactly know what my mother was talking about. I just wanted a piece of her with me, but now it all makes sense. Her words are for us."

He slowly took off his T-shirt and turned around, letting me look at the ink. I ran a hand lovingly over the words, as tears gathered in my eyes. My voice shook as I read out loud, "The queen of your heart can warm you with a fiery flame. Guard each other well."

I remembered the look on his face when we were in the portal searching for Malakian, and I had lit a fire. I had said something eerily similar that night.

"I had it written in Latin. A language that I cannot read fluently, but I knew that it was important that it be in Latin. That's your first language. I also had it be spelled, so no one could see the tattoo. Can you imagine how shocked I was when you first saw it?" He turned back around. "You were meant for me. I will love you until my dying day, and then I will continue to love you from the other side."

The hay with seeing the house. It would still be standing in an hour. I wrapped my arms around my mate's neck. "I'm sure there is a master bedroom?"

His eyes twinkled. "I think I might be able to find it."

He picked me up and carried me through the gigantic house. My hand found the tattoo once again. I was meant for him, but he was also meant for me. Together, we would be unstoppable, and we would anchor each other in the storm. I was finally free of my chains holding me down to something I never truly wanted to be. I was untethered and happy. Something no demon had ever achieved before. I smiled as my anchor impatiently kicked the bedroom door in. Life was finally going to be worth living.

about the author

Brandi Elledge lives in the South, where even the simplest words are at least four syllables.

She has a husband that she refuses to upgrade...because let's face it he is pretty awesome, and two beautiful children that are the light of her life.

Printed in Great Britain
by Amazon